Cast of C

Enid Marley. The ill-tempered advic
determined to avoid a possible charge

Sam Egon. The ebullient editor-in-chi
is indispensable to whatever success t

Kidder. The most dogged crime reporter in London. He now lives in a lift.

Doon Travers. The beauty editor of *You*.

Rex Travers. Her brother, an unemployed ballet dancer, hired to fill in for
Enid with disastrous results.

Ellie Sansome. The frighteningly thin and chic fashion editor of *You*, who
is secretly infatuated with her boss, Sam Egon.

Doctor Felz. A terrified Viennese psychiatrist with dark secrets, who is the
medical editor and all-purpose columnist at *You*.

Gyko Khosrove Melik Mangoyian. A tall, red-headed Armenian, who is
Dr. Feltz's old nemesis.

Mrs. Ryder, Paul East, and **Jimmie Summers.** The cookery, fiction, and
photography editors, respectively, at *You*.

Carstairs. A private detective. He does no detecting.

Inspector Woodman. A Scotland Yarder, recently demoted.

Killer Kayes. A dangerous murderer, Inspector Woodman's old nemesis.

Browneyes. A thief, and Enid's most devoted fan.

Mr. Jackson. Her aggrieved husband, deserted on their honeymoon, who
heads up **Farmer Jepson**, **Mr. Cream**, **Colonel Quincey**, and an entire
army of other Complainers, all seeking revenge from *You*.

Trouble O'Leary. A contentious Irishman, now Mr. Jackson's ally.

Mrs. Pickett. Enid's charwoman.

Mrs. Fred Turner. The unfortunate woman who broke Enid's fall.

Plus an Indian restaurant owner, a stenographer, another charwoman, friends,
colleagues, and the entire da Gongas clan, whom nobody understands.

Books by Pamela Branch

The Wooden Overcoat (1951)
Published in the U.S. by
The Rue Morgue Press
January 2006

The Lion in the Cellar (1951)
Published in the U.S. by
The Rue Morgue Press
February 2006

Murder Every Monday (1954)
Published in the U.S. by
The Rue Morgue Press
April 2006

Murder's Little Sister (1958)
Published in the U.S. by
The Rue Morgue Press
June 2006

Murder's Little Sister

by Pamela Branch

Introduction by Tom & Enid Schantz

Rue Morgue
Lyons / Boulder

For Francis Iles,
with love

Murder's Little Sister
Copyright © 1958 David Higham Associates Limited

New Material Copyright © 2006
The Rue Morgue Press

For information on our titles see
www.ruemorguepress.com
or call
800-699-6214
or write
The Rue Morgue Press
87 Lone Tree Lane
Lyons, CO 80540

ISBN: 0-915230-93-3

Printed by
Johnson Printing

PRINTED IN THE UNITED STATES OF AMERICA

Introduction
Pamela Branch
"The funniest lady"
With major revisions to
the introductions to
The Wooden Overcoat & Lion in the Cellar

Pamela Branch was "the funniest lady you ever knew," according to fellow mystery writer Christianna Brand. Brand was referring not only to her books but to Branch herself, who delighted Brand by sending her countless "postcards with smears of pretence blood on them, purporting to be from her various characters," or "a dreadful squashed box of chocolates with very obvious pinholes into which poison had clearly been injected." That wicked sense of humor permeated Branch's four mysteries as well, leading contemporary reviewers to describe her first book, *The Wooden Overcoat*, as a "delightfully ghoulish souffle" (*The Spectator*) where "even the bodies manage to be ghoulishly diverting" (*The Sunday Times*) graced with "the gayest prose" and a "gloriously gruesome" touch (*The Queen*). *The Spectator* welcomed her second book, *The Lion in the Cellar*, as a "charnel-house frolic." Nancy Spain, to whom Branch was favorably compared, called it a "masterpiece," a blend of "the Marx Brothers, Crazy Gang and the Little Intimate Reviews." *The Times Literary Supplement* strayed from the mystery field to compare her third book, *Murder Every Monday*, to satirist Evelyn Waugh. Her fourth and final book, *Murder's Little Sister*, was published in 1958 and was the only title to see publication in the United States. American mystery writer Carolyn Hart listed it among her five favorite mysteries of all time. It was reissued in 1988 in England as part of Pandora's Classic Women Crime

Writers series after twenty-five years of being out of print. In spite of these extravagant reviews, Branch is rarely mentioned in any of the standard reference books devoted to the mystery genre, perhaps because her career was cut short by cancer at the age of 47.

Nor does anyone have any idea what happened to her fifth book. In 1962, her paperback publisher reported that she had begun the book in the Scottish Highlands and was finishing it in Ghana, West Africa. She would not die for another five years, so either her illness prevented her from finishing the book or she encountered a major writer's block. Or it just might have been that she made a good marriage at last and no longer needed to publish to make ends meet. No one knows for sure because she appears to have left no estate behind. Since she died so long ago, even the literary agency which holds her copyrights doesn't know what happened.

Why she isn't better known among the historians of mystery fiction is perhaps even stranger. She rates an entry in the third edition of *Twentieth Century Crime and Mystery Writers* but is dropped from the fourth edition, retitled *The St. James Guide to Crime and Mystery Writers.* Critic Gillian Rodgerson summed up Branch's writing by saying: "The humor in Branch's books lies in the situations, the outrageous characters and in the dialog which almost makes sense but not quite. This is life viewed through a fun-house distorting mirror where the ordinary suddenly becomes bizarre and then ordinary again." Rodgerson admits that the situations, as in *The Wooden Overcoat,* make for "a very silly book but the writing is seamless and witty and the denouement makes it all worthwhile." It's a fair judgment, though Branch's books are no more "silly" than those of P.G. Wodehouse or Sarah Caudwell. Looking back on her career from a vantage point of fifty years and an era in which humor and homicide have truly come into their own, one could argue that Branch rates as perhaps the premier farceur in a now overcrowded field.

In her own time, there were a few contemporary reviewers who were not enthralled with the idea of introducing humor into crime fiction. English critic Sutherland Scott admitted in his 1953 study of the genre, *Blood in Their Ink,* that writers such as Phoebe Atwood Taylor (aka Alice Tilton) and Constance and Gwenyth Little "serve up a sparkling cocktail" but he questioned if the idea of "mixing hectic humor and even more hectic homicide is entirely to be recommended." Taylor and the Littles were American writers who were very popular in Britain. Scott was somewhat alarmed that British writers might follow suit in turning chills to laughs. "It is interesting to note that the most recent addition to the mix-your-murder-with-plenty-of-fun brigade is also a lady, this time a home product. If you can digest this kind of hot-pot, Pamela Branch's T*he Wooden*

Overcoat and *The Lion in the Cella*r should be to your taste. Some digestive systems may tend to rebel." It's an odd judgment, given that Scott called another, somewhat earlier English female farceur, Nancy Spain, one of the genre's emerging talents.

While Scott merely comes off as being more stuffy than perceptive, it has to be admitted that humor is subjective. Yet, other English writers were known to go for a laugh. There's more than a touch of the absurd in many of the books by Edmund Crispin (*The Moving Toyshop*, 1946) or Michael Innes (*Appleby's End,* 1945). Branch's humor, of course, was a bit blacker ("ghoulish" in an adjective often pops up in her reviews) than either of those two gentlemen. Though a bit more farcical and madcap, Branch may also remind some readers of Richard Hull (1896-1973) who plumbed the darker side of humor in his crime novels, most notably in *The Murder of My Aunt* (1934), a book whose marvelous title can—and should—be read with two vastly different interpretations, or in *My Own Murderer* (1940) wherein a staid Londoner's lifestyle changes when he comes across a murderer in his apartment and decides to hold him captive rather than turn him over to the police. Anthony Rolls's homicidal clergyman in *The Vicar's Experiment* (aka *Clerical Error*, 1932) would be perfectly at home in Branch's world. Her brand of madcap black humor was also present in many of the British film comedies of the 1950s, especially in such Alec Guinness vehicles as *Kind Hearts and Coronets.*

While these British films fared well in the U.S. during this period, American publishers didn't believe that readers on this side of the Atlantic would embrace Branch's odd brand of gallows humor. Of course, one has to remember that the early 1950s were seeing a change in direction among publishers, who were pulling away from the traditional mystery so popular before World War II and replacing it with action thrillers by the likes of Mickey Spillane and John D. MacDonald. The 1970s and 1980s saw a rebirth of the comic traditional mystery. The blackest of these were the early biting satirical novels of English writer Robert Barnard, whose *Death of an Old Goat* (1974) and *Death by Sheer Torture* (1981) remind one of a less frenetic Branch. Even closer in tone to Branch are the recent "subversively funny" (*New York Times*) novels of another English writer, Ruth Dudley Edwards.

She was born Pamela Byatt in 1920 on her parent's isolated tea estate in Ceylon (now Sri Lanka). Her earliest memory is of helping her father persuade an elephant to swallow a homemade aspirin the size of a croquet ball. The elephant did not oblige.

She was educated at various schools along the south coast of England and then went to Paris to study art. She quickly tired of painting the traditional still lifes of "guitars, grapes and Chianti bottles" and returned to England where she studied at the Royal Academy of Dramatic Art for a year, once performing in a modern-dress version of *Hamlet* wearing a mackintosh and gumboots. This flirtation with an acting career led some researchers to confuse her with the actress Pamela Branch, best known for playing one of the nuns in the Sidney Poitier film *Lilies of the Field*.

After she left the RADA, she returned to Ceylon and then moved on to explore nearby India, starting in the north and gradually working her way south. For three years her home base was a houseboat in Kashmir. She trekked across the Himalayas by horse, living out of a tent during the summer months, and went skiing in the winter. She learned to hunt with guns and falcons, once shooting a black bear. During this period she also learned Urdu, with a special emphasis on the racier words in that language, painted several murals, and trained two racehorses.

Or so she claimed. Alice Woudhuysen, a close friend who met Pamela in 1950, said Pam never referred to these adventures. "I did think at that time though that Pam and Newton (her first husband) were both inclined to live in a fantasy world and their tales were somewhat embellished to make an amusing story." Pamela met and married Newton Branch following her return to England. The two of them moved to Cyprus where they lived in a twelfth century Greek monastery poised precariously on the edge of a cliff overlooking the sea. Both tried their hand at writing, Pamela producing *The Wooden Overcoat*, Newton possibly a number of boys' books. During this period, they also lived in a small fisherman's cottage in Ireland where she worked on *Lion in the Cellar*. Back in England, Newton worked as a staff writer for Adprint, a publishing firm, and edited *This Britain*, a collection of essays by various hands written to celebrate the 1951 Festival of Britain. The son of a distinguished judge, Newton qualified as a barrister but never practiced law and lived much of his life in the shadow of his more accomplished father and wife. Writing, according to Alice Woudhuysen, did not come easily to him. "He was not as focused as Pamela, who must actually have worked very hard at her writing but talked very little about it. She may possibly have played down her role as a writer in order not to seem to complete with Newton." Pamela is said to have collaborated with him on film scripts but there is no record that any of them ever were filmed, although Newton was employed by the British Institute of Film Censors. Newton complained about having to sit through innumerable second-rate films but endured it because he and Pamela needed the extra income. The name "N. Branch" appeared on many a movie screen.

Although the two of them gave off the impression of what Alice

Woudhuysen described as a "devil-may-care affluence," money was obviously tight. "In 1950 Pam and Newton were living in a gloomy mews flat in Elvaston Place, Kensington. London was still a depressing city after the war, flats were hard to find, rents were high, food was still rationed and life was rather tough and bleak, especially in the winter," Alice Woudhuysen recalled a half century later. "We were always cold as few people had central heating and the smog made even the daytime seem bleak." Branch vividly recreates that period in *Lion in the Cellar*.

The Branches were able to get the flat in Kensington on the cheap because Newton claimed that a previous occupant had gassed himself in the tiny kitchen. Although these flats, carved out of old stables and carriage houses, were apparently much in demand by bohemians, many were far from pleasant places in which to live. "The sitting room was a long, narrow room with no windows, only a skylight which let in a dismal, yellowish glow," according to Alice Woudhuysen. "I think there was a sort of curtained-off alcove for a double bed. There was also a small dining room with rather heavy, dark furniture where Pamela wrote her books."

The Branches drove about London in an old taxi cab, often accompanied by a young boxer dog named Culley. Alice Woudhuysen said Culley was very affectionate "but slobbered dreadfully" and was known occasionally to have a glass of beer with his owners at a local pub. Later, the taxi cab was replaced by an old tradesman's van in which the Branches installed a mattress for overnight trips. She and Newton continued to travel extensively. Pamela was apparently able to write anywhere. *Murder Every Monday*, her third book, was written in various parts of England, France and the Channel Islands. It was dedicated to Christianna Brand to whom she had once expressed amazement at having readers write her asking for her castoff clothing. These requests so amused Pamela that she has one of the characters in *Murder Every Monday*, a romance novelist, repeat the story.

Her last published book, *Murder's Little Sister* (1958), was written in that mews flat in Kensington. This was a very tense period in her life. By 1954, the strain on the Branches' marriage was beginning to show. Pamela dropped hints to Alice that she was "finding Newton very difficult" to live with. She suggested that he was drinking a great deal at this point and had lost much of his motivation to write. Pamela went from merely helping to possibly actually writing his stuff for him. Friends were not surprised when they parted and eventually divorced a year or so after the release of *Murder's Little Sister*. Newton remarried but the old troubles continued to haunt him and this marriage apparently soon failed as well. He died sometime in the 1970s.

Pamela also remarried, to Wing Commander James Edward Stuart-Lyon, and her final years were apparently lived in relative comfort. With the exception of the rumored fifth novel and a play based on *Murder Every Monday*, written in collaboration with Philip Dale and performed at the Civic Theatre in Chelmsford in October 1964, Branch's career as a professional writer appears to have ended. Ironically, it was during this period that several of her books, originally published by Robert Hale in hardcover, were reissued by Penguin in paperback.

Friends described her as a very glamorous woman. "Beautiful, marvellous Pamela, with eyelashes like bent hairpins," is how Christianna Brand remembered her. Alice Woudhuysen, six years Pamela's junior, was in awe of her. "She seemed incredibly glamorous and sophisticated. She wore a lot of makeup, painting her lips in an astonishing Cupid's Bow above their natural line and she had masses of tawny, blond hair. She was slim and elegant in a casually dressed way and to me she appeared rather dauntingly self-possessed and confident but I soon discovered that she was also very warmhearted, amusing and likable and when she related that she had been voted the most popular girl in her school, I readily believed her."

While the Branches were still together and living in Kensington, Pamela's mother was taken ill and died in great pain. Thoughts of that period were no doubt in Pamela's mind when her own health took a turn for the worse in the mid-1960s. But that marvelous sense of humor which permeated her books didn't desert her.

"No, I can't come tomorrow, darling," she said to Christianna. "We're flying to Geneva." Pamela paused, then added, "My husband wants to buy a watch." That was in 1967. Brand never spoke to her again. Shortly afterwards, Pamela died of cancer. The woman whose books were perfect specimens of gallows humor couldn't resist making a joke in what well may have been her darkest days.

Tom & Enid Schantz
November 2005
Revised March 2006
Lyons, Colorado

Editors' Note: We would like to thank Barry Pike, Alice Woudhuysen and H.R. Woudhuysen for their invaluable contributions to this introduction.

Chapter 1

THE yellow cushion looked too frivolous in the oven, so Enid Marley went and fetched a black one. That did not look right either, but it could not be helped. Since she had no intention whatever of dying, she was determined to make herself as comfortable as possible. Looking into the mirror on the back of the kitchen door, she carefully disarranged her hair so that one strand hung over her forehead in a desperate manner.

While of Unsound Mind, she thought, suppressing a smile as she slightly smudged her lipstick.

She had thought it all out with great care, planned each detail, revised it, scrutinized it from every angle. She knew well that it was a drastic ploy, but it was the only one left untried. Somehow, she had to recapture her husband. It was not that she loved nor even liked him, but to be deserted by no less than three men – all of whom had quite frankly married her for her money – was ridiculous, humiliating, monotonous.

She arranged the three farewell notes artistically on the refrigerator. One was addressed to her husbands; one to the editor of the magazine, *You*, for whom she worked; one to the coroner.

Glancing at her watch, she lay down on the floor, turned on the gas and placed her head on the cushion inside the oven. There was no danger, she reassured herself. Her charwoman, always punctual, would arrive in four and a half minutes, in plenty of time to save her.

Closing her eyes, she breathed deeply, cooperating with the gas, thinking of Harold's fat, silly face when he heard the news. It was essential to be unconscious before Mrs.. Pickett arrived.

Four minutes…three and a half…three…two and a half…two…

Mrs. Pickett, for the first time in six years, was eight minutes late. "'Ere I am!" she shouted in the hall, as she did every day, going through into the kitchen, taking off her baggy coat. Then she saw her inert employer sprawled before the oven. Involuntarily, she asked herself, *Now didn't I tell Sid this was a black day? Yes, I did. On the stairs.*

Accustomed to appalling and recurrent disasters among her own large brood, she was not unduly surprised. She therefore hung up her hat before lumbering down on to one knee to inquire, "You dead, dear?"

Enid Marley opened her eyes and sat up, pale with rage.

"No, nor you are," said Mrs. Pickett, rising, disappointed that she no longer had a topic of conversation for the long bus journey home. "An' you know why?" She reached for her overall. "'Cos the Gas Workers' Union's out again. They been Goin' Slow since last night. 'Smornin' – an' you can call me a liar but I'm not – it took me solid forty minutes to boil a *kettle* . . ."

Ten minutes later, Enid Marley, nursing a throbbing headache, adjusted her hair and lipstick, put on her hat, coat, and gloves, slammed the front door behind her, and began to walk towards the main road and the bridge.

Damn Mrs. Pickett, she thought. *Damn Harold! And to flaming hell and perdition with each and every pig-faced member of the Gas Workers' Union!*

"Morning, madam," called the local butcher, wrestling with his awning. "Now weren't those chops a treat?"

She walked on without answering him for two reasons. First, she did not believe in speaking to her social inferiors unless it was absolutely imperative. Second, because she was again reviewing the most popular methods of suicide.

Most of them, if one intended to survive them, were horribly dangerous. Even those which allowed a margin for error or rescue were notoriously chancy. Aspirins and sleeping pills were unpredictable. Guns misfired. Drowning was out of the question since she could not swim . . .

She crossed the road with even more than her usual caution. If she were to be run over now, how relieved Harold would be! Harold and the dull, plain, hairy girl for whom he had deserted her! Halfway across the bridge, she paused and looked down. The high jump? No, the river looked cold and dirty and there was always the chance of landing shamefully on one of the darting skiffs below. Nor could one rely on rescue, and there was nobody near enough to woo her off the parapet. Moreover, she intensely disliked heights. She walked on.

As she waited for the traffic lights to change, she unwillingly considered high places. Mountains, airplanes, penthouses; scaffolding, windows, cliffs. *Windows?* High windows? Dignified, dramatic, *safe!* Alarming, of course, but in order to teach Harold a lesson, she was prepared to suffer almost any discomfort.

She saw herself teetering on a high sill, saw the scene below. The silent, upturned faces of the crowd; the press photographers; the men in helmets straining at the fire service nets; the expanding scarlet ladder of the fire engine rearing towards her; the bluff, gruff voices of the policemen in the neighboring windows.

Ah yes! Splendid!

But *which* high window?

Her own flat was useless, on the ground floor. A large store or hotel seemed impersonal and therefore risky. Would a complete stranger be prepared to cajole and persuade with enough passion to enable her to retreat without loss of face? One of her fans, yes, certainly. But the photograph which dominated her weekly column was eighteen years old, and none of her fans ever recognized her.

Where then? Her husband's office? No. Sir Francis might be present, with his impatient, hooting laugh, his brusque air of no-nonsense. Anyway, Harold would probably be playing golf.

Her own office then? Why not?

It was on the fifth floor. The window had a broad, sturdy sill and overlooked a busy thoroughfare. The staff would surely plead with her. Or would they? She knew that her colleagues hated her almost as much as she hated them. But she also knew that her column was the life blood of *You*. Without her, the small, unsuccessful magazine would certainly slide into bankruptcy. Yes, the staff would plead . . .

She hailed a taxi, sank on to the hot leather seat, and wound up the window. "*You*," she told the driver.

He looked at her over his shoulder. "Look, lady," he said. "This cab's me own, see. If that's your attitude . . ."

She resisted the temptation to grab at his face. "Croissant Street, you dolt," she snapped. "And hurry!"

That week, only 50,000 people bought *You*, an estimated readership of less than 200,000. The orders for the next week's issue decreased by eighty-one copies, thus losing some ground upon the sales figures of the sister magazine, *Me*.

You had been launched some ten years before by a spent dynamo named Sam Egon. Having floated out of the editorship of various Far and Near East publications on a tide of gin, he had finally returned to England and cast about for employment.

Among his few contacts had been one of his former proofreaders, now the editor of *Me*. Egon had visited him. To his annoyance, the upstart had not risen when he entered. He had called him Jack-no-Sam-isn't-it without apology. He had not only not invited Egon to sit down but had also dismissed him almost immediately, suggesting with ill-concealed sarcasm that he visited the Chairman of the Board.

Egon, in a rage, had done so. He considered himself to be a plausible fellow of wide experience and a certain wild charm, an acquired taste. If the Chairman acquired it, it should not be difficult to oust his former underling and take over the editorship of *Me*.

The Chairman of the Board, having consumed a shock-absorbing City lunch, had entirely failed to understand Egon's cautious innuendoes. They had talked for some time of the Far East, of a certain evil nightclub in Hong Kong, of Murray whisky, of the indiscretions of two colonels, before Egon said desperately, "Well, I felt I ought to give you first refusal, sir."

"Damned white of you, my boy," the Chairman had said. "Call me B.F., they all do. Must come down to my place in Kent. Golf."

"There's a lot of unnecessary wastage going on in *Me*," said Egon. "You're the judge, B.F., sir, but I do feel that Larkin . . ."

"Quite." The Chairman had risen, placed an arm around Egon's shoulders. He said with sudden suspicion, "Not Meg's boy, I suppose?"

"No, sir."

"Thank God."

A week later, Egon had received a letter inviting him to inaugurate a new magazine. It was to consist almost entirely of *Me*'s waste products, was to be run, at first, with an ill-paid skeleton staff, and was to share the printing, layout, advertising, and secretarial facilities of the senior magazine. Could Egon prepare a dummy within three months? Could he suggest a title?

"*This and That*," suggested Egon.

"No woman appeal," said the Board.

"*I*," suggested Egon.

"*Eye?*" said the Board. "Eyebrow, highbrow, intellectual, *out!*"

"*Us*."

"Too political."

"*It*."

"No sex."

Egon hesitated. *It* was the title which he himself favored, but he wanted them to think that they had talked him into it. "Well," he said slowly, "I suppose you . . ."

"Yes!" roared the Chairman. "I'm for it! I like it! It's got everything!

You! What the hell's the matter with *You?*"

Crippled by a minute budget, Egon nevertheless determined to outdo and humiliate his bumptious rival, Larkin. It might take several years, but sooner or later the circulation of *You* must be at least double that of *Me*. Long before the first dummy had been approved or even planned, this had become an obsession.

Egon placed an advertisement in the *Situations Vacant* columns of various daily publications, but the salaries he offered were so low that he was about to despair when Enid Marley presented herself. He took an instant dislike to her, to her small, shrewd eyes, to her rigidly corseted figure, to her obvious efficiency. Grudgingly, he accepted her as Assistant Editor, and explained his project.

You was to have wide family appeal. There was to be a dash of sex, but nothing torrid. There was to be a serial, short stories, a letter page, fashion, gossip, interviews, reviews, news.

"I can't lose!" he had cried. "I've got the lot!"

Yet ten years later, *You* still wavered on the edge of bankruptcy. At the beginning of each quarter, Egon received a letter from the Board inviting him to justify his publication's existence. For *You*, as though contaminated by Egon, had about it an aura of failure. It was a periodical of marked indifference. It was broke and in constant danger of extinction.

Only the inclusion of the Enid Marley column – a double page spread featuring and answering readers' problems under the legend *Can I Help You?* – kept it from broadcasting the death rattle which had been in its throat from the start . . .

Enid Marley got out of the taxi in Croissant Street and since, ostensibly, she was about to die, omitted to tip the driver.

She passed through the archway entrance of the vast, square *You* and *Me* building which also housed a travel agency, two furriers, an Indian restaurant, an export merchant, a Hungarian photographer, a dancing school, an escort service, a private detective, and a firm called da Gongas about which nobody knew anything.

The dangerous lift slid up from the packaging department, still full of pieces of straw. Enid Marley eased open the frail gate, closed it behind her. A shaft of light fell on the typed notice above the Emergency Stop.

If you are TRAPPED, it read, *do NOT attempt to force the gate. Stand STILL. Press the red bell, summoning the janitor.*

She pressed the button marked 5.

Between the third and fourth floors, the lift hesitated, then stopped. Enid Marley knew it in all its moods. Clenching her hands, she waited. Presently it shook itself like an old dog coming out of water and rose unsteadily to the sixth floor. Enid Marley stepped out with relief. She went down the stairs to the fifth floor, turned right down the dark corridor which led past the offices of *Me* to those of *You* and her own.

Two girls clicked past her on high heels. They had come from the model kitchens. They wore pink smocks with *Me* embroidered on the left breast. They did not greet her. One whispered, deliberately before she was out of earshot, "Old cow! I love her like a snake."

Enid Marley stalked on. She knew that she was unpopular and was proud of it. She passed the notice informing the staff of the nearest shelter in the case of atomic warfare – over which was painted jauntily in green *Welcome to YOU and ME!* – the Art Editor's office which marked the boundary between the two publications. She was obliged to pause behind a crouching charwoman who was plucking cigarette butts from a bucket of sand and putting them into an envelope.

It occurred to her that the woman would later become a witness. She assumed a tragic expression and said in a low, haunted voice, "Good morning, Mrs. Barker."

Mrs. Barker brushed a strand of hair off her forehead with her wrist. "My back says rain," she mumbled.

Enid Marley edged past her. The door of Egon's office was open. He was pacing up and down and shouting into a telephone. Next door, Ellie Sansome, the Fashion Editor, was sitting on her desk touching up her silver fingernails. She looked up and nodded distantly.

Outside her own office, upon whose door was painted *Can I help You? KEEP OUT!* Enid Marley hesitated. Then she went in and closed the door behind her. She realized that she ought to lock it. But if she did so, her rescuer would be unable to reach her. She removed the key and forced it between a crack in the floorboards.

It was a small room with a large window. There was a flat-topped desk, two telephones, nine filing cabinets. The huge charts which represented years of hard labor, which were the secret of her success, were plastered all over the walls. There was coconut matting on the floor. The window was dusty and, as usual, closed.

In the IN tray was a great splaying heap of letters. Slumping into the chair behind the desk, Enid Marley noted that the topmost one came from her most ardent, most hated fan, Browneyes. Automatically, she reached for it. She had dictated Browneyes's life for the past eight years. She had advised her to leave home, to break her two engagements, to sue her employer, to inform her father in a tactful manner of her mother's infidelity.

Dearest Enid, she read. *I don't know what suddenly came over me. You'll be ever so wild but I've married that Mr. Jackson I asked your opinion about. Now I know you were right when you said show him the door. Whatever can I do? Only last night . . .*

Enid Marley pushed the letter aside. Even the delight of leading Browneyes into increasingly chronic plights had palled. She drew from her bag the three farewell notes. She had propped them against the ink well before she remembered that in each the word gas appeared. They would no longer fit the circumstances. She fumbled for a match, burnt the letters carefully and crumbled the ashes.

She took a sheet of headed notepaper and fed it into the typewriter. As she did so, it occurred to her that she could cause infinitely more alarm, far more despondency, if she were to address her supposedly last communication to an all-embracing *You*.

Yes, a brainwave! If the letter were published, it would make even the-man-in-the-street feel subtly guilty, vaguely responsible.

But in what style should she write it?

The one in which she answered her readers' queries? *My dear, I know that you will be so sorry to hear of my desperate plight . . .* No, it would madden her husband, drive him perhaps even deeper into the arms of his lumpy concubine.

Why not the style in which she commented upon prize-winning letters on the *Hullo, Hullo!* page? The light touch? *When, last week, we told a friend that we had reached the very, very end of our long-suffering tether, her son, aged four, said . . .* No!

Pathetic? Hysterical? Accusing?

No. None of these. Noncommittal was the safest, the style in which she wrote to her bank manager.

Dear You, she tapped. *The present situation, obviously, is intolerable. I can no longer bear so heavy a burden. I have, quite calmly, given this matter considerable thought. I have been forced reluctantly to the conclusion that the only solution lies in the final severing of all old ties . . .*

She stopped, considering the last five words. She saw momentarily two music hall comedians cutting off each other's ties with scissors, a surefire holiday laugh. *No!*

She ripped the sheet of paper from the typewriter, burnt it, trampled the ashes into the matting. She retyped the first three sentences. *I have been regretfully forced to the conclusion*, she tapped, *that the only solution lies in a swift, final . . .*

A swift, final what? *Escape from this scene of unequal combat?* No, it sounded somehow as if it had been translated from the Latin. *Farewell to all those who . . .* No, no, none of that! Why should she say good-bye to any of them, damn them? Anyway, she'd still be here tomorrow, like an unwelcome guest who said good-bye yet stayed the night. *Journey into oblivion?* That wasn't bad, it had a nice rhythm. But had it got that fatal touch of the *ham?*

Ah, to hell with them all! She'd be here all day, and at any moment now Sylvia would appear to collect the mail. She wasn't trying to win a Nobel prize. *Exit*, she wrote.

She drew the paper from the typewriter, fumbled in her bag for the rubber stamp of her signature which she always kept on her key ring. She had stamped the letter before she remembered that her own handwriting, perhaps a trifle smudged, might have been more effective. Should she type the damn thing again?

No, she could not be bothered. She replaced the key ring in her bag and laid the letter elegantly in her OUT tray.

Smudging her lipstick for the second time that morning, loosening the strand of hair, she rose and crossed to the window to assess her potential audience.

The pavements below were crowded. A crocodile of buses was held up by the traffic lights. A four-piece street band played mournfully in the gutter; an old monkey sat on the drum holding out a hat. A policeman argued with a barrow-boy selling oranges.

Perfect!

She knew that she was going to detest the next few minutes, but, she comforted herself, they would be spent in an excellent cause.

She opened the window and squirmed through the narrow aperture.

The sill, as she straightened up and felt the summer breeze around her, seemed to be horribly narrow and much, much higher than she had remembered. She gripped a drainpipe and held on tightly. She edged a few inches, not daring to look down. How much safer she would have been if only she had not forgotten to take off her shoes! And why, why, *why* was she clutching her handbag?

Five minutes later, when her hands were beginning to whiten around the knuckles, when she was wondering whether to retreat, to wait until the end of the gas strike, to try some other less spectacular gambit, she heard a shrill scream in the street below.

With profound relief, she knew that rescue was imminent.

She heard a squeal of tires as a car stopped, then another, and another. A voice cried, "Cor! *Look!*" There was a sudden silence. Except for the dull roar of the distant traffic, the hum of the wind in the telegraph wires, the throb of a record from the dancing school on the fourth floor, it seemed that for an instant the neighborhood held its breath. Then there was a sudden babble of talk, followed, equally suddenly, by an even deeper hush.

An authoritative voice in the street shouted, "Get back there! Now move on now!" Another, "Oh, Fred Turner, *do* something! Get a rope!" Another, "Don't look, mother! Taxi! Taxi!" The dancing school record stopped abruptly in the middle of a bar.

She looked down. She had to. She knew it was unwise, but she could not resist it. She had suffered five hellish minutes. Why should she not now enjoy somebody else's discomfort?

Two constables were attempting to control the traffic. Buses and cars were parked haphazardly all over the road. People were swarming out of them, gazing upwards. The street band had lowered their instruments; the monkey had fallen off the drum. The barrowboy was running forward, yelling, "Go on, ma! 'Ave a bash!"

It was all much as she had imagined. At any moment now, the fire engines would arrive, the photographers, the reporters. She saw a man aiming a box camera. It was not enough. *Hold on! Wait for the Leicas, the Speed Graphics, the Long Toms, the flashes and the telescopic lenses! I can't! I'm terrified! Nonsense! You're perfectly safe, and you've got to!*

In the room behind her, she heard the door slam, then a crash. Somebody had knocked one of the telephones off her desk. She heard the dialling tone. Then a hand gripped her ankle, another grabbed a handful of her skirt.

A breathless, unrecognizable voice panted, "It's all right! I've got you!"

But it was much too soon to retreat. She threshed away from the clinging hands, kicked out at them. In the distance, she heard the clamor of a fire engine. She crouched, jabbed at the hands with her elbows, kicked again.

One of her shoes flew off. It fell in a slow arc, turning over and over. She was unable to take her eyes off it, mesmerized, for the first time giddy.

Her hands slipped on the rusty drainpipe. She snatched at it, and her hands slipped again. *Danger!* she thought. *Real danger! Must have been mad! Unsound mind! Get back! Get back while there's still time!*

Again, she reached wildly for the drainpipe and her fingers closed on nothing. Panic swept over her.

"Hold on!" she shouted. "Help me! *Save me!*"

Again the hands dragged at her, tugging at her knee, at her ankle, at her clothes, pulling, trying desperately to haul her to safety.

Whose? But she could not turn around. Her head felt as if it were revolving slowly a long way from her body. She felt the strength draining

out of her, falling, turning after that falling, turning shoe. There was nothing to hold on to. She was losing her balance, swaying towards nothing,
whirling nothing. Her head cleared for an instant, but it was already too
late. She was beyond rescue.

Incredibly, she was about to die! For a second, she thought of Harold's
relief and tried again without hope to save herself. For a second, she felt
the hot, frantic grappling of somebody's hands.

She flung out an arm and heard the window shatter behind her. A voice
said, "Here! Here! Quick!" She felt a tug at her skirt, then heard the
material tear.

"No!" she screamed soundlessly. "No, no, no, *no!*"

Then the sky and the earth and the buildings spun towards and away
and around her and she gave up all hope and flopped into space.

Chapter 2

THE proprietor of the Indian restaurant five floors below spoke with an
almost Welsh lilt. "I cannot tell you," he was saying, "how much animosity
is generated during my conversations with that chap."

His fat old mother glanced at the Singhalese waiter and nodded. "He is
a low category fellow," she agreed.

Then several things happened almost simultaneously.

A trailing, bubbling scream coincided with a sharp report, a grinding of
metal, a loud ripping of canvas. Another and louder scream rang out.

The two Indians, swinging around abruptly, for the first time noticed
the traffic jam, the jostling crowd beyond the plate glass windows.

A woman cried, "Fred! Oh, *Fred!*" rushed forward, her mouth wide
open, tripped on the curb, and fell on to the pavement.

Then the awning above the restaurant collapsed. Among its gaily striped
folds, Enid Marley lay still, white, twisted, clutching her handbag.

The Indian proprietor, after a moment of complete paralysis, seized his
mother by the shoulder and gave her a push which sent her reeling. "Now
ascertain the dame's demise and step on it!" he shouted. With his other
hand, he snatched the telephone and rang up Egon.

"Good gracious now!" he keened. "Such a *tamarsha*! Calamity, by
jingo! Marley memsahib has surely bitten dust! Now action there, man!"

Twelve seconds later and five floors above, Egon dropped the receiver
and left it swinging against his desk. "Why me?" he asked himself quietly.

"Why does everything happen to *me?*" *And naturally it had to be dear Enid*, he thought bitterly. *Typical, absolutely typical!*

Then the full horror of the catastrophe struck him. He sprang up, knocking over his chair, clamored into the passage, and bellowed for his staff.

Ellie Sansome, the Fashion Editor, looked around the neighboring door inquiringly. She wore pale corduroy and a green hat with a false apple on top of it. She was flapping one hand, trying to dry her newly applied silver nail varnish.

"What now, Mr. Egon, dear?" she asked.

Egon beckoned speechlessly, dragged at his tie, and stumbled back into his office. Ellie followed him. He was at the open drawer of a filing cabinet, pouring gin into a teacup. He waved a hand mutely towards the window.

Ellie raised her eyebrows. She perched on the sill and looked around. She saw the offices above the shops on the opposite side of the road, the blind walls of the buildings around the bomb site which was now a car park, an airplane trailing a plume of vapor in the sky.

"Ingenious, aren't they?" she said. "I can't think how they stay up."

Egon pointed downwards convulsively four times with his index finger.

Ellie looked down. She saw the crowd, three policemen trying to form a cordon, a man standing on the radiator of a car, craning. She leaned further out of the window and saw the crumpled awning on the pavement. A woman's leg and a piece of skirt stuck out from underneath it. The proprietor of the Indian restaurant, his pink turban askew, and a man in a duffle coat were trying to raise a snarled piece of metal, struggling with the canvas.

"My God!" she said. "What happened?"

"Zoom!" said Egon. He gulped gin and added, "*You* didn't deserve this. Splat!"

"*You?* Who is it?"

Egon passed a shaking hand over his unruly hair. "Enid," he whispered. "*Enid.*"

"Oh." Ellie noted the relief in her voice and said quickly, "Well, well!"

"Blease?" said Doctor Feltz from the doorway. "You gall me?" He was barely five feet tall. He had a fine head, a flurry of soft gray hair. He might have been any age from forty to eighty. One of the most valuable members of the staff of *You*, he wrote four columns under the names of *A. Friend, Sigmund Feltz (Viennese Psychiatrist), G.P.*, and – under an agency picture of a man with a ring in his nose – *Romany Nemo, Astrologer*.

Doon Travers, the Beauty Editor, was behind him, trying to sew a button on to his cuff. An inch taller than Doctor Feltz, she wore jeans and a red sweater. She said, "Doc, ducky, do keep still!"

Egon stood with his back to the window. Gray-faced, he signaled them forward, the gesture of a tired policeman waving on approaching traffic.

Doon went across to the window and peered out. She was determined, in the presence of Egon, not to put on her spectacles. This habit dated from an occasion, some years before, when he had ordered her to stop staring at him like a ruddy owl. She could therefore see downwards only as far as the fourth floor.

"Well," she said, carefully ambiguous. "That'll teach them not to cough in church!"

Doctor Feltz took her place. He looked down, drew a sharp, hissing breath, then sank into a chair holding on to his forehead as if it might fly apart.

Doon touched Ellie's hand. "What's the flap?" she murmured.

"She must have jumped."

"Jumped?"

"Yes, dear. Not to be tiresome."

"Who jumped where?"

"Madam. Window. Out of."

"Oh, corks!"

"Precisely."

Egon dragged a hand over his face, marched back into the passage, and broadcast a wordless roar.

Mrs. Ryder, the Cookery Editor, stumped from the corridor leading to the model kitchens. Her coarse white hair was, as usual, dishevelled and there was a smear of flour on her cheek. "Snap out of it Egon," she ordered gruffly. "What's up?"

In the room behind, two of the telephones began to ring simultaneously. Nobody answered them. Mrs. Ryder pulled off her food-stained overall and pushed past Egon.

Doctor Feltz was at the window, staring downwards, whispering to himself in some central European language. Mrs. Ryder looked over his shoulder. A tiny gasp escaped her, then her lips tightened. Calm as always in the face of disaster, she said briskly, "I'll make some tea," marched back into the corridor, and disappeared.

"You node?" Doctor Feltz asked hoarsely. "In sdade of shogg, we reveal always the vundamental . . ."

Paul East and Jimmie Simmons appeared in the doorway. Paul was *You*'s most popular fiction writer. He looked very much like one of his own lean, dangerous heroes. He said, "What gives? Who was baying?"

Jimmie, who was in charge of the photographic department, was, as usual, whistling soundlessly through his teeth. He raised toast-colored eyebrows, and waited.

Ellie jerked her head backward. "Madam passed thataway," she said.

Jimmie leaned out of the window. "Blimey!" he said, awed.

One of the telephones stopped ringing and immediately started again. Egon picked it up and shut it into a drawer.

Paul took Jimmie's place. "Oh, God!" he said. Then, "Who pushed her?"

Egon glared at him. "If you say that again," he growled, "No, no, *no!*"

"*Pushed?*" said Ellie. "You're mad, dear. Nobody would have touched her with a bargepole."

"She vell," said Doctor Feltz. "By aggzident."

"Maybe she jumped," suggested Jimmie.

"Mizadventure," pleaded Doctor Feltz.

"Suicide?" said Jimmie.

"Murder," said Paul East.

"*Shut up!*" roared Egon. He shut his eyes, laid hold of the lobes of his ears, and shook them. "Now listen, chums," he said slowly. "She *fell*, get it? We want a Misadventure verdict or we're out of business." As usual when trying to convert others to his way of thinking, he immediately began to doubt his own reasoning.

Inside the drawer, the telephone continued to ring. Egon opened the drawer and removed the receiver.

"You mean she just kind of sort of overbalanced?" Paul asked sarcastically. "Madam never opened a window in her life. Fresh air brought her out in a rash."

Egon glared at him. "If you say that again," he growled, "you're going to be out of a job quicker than I can fire you." He pointed his cigarette at each member of his staff in turn. "We're a fine team," he said warmly. "I love you, I love you all. Are we going to let a little thing like this bust us up?" He did not wait for an answer. He knew that the moment he stopped talking he would be gripped by doubts. "She was happy, she was drunk, she had vertigo. Is that so unreasonable?" He spread his hands. "You want *You* to fold? You want us all to starve? You want us to spend our cold and hungry nights on the Embankment wrapped up in somebody else's crummy publication?" *ME, for instance*, he thought, and clenched his hands. "Be fair, be reasonable! Will you please forget this fresh air stuff? Will you do that little thing?"

"Her husband won't," said Paul.

Egon lost his temper. When this happened, he either turned an apoplectic mauve or went a ghastly gray. Either he started smashing up his office or he succumbed to immense lassitude and a partial rigor. Now, he paled, fell into a chair, and sprawled listlessly across his desk.

"We musd dezzend," urged Doctor Feltz. "Ad wunze."

"Chums," said Egon, rearing like a tired cobra. "Please, please, watch yourselves. Say how awful, how sad, how terrible, then keep your traps shut. By this time the Big Five will be there. As a team, let's have a stab at Misadventure, mm? If some swine's found a clue, we gradually introduce Suicide. Soft pedal it. Nothing of interest to a lurking journalist. Nothing definite, nothing chatty, nothing squalid. Remember we don't want Suicide, and I absolutely refuse to have Murder."

"You'll get Suicide if she left a note," said Paul.

Egon looked at him with sudden respect. "Ah, yes, indeed," he said. "Go up top, old man." He rose and left the room, turning right towards Enid Marley's office.

Paul ground out his cigarette. "Would he tamper with evidence?"

"He'd burn down the whole block to boost *You*," said Ellie. "Hands up who cares."

"We'll care good and proper if we get a Murder verdict," said Paul. "This is no Misadventure. And if there's no note, it's not Suicide." He ran into the corridor. "Egon!" he shouted. "Egon, *wait!*"

"This I *must* see," said Ellie. She adjusted her hat and departed.

Doctor Feltz followed her without a word.

Doon looked at Jimmie. "Ducky," she said. "Isn't it awful? Nobody gives a damn."

"Egon does."

"Only because *You* may pack up."

"And Doc does."

"Only because he hates rough stuff."

"And I do."

"You do not."

Jimmie scratched his sand-colored crew cut. He said defensively, "Well, how can you mourn for Madam? How *can* you?"

Doon said, "*I* can't, I admit it freely. She was *nause*." She took his arm and blinked up at him. "Shall we go and look for helpful clues?"

"You mean Misadventure clues?"

"I don't know. Whatever."

"Some clues are absolutely tiny. You'd better wear your specs."

"No. You can ferret around for both of us."

In Enid Marley's office, Egon was shouting above the persistence of the telephones, haranguing a dark, plump girl named Sylvia, a secretary from *Me*. Paul had emptied the wastepaper basket on to the floor and was purposefully going through its contents, smoothing out the crumpled papers, attempting to piece together the torn-up shreds. His attitude and fierce expression were based upon the illustration printed opposite to his latest short story. The difference was that Spike Raven, the toughest of his three sleuths, always found what he was looking for.

"Oh, *no*, Mr. Egon," Sylvia was saying. "There were just two letters in her OUT tray. One from that Browneyes, and the answer. But nothing else, not a sausage. I addressed the answer and posted it just a moment ago."

"Okay, scram, dear," said Egon absently, patting her round behind.

"All that mail every day," she said. "Whatever are you going to do?"

"I said scram, dear." Egon leapt suddenly to his feet, crouched slightly and yelled, "*Go on! Beat it, you cretin!*"

She waggled her hips angrily and left, slamming the door behind her.

"Now, blease," said Doctor Feltz. "We musd, I rebead *musd*, dezzend. The boleeze will thing id is too fonny. Blease! *Ad ones!*"

Going down in the shaking lift to the scene of the disaster, it suddenly occurred to Egon that, in fact, Murder might not be the most punishing of the three possible verdicts. Dragging at his cigarette, he pondered.

Misadventure, at face value, was obviously the most desirable of the three. WEST END DEATH FALL, the headlines would shout. Or, JOURNALIST PLUNGES FIVE FLOORS! Neat, but not gaudy. Bad, in that Enid Marley's publicized death would strike a telling blow at the London circulation. Good, in that the news might not reach the roots of *You*'s dodgy existence, the provinces.

But slowly, surely, the story would seep down shaggy country lanes, over wind-torn moors, to the last strongholds, the islands where mail was dropped once a week from helicopters. Within six weeks it would have reached the last survivor in the last marooned lighthouse – desperate not for food, but for Enid Marley's advice. But long, long before that *You* would be dead and buried.

Anyway, Misadventure, if Paul refused to cooperate, was no longer feasible. Egon smeared out his cigarette down the wall of the lift. Suppose he somehow got rid of Paul, now, immediately? Suppose he fired him? Suppose he kidnapped him, locked him up somewhere? Suppose he doped him, trussed him up in a crate, and sent him to his aunt in Wales?

No, Misadventure was out.

Suicide, upon reflection, would from every point of view be disastrous. ORACLE CAN'T TAKE IT, JUMPS! Or, worse, a White Paper issued by the

Stationery Office – *The Press and Applied Psychiatry*. Being the better story, it had a better chance of reaching the provincial papers. It would not only cripple circulation everywhere, and immediately, but it would also be an astringent comment upon staff conditions.

But anyway Suicide was also out. Suicides left farewell notes, and Enid Marley had not done so. And she, of all people, would never have missed the opportunity of giving Egon a final piece of her mind.

No Suicide.

All right, then, Murder. If it had to be Murder, then he must take it and like it. But what was there in it for *You*? Sage Hurled Sixty Feet! Or, Mystery Slaying Of Ask–Me Columnist! A splendid story rating front pages all over the country! The publicity! Overnight, the names of the staff, all under suspicion, would become household words. Until the fatal phrase, "The police believe that somebody or other may be able to help them in their inquiries," the word *You* would be on every tongue.

Silent or perhaps booing crowds would loiter outside the building. How many, from morbid curiosity, would buy the magazine? How many, caught like flies in amber, would become lifelong subscribers? Would *You*, publicized on such a scale, at last have the chance which had been denied to it at birth? Would *You*, finally, oust *Me*? Would *Me*, eventually, be transferred to the smaller premises and forced to accept *You*'s rejected material?

Egon lit another cigarette. "Listen, kids," he said, making up his mind. "Let's face it, she was unhappy, she didn't drink, and she never had vertigo. Let's tell 'em the truth."

Paul said, "What about the fresh air?"

"The air too," said Egon smoothly. He blew smoke up his nostrils and distributed his sudden brilliant smile. "But remember to forget the drink, mm?"

"That's Murder," said Paul. He nodded approvingly.

Egon did not answer. As the lift shivered to a stop, he pulled open the gate. "Scrub the drink," he warned fiercely, and headed for the archway and the street.

Around the Indian restaurant, there was a small crowd of people talking in low voices. A policeman was calling without hope, "Now come on now. Nothing to see. Now move on now."

Egon pushed forward impatiently, causing some resentment.

"Plain clothes written all over 'im," murmured a woman on his left.

"Would of been the spleen, see," remarked her neighbor. "Everything ruptured, the *lot*. Mean, drop a grapefruit off a roof an' . . ."

"Said they was takin' 'er to St. German's, sir," volunteered a man in dungarees. And added, shaking his head slowly, "That's where they killed my two."

Egon stepped into the clear space in front of the restaurant. The policeman surged towards him. "Keep back there, sir," he said. "Right back, please."

"I'm *You*," said Egon.

The crumpled red and white canvas and the buckled steel of the awning still sprawled on the pavement. A small bay tree lay overturned, the soil spilt out of its tub. The stubby heel of a woman's shoe lay in the gutter. There was no body, no blood.

"The sergeant's inside, sir," said the policeman, "This way, sir."

Egon looked back. His staff hesitated on the fringe of the crowd, waiting for orders. Paul raised his eyebrows. Egon shook his head, turned, and followed the policeman.

Inside the restaurant, there was an overpowering smell of burnt curry. The proprietor, highly excited, was alternately telling the sergeant what he had witnessed and crying, presumably to himself, "Please now! No bedlam there!" The Singhalese waiter lolled in the service hatch, scratching his armpit.

The proprietor saw Egon and waved a speckled menu. "What ho!" he called. "I warned you to look slippy! You have missed the entire occurrence. Body transported, ambulance vamoosed! Impossible to describe the horror of the occasion! She descended upon her like a sack of mangoes . . ."

"What? Who?"

"Me, naturally, I am insured, but . . ."

"Who descended on who? What do you mean?"

"Retain your hair, man! The other, of course. Oh, good gracious, what a spree!"

Egon seized the man by the lapel. "*What* other?"

"One she fell on, sir," said the constable.

"Oh, yes, indeed!" said the Indian. "She will pushing up daisies in two shakes now."

Egon began to dance with anxiety and frustration. "*Who* will, damn you?"

"So dense, man? The other, the *other!*"

"Afraid she bought it fair and square, sir," said the constable. "Slap underneath. Mrs. Fred Turner, the name was."

Egon drew a long breath. "Where's Mrs. Marley?" he demanded in a carefully controlled voice. "St. German's, mm?"

"Oh, some people!" said the Indian, rolling his eyes upwards. "No, man, *no!* That was the *other*."

"Mrs. Marley's all right, sir," said the sergeant. "Not a scratch! Canvas and Mrs. Turner between them broke her fall. She grabbed a taxi and made off. Bad show, that."

"Ah, but other ill-starred dame!" cried the Indian. He raised his shoulders and spread his hands. "Trapped beneath my awning, bashed by the joists, snuffed like a candle!"

The sergeant told Egon, "We have an inspector coming from the C.I.D., sir. He'll want to ask you a few questions."

The Indian clasped his hands and remarked with satisfaction, "Oh, jiggery-pokery! What a case for the dicks, eh? Tell me now, what *is* it by the Law? Homicide? Suicide? Or good old Accident? Me, personally, if asked, I would say it was surely all three. Like we used to say in college, *the whole bloody works!*"

Chapter 3

FIFTEEN minutes later, the staff of *You* had retired upstairs again. They sat behind the closed door of Enid Marley's office, waiting for the man from the C.I.D. They spoke in low voices because there were reporters in the corridor.

Egon sat at the desk, propping up his cheekbones with his thumbs. Two cigarettes smoldered in the ashtray between his elbows. Mrs. Ryder stumped around dispensing hot, red tea.

"She was pushed," said Paul for the third time. "I'm not being difficult or blaming anybody . . ."

"Who wouldn't have grabbed the opportunity to bump her off discreetly?" asked Doon with her usual appalling honesty. "Name one."

Mrs. Ryder hovered. "Sugar? Milk?"

"It was *not* Murder," Ellie said impatiently. "She's not dead."

Paul said, "That doesn't alter the principle of the thing."

"By now," Jimmie remarked heavily, "this Mrs. Fred Turner will have kicked off. Now is *that* Murder?"

"Assuming that it is," Doon said, "then who's responsible? Madam? Or whoever pushed her, or somehow sort of both, if you see what I mean?"

"Suicide's a felony," murmured Egon. "I wish we could make Suicide stick."

"You haven't a hope," said Paul.

"Sugar? Milk?"

"Suppose we assume that the second one was Suicide," Jimmie began helpfully.

"Oh, shut *up!*" snapped Egon.

There was a long pause.

Doctor Feltz asked faintly, "What hoff we levt, blease?"

Paul consulted his notebook, ticking off each item with a pencil. "Attempted Murder and Misadventure, Attempted Murder and Manslaughter, Attempted Murder and Murder; Attempted Suicide and Misadventure, Attempted Suicide and Manslaughter, Attempted Suicide and Murder; Misadventure and Murder, Misadventure and Suicide, and double Misadventure."

"Milk?"

Egon lit a cigarette and laid it between the other two in the ashtray. "Naturally she had to pick an office cleaner," he said bitterly. "Where's the story? Where's the drama? Why not a deb, or a film star, or some chap from the Gas Workers' Union? But no! No, she has to dive at some drone unknown to science."

"Dive?" said Ellie. "Are you still hankering after Suicide? It won't *do*, Mr. Egon, dear. It simply will not do."

The phone rang.

Egon removed it from the drawer and scooped up the receiver. "Wrong number," he said sternly. Then, "Who? Oh. Yes, good morning." Behind his hand, he informed his staff, "This is it, kids. It's the Holy Hun Hospital. The latest on Mrs. Fred expendable Turner."

Doon reached for Jimmie's hand. Mrs. Ryder stood with a teacup halfway to her mouth. Doctor Feltz took an involuntary step forward, bumped into Paul, who said, "Sorry, Doc." Ellie sat pale-faced, staring at Egon.

"Yes, of course," Egon told the telephone. His face seemed to have grown smaller and there were beads of sweat on his forehead. "That's tough. Too bad. Rotten. Lousy. Terrible. *What?* Oh. That's fine. Good. Grand. Splendid. Marvelous. Goodbye." He replaced the receiver and lay back in his chair. He closed his eyes and rubbed the bridge of his nose with his middle finger.

"Mrs. Fred Turner," he said in a stifled voice, "has a broken arm, no more. It's been set very satisfactorily and she feels fine. Cross off Murder."

In the casualty ward in St German's Hospital, Mrs. Turner floated reluctantly back to consciousness. Dreamily, she noted the dark green walls, the rows of white-enameled beds, her husband sitting on a chair beside her and watching her with unblinking awe.

She attempted to sit up. "Fred," she said weakly. "I got struck by lightnin'. What's all this white muck on me arm?"

"That French plaster." He added, "I come 'ere in a police car. Sat in front."

She struggled with the sheets. "Don't 'alf feel queer, Fred. 'S not 'ypochondria, honest. Feels quite different."

"She bust your arm," he said. A shrill note crept into his reedy voice. "Jumps at you off the roof."

She sat up, her mouth ajar, gazing at her arm. She realized slowly that it stood for a prolonged rest from her office cleaning and the horrible mess at home. "'Ow long do they take?" she asked, smiling, unable to conceal her delight.

He had asked the same question of the matron and had not understood her answer. "Depends," he said.

She settled herself comfortably back among the pillows, said, "Well, I don't know," then sat up again with a jerk. "Oh Fred," she wailed. "Whatever'll we do about *Tinker*?"

By half past two the pile of mail addressed to Enid Marley had swamped her IN tray and was flowing over her desk. The man from the C.I.D. had been and gone. He had introduced himself as Inspector Woodman. He had asked few questions. Since nobody had been killed or even seriously injured, he clearly thought that the affair, at this stage, deserved no more than fifteen minutes of routine inquiry. He had examined the broken window, advised Egon to put up bars, demanded Enid Marley's home address, and departed.

The reporters, however, scented a story. Five of them still lounged in the corridor occasionally kicking the closed door and baying for Egon. The only woman among them had three times gone downstairs and rung up *You*, but each time the girl at the switchboard had crooned, "Sorry, they don't *arn*-ser."

From time to time, the youngest and most impatient of the reporters tried to force open the door, but Mrs. Ryder was sitting on a chair just inside it. Once she had snapped, "Where are your manners, you young puppy?" and he had retired abashed.

In Enid Marley's office, the telephones, both shut into drawers, rang, stopped, clamored again.

Egon sat hopelessly. He knew that his staff was watching him, waiting for his decision. Once, Paul had suggested that everybody went back to work, but Egon had shaken his head. He realized that the fate of *You* hung in the balance, that he must rouse himself, shake off his confusion, give orders coolly for some fearful yet calculated risk.

He could not afford to offend the Press. Therefore he dared not allow anybody to leave the room until he had decided upon the most tactful, the most profitable story. He knew that he must think, hard and at once. But he was unable to concentrate upon anything except the fact that tomorrow was his birthday.

Sooner or later, he would have to face the hyenas in the corridor. They would greet him with a barrage of questions, insist upon taking photographs of Enid Marley's small, bleak office, which only last week he had described in an editorial as "luxurious."

He wondered whether the five outside would become intimate acquaintances. If he refused to talk or tried to fob them off with some noncommittal statement, would they follow him home? Would they invite him to sit down in his own flat, cook his food, open his letters, use his toothpaste? Would they doze like dogs, one eye open, on the floor around his bed, in case he should talk in his sleep?

It was possible. Therefore he had to talk and at some length. No "Sorry, no comment," no dumb crambo, no "Look, kids, give me a break – right now I spikkit only da Angostura." No, he had to talk.

But what the hell was he to say?

The story, without even one death to lend it dignity or drama, was absurd. Worse, it was downright comical. It would provoke the surrealist in even the most sober journalist.

"Huh!" he sneered.

"Yes?" said Mrs. Ryder. "Seen the light?"

Egon scowled at her. A sudden urge for action, the imperative need to do something, however unpromising, made him snatch up one of the ringing telephones. "Yes?" he barked. Then, clearing his throat, "Oh, good afternoon, matron!" He sat listening barely breathing then nodded politely and replaced the receiver. "Our broken arm has just eaten some steamed fish," he told his staff tonelessly. "It is now asking for Tinker."

Paul frowned. "Tinker?"

"I don't know," said Egon. "I don't *care*. Don't ask me."

The youngest of the reporters forced the door open and inserted his head. "Have a heart, buddy," he said. "I have to cover this flood in Essex."

Mrs. Ryder threw her weight backwards on her chair. The reporter withdrew his head hastily. The door slammed.

Egon picked up the first telephone, demanded a number. He heard the girl at the switchboard knitting, wondered for an instant whether to sack her, and decided against it.

"Private residence of Mrs. Enid Marley," came the voice of Mrs. Pickett, the charwoman. "'Er 'usband's gone off with this girl an' she's got an 'eadache an' she can't talk to nobody. What you want?"

Egon said, "It's important. This is Doctor Palmerston."

"Well, I dunno," said Mrs. Pickett. "I'll see."

Egon waited, glaring at the ceiling, knowing that he was probably about to make a disastrous mistake, yet quite unable to contain himself.

"'Ere I am," announced Mrs. Pickett. "She says to say you aren't Doctor Palmerston at all 'cos 'e's washin' 'is 'ands in the toilet."

Egon at once assumed a falsetto voice. "Was just a joke," he lisped. "Course I'm not Doctor Palmerston, you silly thing! I'm Mags, Cornwall."

"Orright," said Mrs. Pickett placidly. "I'll see."

Egon found himself trying to bend and break a kirbigrip in Enid Marley's pen tray. He considered it, wondering whether it was a clue, then threw it out of the broken window.

"Mags, my dear," cooed Enid Marley's public voice in his ear. "Now what are you up to this time?"

"Ah, Enid," said Egon pleasantly. "How do you feel, dear? Aren't you a *one*, though? And landing slap on your feet like a ruddy cat! Well, eight lives to go, mm? What?" He knew that he was about to lose his temper. He closed his eyes, fighting against it, but he knew that it was inevitable. "Yes," he said. "Yes indeed, little Mags is right beside me being sick into her handbag." Suddenly, convulsively, he bellowed, "Listen, you phony know-all, you electroplated mother-figure, you double-breasted hag! You're fired! Fired, fired, fired! BANG, get it! Mm? *Mmm?*"

Enid Marley's migraine and her hatred of Egon were both so stupendous that this news had little effect on her. She went back into her bedroom, slid beneath the eiderdown, ate three aspirins, and forced herself to think.

On her wild escape from Croissant Street, bruised, in a state of shock and rage, she had thought only of reaching the privacy of her own home. The fact that she had been recognized by the proprietor of the Indian restaurant had automatically made her pause briefly to apologize to the unconscious woman trapped beneath the awning. Then she had staggered to her feet and lurched through the gathering crowd. Hobbling, one shoe lost, she had clawed open the door of a taxi and panted, "Get me out of here! Faster, *faster!*"

Oh, the shame, the humiliation!

Enid Marley, symbol of hope and sanity to a million lost souls, had at last fallen from her fifth floor pedestal! She had flopped on to a littered pavement, ungainly, uncouth, ridiculously alive!

She remembered one of Browneyes' – or was it Mags's? who cared? to hell with them both! – early letters. *I know you'll laugh, but you're so good and wise. I always think of you sort of sitting on a cloud!* No, she had not laughed. But now Browneyes and Mags, and the others in their countless thousands would forever think of her scrabbling in the gutter, a buffoon. *They* would laugh.

What a fool she had been! While of Unsound Mind *indeed*! Why, oh why, had she not looked at her problem objectively, as she had looked at so many other identical ones? Why had she not consulted her charts? What splendid advice they would have given her! Or would they?

My dear, they would have told her. *The tone of your letter suggests that you may be "run down". It could do no harm to consult your medical advisor. Could you not get away for a short holiday? Nobody is indispensable, you know! I'm sure that a change would make you see things in a different perspective!*

Good God, what nonsense!

Rubbish! Of course it wasn't nonsense! It was URG 8/4, the most popular, the most successful of all her replies, the one which had won her at least five hundred slavish fans.

But suppose, as a fan, she had written to herself and neglected to enclose a stamped, addressed envelope? Then she would not have answered herself for several weeks. And even suppose she had answered herself by return of post, had rushed off for some infernal holiday, would that, in the long run, have really helped either?

Yes, of course!

Honestly?

No. But she would have done her best. For how could she possibly have assessed her circumstances from one wild letter? How could she have known that this one, calmer in tone than nine hundred and ninety-nine others, was the one which meant business?

But she was one of the nine hundred and ninety-nine! She had *not* meant business. And if she had written to herself, at length and disclosing all, declaring that she intended to fake a suicide, then she would have sighed and wearily reported herself to the nearest police station. For Attempted Suicide, legally, was a criminal offense. She, Enid Marley, grinning benignly on her cloud, had committed a crime!

Impossible!

Damn Harold! Damn him!

Let them prove it! She would deny until she was black in the face and hell froze over that she had had any intention whatever of committing suicide.

It had been an accident, a horrible experience which might have happened to anybody, anybody at all. *Just bad luck, Inspector! Thank God, Inspector, that I was spared . . .* and so on and on and et cetera, et cetera.

No crime, no shame, no prosecution.

Accident.

But would Accident hold water? *Think, think!* Suppose she claimed that she had been at her window, enjoying the sunshine? No, there were fifty witnesses who would testify that she hated and feared drafts, that she avoided fresh air like the plague. Why, then, had she opened that blasted window?

Why?

It was because of a bird, Inspector, a baby bird. I can't watch suffering, Inspector, I just can't. The poor wee mite had caught its little foot – beak, neck tail? – in . . . in something or other. I couldn't stand it. I just had to save it, I *had* to. And so on.

Too implausible? No. The British public were incurably sentimental about all the birds they did not shoot.

Just a fledgling, Sir, Your Lordship, M'lud, Your Good Honour, or whatever you called the old fools. It only had one leg – wing, eye, head? Then, ringing voice, "Your et cetera, I believe, indeed I *know* that every human man and woman in this room – Court, country, lovely land of ours? – would have without hesitation done exactly as I did . . ."

Yes?

No. For how could she explain the farewell note laid so prominently in her OUT tray?

And what – a new and shattering thought! – about the owner of those hands which had tried so frantically to save her? Whose, *whose*, WHOSE?

Somebody knew her shameful secret. Somebody knew that she had had not the remotest intention of committing suicide, that there had been no bird, that she had cried, "Hold on! Help me! *Save me!*" Some monster *knew*.

Who?

Perhaps he or she had already blurted out the silly story. *She was just standing there, Inspector. I suppose she was going to jump, but she can't have been because she yelled, "Save me!" But she must have been because when I tried to, she kicked me!* Or was he or she nursing the knowledge, waiting to blackmail her?

Wait!

There *was* a way out. One, only one.

The farewell note? It was typed, signed with a rubber stamp. Obviously, she could claim indignantly, a forgery! And her charwoman, Mrs. Pickett? The episode of the gas oven? That too could be dealt with. The old doxie forgot most things immediately and would forget anything she had ever known in her entire life for ten shillings.

Yes, it might work. It *had* to work. It was the only way.

Enid Marley ate two more aspirins, relaxed among her pillows, and smiled.

Twenty-five minutes later, Mrs. Pickett ushered in two men in no-colored mackintoshes. Enid Marley lay limp and pale. There was a hot water bottle at her feet, an icebag on her head. By the window, Doctor Palmerston was sawing the head off an ampoule.

"Couple o' rozzers, dear," announced Mrs. Pickett. She was in no way alarmed by the presence of the police. She saw too much of them. They were always in and out of her house, bringing catastrophic news about one of her clan, expecting tea, mucking up the lino. She looked pointedly at the boots of these two, cleared her throat in a menacing manner, and left the room.

"Do sit down," murmured Enid Marley faintly. "Please don't scold me for running away. I know it was unforgivable. I'm so ashamed." She pushed the hair off her forehead, an infinitely weary gesture, drew a long, shuddering breath, and added hoarsely, "I was at my window, enjoying God's sunshine. Such a beautiful day! It was good to be alive. Then, to my horror, I saw a sparrow . . ." She knew a moment of horrid doubt. Why had she said a *sparrow*? Hadn't the damn things migrated? Or was that larks?

"A sparrow," prompted the older one.

"Yes," she said, reassured. "Just a fledgling, Inspector." She gave him a small, sad smile. "Inspector *what?*"

"Woodman."

"I adore birds," she said. "Humble robins, soaring hawks, great proud eagles."

The two men had remained standing. Woodman looked at her through half-shut eyes. "And this sparrow?" he asked.

"Poor sweet, it fluttered on to the drainpipe. It got its tiny foot caught somehow. It was terrified, desperate. Tweet, tweet, tweet!" She laid a hand along her right cheek and bit her lip.

Woodman watched her impassively.

"It was terrible," she whispered. "Terrible." She blew her nose, blinking, and said, "I'm sorry. I'm dreadfully upset. I had to save it, I just *had* to. I opened the window . . . and before I really knew what I was doing, I'd climbed on to the sill. . . ."

They waited. Woodman asked, "You're not affected by heights?"

She clasped her hands together. "Yes," she sighed. "Yes, I am. I know it's silly. I just can't help it. I grabbed the drainpipe. I held on tightly. I couldn't move. I tried to scream but . . ."

"Yes?"

"My voice had gone."

"I see."

"And then . . ."

"Go on," he said.

"And then . . . oh, Inspector, if you were a woman, you'd understand! I was suddenly conscious of a . . . I can't describe it . . . of an uneasiness, a prickling of the scalp, a definite alarm, of a malign *something* behind me."

"Oh?"

"Before I could turn round . . ." She clutched her throat and said tragically, "I'm sorry, I can't go on."

"Take your time, my dear," said Doctor Palmerston.

She took it. She counted slowly up to three hundred and fifty before she raised her head and levered herself, grunting, on to one elbow. "It's incredible," she said in a choked whisper. "Unbelievable! I just . . . I just know . . . I just know that . . ."

She fell back among the pillows and lay there breathing heavily. "I hate to make this terrible accusation," she panted. "But I must tell you, Inspector Woodman, that I have good reason to believe that . . . *that I was murdered!*"

Chapter 4

HALF an hour later, as Inspector Woodman left Enid Marley's office in the *You* and *Me* building for the second time that day, Egon reached for his gin. So it was Murder again, was it? So he had spent the last two and a half hideous hours talking himself back into Misadventure, had he?

"Kids," he said, eyeing his staff. "Are we going to give up Misadventure without a struggle? It's only Enid who's yelling Murder. She's outnumbered seven to one."

"Six," said Paul.

"What?"

"Six to one. I'm for Murder."

Egon ran a hand through his hair. "All right," he said, glaring around the room. "Let's get this straight, let's know how we stand. Hands up for Murder!"

Paul raised his cigarette. Nobody else moved.

Egon stared at Paul. He said persuasively, "Come on, old chap! Change your mind. Be a rotter."

Paul said, "I'll play ball. I just want you to know that I know that you know it's Murder."

"Well, now I know."

"I'm glad."

"I'm glad too."

"Good."

"Have you quite finished?"

"Yes."

"Fine." Egon lowered his head and began to pace around the desk. He was halted by the huge pile of mail addressed to Enid Marley, which had now overflowed the IN and OUT trays and was stacking up on the floor. He stood making popping noises with his mouth, looking at it hopelessly. Who was to deal with it?

Ellie said helpfully, "You'll have to hire someone, Mr. Egon, dear. Now comes fascinating problem. Who do we know who couldn't possibly be a reporter or a police spy? Who can we trust implicitly? Who loves long hours and hates money? Who wants to meet a murderer?"

"How about a relative?" suggested Paul.

Egon thought briefly of his kind, helpful aunts, and the hair rose on the back of his neck.

"A reladive?" sneered Doctor Feltz explosively. "Drust a reladive? Very fonny! Ha!" He realized that his colleagues were staring at him, flushed, and added gently, "Of gourse id is nod the same here."

There was a heavy pause.

"I know!" said Doon suddenly. "My twin!"

"Of course!" said Paul and Ellie simultaneously.

Egon drummed his fingers on the desk. "Loyal?"

"An absolute darling," said Doon.

"Intelligent?"

"Oh yes, terrifically."

"Egghead?"

"No, no."

"Do this or that as told?"

"Well, mostly."

Egon hesitated. Doubts buzzed in his mind like a swarm of bees looking for a new hive. "Available immediately?"

"Yes." Doon understood Egon's difficulty. Every member of the staff knew that although he had fired Enid Marley, he had also fired her, with equal relish, fifteen times before. It had long been understood that after each dismissal she would wait a decent period, then return to her office as if she had never left it.

Ellie said tactfully, "But only temporarily."

"Suspended," Doon explained.

Egon frowned. "I don't understand you."

Doon said, "Well, there was this barking great row backstage. You know how it is."

"No." Egon was past caring. He clicked his fingers impatiently. "Okay, okay! Get her."

"Him."

"What?"

"Him. Rex. My brother."

A pulse began to beat steadily in Egon's right temple. He knew that this was the last straw, that he must escape at once to the quiet, healing squalor of his own home before he lost his temper. He blundered around the desk, through the pile of spilt mail, towards the door.

He grabbed it open and stormed into the corridor. He stood for a moment expecting trouble, prepared to knock down anyone who so much as glanced at him.

Countless cigarette ends were scattered over the linoleum. A torn playing card, an afternoon paper, a broken pencil, and an empty bottle of whisky lay abandoned. But the four male reporters had disappeared. The woman, who had been leaning wearily against a fire extinguisher, darted forward.

"Mr. Egon!" she cried. "Give a girl a break! What was she *wearing*?"

"Tweed rig," said Egon at random. "Seed pearls, army boots."

"Thanks, pal." She streaked ahead of him down the passage.

When Egon arrived at the shaft, he stood listening to the slow, rasping descent of the lift. It was an antique contraption. Only one man in London, the janitor, equally old and temperamental, had any affection for it or knew how to deal with its senile tantrums. Egon heard the cage clanking and wheezing past each floor. He heard it crunch to a standstill at street level. He heard the woman reporter hurriedly clash the gate. He was propped against the wall, a hand over his eyes, when he heard the almost inaudible sound which he had been dreading – the soft little double click as the faulty grille slipped its catch and creaked open that half inch which was enough to put the lift out of action.

He had started down the stairs when he heard voices around the corner in the corridor above him.

"I *told* him it was Murder," said Paul. "Didn't he get quite keen on it?"

"Absolutely," said Doon. "Keen as mustard."

"Really, loves, you are peasants," said Ellie. "Didn't you notice Misadventure double back on him?"

Doon said, "Well, personally, I don't think bumping off Madam *counts*."

"Tut, my dear!" said Ellie. "You must not, absolutely *not* tell that to the dicks. You'll wind up in jug quick as a flash. Mugs, tin plates. And, oh God, think of all those carbohydrates!"

It was the rush hour. The bus queue was a long one. Three buses roared up, all full, and roared off again. Doon, Paul, and Ellie got on to the sixth. "No standin' on top!" shouted the conductor. "Sorry, dear, no dogs."

A man in a bowler hat offered Ellie his seat. Paul and Doon stood, Doon clinging to the belt of his mackintosh. Paul stared out of the window, reviewing the events of the disastrous day. Murder! And no ordinary, decent, straightforward Murder, either! A sloppy job which left the corpse alive and kicking, in a position of new power.

Doon said, "That man's paying Ellie's fare."

"I'll pay yours."

"It's not the *same*."

Ellie was not listening to the man in the bowler hat. She carried a large manila envelope containing the photographs of the Rome winter dress collections and a roll of the Marley charts in a cardboard cylinder. But her mind was not upon the article she had to write that evening, nor on the Marley affair. She was praying silently that she was not about to fall in love with Egon.

Although nobody studying her fashionably angular profile would have suspected it, she was subject to sudden and devastating infatuations. While outwardly composed, she would swoon and yearn inwardly for the most unlikely people. These maladies, if not encouraged by the object of her affections, lasted from three to eight days. She would lose weight, mostly off her face, neck, and bust.

Egon had said, "I love you." It was a habit of his. He said it many times a day, to all and sundry. That morning, just after the Murder or Misadventure or Suicide or whatever it was, he had been speaking to the entire staff. But had he not smiled at her in a private manner?

Ellie was not sure. But she was prepared for at least a week of exquisite torture and the loss of about eight pounds, which in her present state of emaciation she could not becomingly afford. She did not want to go and have a drink with Doon and Rex. She would have preferred to go home and type out a list of reasons why Egon was awful.

But she got off the bus with the other two in silence. They turned right. Paul bought three newspapers on the corner.

The front page of the first was dominated by a large, streaky photograph of a murdered man lying behind a bush with an eminent pathologist bending over him. The Marley story was in the Stop Press column. *Mrs. E. Marley*, it was announced, *fell uninjured today from a window in Croissant Street, W 1. Mrs. F. Turner was detained in hospital.*

"*Fell*," noted Ellie. "Egon *will* be pleased. That's Misadventure."

The second paper was preoccupied equally with the gas strike and what it called the THIRD BUSH MURDER! A small paragraph at the foot of page three was headed *Columnist Dives Ninety Feet Unhurt!*

"*Dives?*" Doon polished her spectacles. "Oh corks! That's Suicide!"

In the last paper, the banner headline concerned the flood in Essex. There was a photograph of a man named Guy Kayes whom the police wished to interview in connection with the Bush murders. Tucked away towards the bottom of the page, in a small italic type, were the words *YOU Fall Mystery.*

At 9.30 a.m. this morning, reported the column beneath, *Enid Marley, well-known solve-your-problems consultant, plunged eighty feet from the fifth floor window of her office in London's fashionable West End. Tragedy was averted by an awning which broke her fall, saved her life. She reached the pavement miraculously unharmed. Mrs. F. Turner, however, office cleaner, of Abbingdon Road, SE, was trapped beneath the fallen structure, removed to hospital with multiple injuries. The police have issued no statement, but it is understood from reliable sources that they have not yet discarded the theory of foul play.*

Paul stuffed the paper into his pocket. "Well, there it is," he said. "Our old chum, Murder."

They walked on. They crossed the road and turned left into a quiet square with a trim garden in the middle of it. The house which Rex had inherited from his dreadful stepmother was the third on the right. It was tall, ungainly, with steps up to the front door. In startling contrast to its sober neighbors, it was painted pink. Its woodwork was a brilliant lime green, and yellow flowers sprouted in the window boxes.

They climbed the steps. Doon fumbled for her key. For the first time she began to wish that she had not suggested that her brother should take over Enid Marley's job. If he refused, she would have to face Egon's fury in the morning. And Rex, at times, could be extremely difficult and stubborn.

"We may have to work on him," she murmured.

"It's for his own good," said Paul as if he had been contradicted.

"And Sammy's, I mean Egon's," said Ellie, and added quickly, "And ours."

"Best all round," said Paul without conviction.

"Yes."

"Well then."

"Make it sound *gay*," said Doon. "And frightfully *easy*."

"We start with the oblique approach?"

"No, no. Velvet-fist-in-iron-glove."

Rex was in the sitting room. He was lounging on a saffron, tweed-covered couch and darning a pair of black tights. His bright hair was ruffled and his mouth drooped. Since he had been suspended from the ballet company in which he had played second leads for a number of years, he had been plunged in gloom. He was deeply depressed. He felt ill-treated, unwanted, unloved, lonely, bored, old, ugly, fat, and doomed.

He glanced at the clock. It was the time when he normally began to think about leaving for the theater, the time for the last hectic rush, the hurly-burly of the Underground, the quick appraisal of the queue outside the Pit, the backstage bickering, the makeup, the limbering up in the wings . . .

And worse, far worse, his friend and rival, Neville, had taken over his roles and was, one critic had said, dancing them quite adequately. Rex sighed. *Tonight*, he prayed, *let Neville muff the lift! Let him get his legs snarled up in the* pas de quatre*! Please, please, let him come a clanging great purler right at the beginning of the solo!*

He was re-threading his needle when he heard voices in the hall. He sprang up and flung open the door with an expansive gesture. "Paul!" he beamed. "Ellie! Rush in, you delicious creatures! Let me give you a handful of jolly gin!"

Half an hour later, he stood staring out of the window at the darkening square. A good listener, he had heard out the Marley story in silence. "Who pushed her?" he asked as Paul finished.

Paul looked at Doon. "You notice he immediately assumes it was Murder?"

Rex defended himself. "Madam's got Kill-Me written all over her. Who did it?"

Ellie said, "If I knew, dear, I'd knit him a cake."

"Well, it wasn't Doon," said Rex. "I should have *known*. Twins *do*. About a year ago, there was this tram in Birmingham. Doon fell off it at 3:14. And at precisely the same moment, but *precisely*, I tripped during a matinee performance of *Giselle*. And where was I? *London*!"

"And the job?" Paul asked impatiently. "Will you do it?"

"No," said Rex firmly. "Not. You're wasting your time. It's just not *me*.

No good to look for conker under oak tree, Chinese proverb."

The other three all began to talk at once.

Doon agreed that the theater management had been monstrously unfair. Rex's backstage dispute with Neville had *not* been audible in the upper circle, only in the first twelve rows of the stalls. Anyway, Neville had started it and it had been he who had used the words which had caused the *corps de ballet* to falter and stare into the wings. But, she pointed out, unfair or not, Rex had been fined a week's pay. He would receive no further salary until his period of disgrace was up. He was not only broke, but he owed her four pounds, six and threepence.

"As you very well know, ducky," she added, "I would love to support you in luxury until you're an old, old man. But I'm broke too." She polished her spectacles and gave him a bleak look.

Paul took over. Conscious of the fact that he was behaving exactly like Stephen Ambler, the blind hero of his most successful serial, he leaned forward and stretched out a hand palm upwards. "Think, friend, *think*," he appealed. "The fate of *You* depends on you, the fate of thousands of readers into whose lives it has brought a ray of sunshine. Egon depends on you, and Doon, and Ellie, and poor old Doc, and . . ."

"Yak, yak, yak," said Rex rudely.

Paul changed his tactics. He abandoned Stephen Ambler and degenerated suddenly into the volcanic Spike Raven. "Hear this, punk," he snarled. "If you rat now . . ."

"Bogey, bogey!" Rex yawned. "Save your breath, dears. I couldn't cope."

"Of course you could, dear," said Ellie. "Madam's got this staggering system of cross reference. It took her nearly ten years, but she's finally got it absolutely taped. Now, any old fool could do her job with a sack over his head."

Rex looked at Doon. "True or false?"

"True."

"Swear?"

"Swear."

"Even me?"

"Even Neville."

"How?"

Ellie rushed into an explanation. In the filing cabinets and all over the walls of the Marley office, she said, there were huge, scientific, and completely comprehensive charts. A moment's study of these would produce the answer to the most intricate problem. "Take, for instance," she suggested, "an Illegitimate Baby."

"No," said Rex. "I don't want to."

Ellie ignored him. She reached for the cardboard cylinder which she had brought with her to prove her point. She removed the roll of charts, selected one, and spread it on the floor. She produced a ball of string and cut off two yard lengths.

Rex watched her suspiciously.

She drew a breath and began to elucidate. If Rex's advice was demanded about an illegitimate baby, all he had to do was to choose the appropriate chart, then place one end of the first piece of string on *Born* or *Unborn*. The other end he would stretch across to *Mother Married, Mother Unmarried, Mother Married White, Mother Married Black, Mother Unmarried White, Mother Unmarried Black, Mixed*, or *Lascars* as the case might be.

"Are you with me?" she asked.

"Go on."

Ellie went on. With string A fixed in position, Rex would merely have to take string B and place it on *Father Willing, Father Unwilling*, or *Father Hesitant*. The other end of B in turn stretched across the chart to a wide variety of contingencies which included *Divorced, Separated, Unknown*, and *Dead*.

"You get the sketch?"

"I'm not a clunk."

"All right. Now watch. Where the two strings cross, you get the opening paragraph of your answering letter, and a formula. The formula refers you to another even bigger chart which copes with the various complications, such refinements as *Racial, Religious, Minors, Pensions, Larceny (Br. or U.S.A.F.), Kleptomania, Drink, Ignorance of F.O.L., Impotence, Frigidity, Industrial Diseases, Hereditary, Insanity, Spastics, Mongols, Schizoids*, and so on."

"In fact, ducky," Doon interrupted, "Madam has solved the problems of the human race in one hundred and sixty-three pages of cross reference."

Ellie unrolled another chart. "I'll prove it," she offered. "Ask me something, anything at all."

"What sort of thing?"

"Anything. The trickier the better."

Doon, whose flights of fancy were well known, challenged immediately. "I am a Siamese twin," she said. "Having drugged me, my sister murdered my husband. Can they hang us?"

Ellie stretched the strings over a chart. " 'My dear,' " she read. " 'I am so sorry to hear of your terrible plight.' Hold everything, I want V5." She pored over another chart. " 'You're lying' " she said. " 'Your sister would have been drugged too. You must persuade her to confess. You'll both go to jug. Two years in Siam, five in India, ten in England if you're model prisoners, acquittal in France provided you can prove that your husband was habitually unfaithful.' Paul?"

Paul thought for a moment. "I am a refugee," he volunteered. "Traveling on a Turkish *laissez-passer*, I went through a form of marriage in 1942 with a passing soldier. He went off at once. I have not seen him since. Anyway, he was a Mormon and only had a Mexican divorce from his first wife. I got an affidavit from a man in Tiflis and have since married him. He is a Moslem and very cruel to me. He has five other wives all living in the same house. My first husband's first divorced wife has now married my present husband. Are our children any relation?"

Ellie said, "Pass me CX2. 'If you will send me a stamped, addressed envelope, I will answer you privately.' Rex?"

"I'm not playing."

"Yes, you are, dear. Come along. Jolly game."

"Well," said Rex. "There are three chums nagging me. I dote on them all, but if they don't shut up soon, I'll scream."

Ellie reached for a new chart. " 'Try to take a more lenient view,' " she read. " 'The friends you complain of are probably only trying to be cordial. If, however, you believe their attentions to be malicious in intent, speak to the one who appears to be the ringleader.' "

"I have."

"Then, 'You should ask somebody respected by your tormentors to tell them frankly that their conduct is unwelcome. Do you know the vicar?' "

"No."

"Well, 'You should consult your solicitor. A firm letter from him should make these people mind their manners.' "

"I want them to shut up *now*."

"Oh. All right, pass me URG. 'My dear, the tone of your letter suggests that you may be *run down*. It could do no harm to consult your medical advisor. Could you not get away for a short holiday? Nobody is indispensable, you know! I'm sure that a change would make you see things in a different perspective.' "

In spite of himself, Rex was impressed. "It doesn't say all that."

"Yes, it does."

"Where?"

"There."

"That's only the first bit."

"Not to be a bore, dear! Look. H to 3, opening para. Now, formula W

+ 5a. You read me? Where's G8? Now put that here and this there and what do you get?"

"What's that asterisk?"

"Whether you get paid while you're away. Want to know?"

"No."

"Catch on?"

Rex hesitated. "Ask them about Neville," he said. "Tell them he's one of my best friends yet I can't wait for him to break his leg tonight. Whose fault is this?"

When, half an hour later, Paul and Ellie left, Rex was still refusing to commit himself. Preparing the supper in the kitchen, Doon heard him padding around his bedroom overhead. Presently, she went up and looked in at him. He was sitting before the mirror trying on all his ties. Three suits were laid out on the bed, and four waistcoats.

"Even if I did go, which I'm not going to," he said, "what would I *wear*?"

Doon went downstairs and rang up Paul. "It's all right," she whispered. "He'll go."

"Fine," said Paul. He rang off and dialed Ellie's number. "It's okay," he said. "We've won him."

"Thank God," said Ellie. "Sa . . . I mean Egon *will* be relieved." She replaced the receiver, lifted it, and rang up Egon. "Not to worry, dear," she said. "It's all fixed."

"I love you," said Egon warmly. "What? What is? Who's that?"

Chapter 5

ON the following morning, in the ninth best hotel in Bournemouth, Browneyes, Enid Marley's most devoted fan, woke abruptly. She sat up in bed and eagerly snatched the envelope with the stylish green lettering from her breakfast tray. Turning her back on her sleeping bridegroom, she ripped open the envelope and drew out the letter.

She bit her lip, apprehensive, trembling slightly. Surely darling Enid would be angry that, without advice, she, Browneyes, had so suddenly married Mr. Jackson?

Her eye sped to the bottom of the page. Her fears were instantly realized. Enid was annoyed. She had signed her letter with a rubber stamp. Browneyes wiped her nose on the back of her wrist and began to read.

Dear You.

You! Where was the usual, heartwarming *Brownie, my dear*? Through-
out the last eight tumultuous years, Enid had never been curt, never been
shocked, never been anything except absolutely marvelous. But now she
was downright unfriendly. Scrabbling under the pillow for her handkerchief, Browneyes read on.

The present situation, obviously, is intolerable.

Browneyes looked guiltily over her shoulder. She moved quickly away
from the steady warmth of her husband's back. She had never met her
heroine, but she had written to her nearly five hundred times and had
always been comforted and reassured by return of post. Suppose Enid
deserted her! For the rest of her life, she would have no idea what to do
next. She saw herself swept anchorless from one blunder to the next. In a
panic, she clutched at the sheets.

*I can no longer bear so heavy a burden. I have, quite calmly,
given this matter considerable thought. I have been regretfully forced
to the conclusion that the only solution lies in a swift, final exit.*

Browneyes began to shake all over with relief. It was all right! Enid
had not forsaken her! She was angry, upset, but she had not withheld her
lifeline of advice.

Browneyes clambered out of bed. She knew again what she had to do.
She struggled into her clothes, pulled on her stockings. She clapped on her
hat and powdered her nose. After some thought, she found a pencil and
licked the point of it. She turned over Enid Marley's letter and wrote on
the back, *I know I only married you yesterday, but I have already
repented of this. P.T.O. – Like Enid says I must go off and atone. Do
not try and find me. I will be far away. Good-bye for ever. Your wife
no longer, Browneyes.*

She propped this communication against her husband's plate of cornflakes, then, her pallid, pretty little face alight with righteousness, she
stepped into her shoes, placed Mr. Jackson's wallet in the pocket of her
coat, and tiptoed from the room.

By the time that Mr. Jackson woke to discover his bride's farewell
note in Bournemouth, the office cleaners were beginning in Croissant Street,
London.

The old janitor watched them. He never allowed them to use the lift,
nor even to set foot in it. When they complained, he would suck in his
gray, sunken cheeks and say with feeble finality, "She's not for the likes
o'you." If he had had his way, nobody except himself would have used
the lift, ever. They treated Her without sympathy, without kindliness, without respect for Her great age. He was delighted when She trapped some-

body and took as long as he dared to repair the faulty mechanism.

He stood in the shadows watching Them arrive, the many-faced enemy who worked from nine until six. He cringed, suffering, as they overloaded his darling, tracked mud over Her shining floor, stubbed out their cigarettes on Her gleaming rosewood panels, clashed Her frail gates. Once, somebody had trodden on an orange in Her. He had been off color for a week.

Paul and Rex turned in under the archway, with the Hungarian photographer. Hating them, the janitor ushered them into the lift and closed the gate tenderly. "Go easy with Her, gentlemen," he begged without hope. "We're moody today."

Paul jabbed the button marked 3 with the corner of his portfolio. The lift lurched and began to rise sluggishly.

The photographer said with a heavy but unconvincing American accent, "I hear some guy finally slung old Ma Know-all from a window, and about time. You got that one for a friend, you need no enemies. You get nailed by this reporter?"

Paul stiffened. "No. What did he want?"

The photographer laughed, a sound like the rattle of dice. "Aa-aah!" he sneered. "Stuff. You know. Just how's it feel, a killer in the block?"

"What did you say?"

"I said, 'Me, brother, I gotta built-in bodyguard. My wife has me trailed by a shamus. You wanna lose your job, you print that.' "

The lift juddered to a standstill at the third floor. The photographer got out and stalked through a purple-painted door immediately ahead. As he slammed it behind him, the half-open door diagonally opposite swung wide. On it was embossed in gold *CAR TAIRS, Investigati ns*.

The private detective slouched out. He was a pasty, thickset man who looked as if he had been born wearing his hat. He got into the lift and shut the gate with his knee, nodding after the Hungarian photographer.

"He'll keep for half an hour," he muttered. "Slippery, he is. Been trailing him three weeks now. Eight girls he's got, all over the shop, but you can't catch him *in flagrante*. Wife's getting wild." He propped himself against the wall and with a great deal of jaw movement ate something from a paper bag. He kept his small leaden eyes on the hand which was transferring the food to his mouth. Although he had apparently not so much as glanced in Rex's direction, he told himself, "Haven't seen that face before. He's new."

"How do you do," said Rex brightly.

"I'm Carstairs," said the detective. He hooked something from under his upper lip with his tongue, placed his little finger in his right ear, and jiggled it savagely. He did not look up but the oblique slant of his heavy features indicated that, having lost interest in Rex, he was now addressing himself to Paul. "Marley dame coming in?" he asked his paper bag.

Paul hesitated. "Not today."

Carstairs pushed a handful of food into his mouth with the palm of his hand as if he were feeding a horse. "Never cared for Murder," he said indistinctly. "Clues and that. Quit the Force on my second case. Never cared who killed 'em, see. Good riddance, I used to say. Give the chap a medal."

"This isn't Murder," Paul reminded him. "She feels too well."

Carstairs shrugged. "Many a good man's muffed it first shot," he said. "No fault of their own. Lack of experience, bad luck, plain fate. Nasty position. What do they do? Have another bash? Their right mind tells 'em, 'Come on, mate, pause and water the horses,' but they don't listen to their right mind. They barge on and get topped."

"Somebody said she might have jumped," said Rex.

Paul kicked him. "No, they didn't. Nobody did."

"Nor they did. Sorry."

"It was just you who said it."

"So it was!"

"And you were drunk at the time."

"Paralytic."

Carstairs pushed the button for the fifth floor. "Know I handled her first divorce for her?" he asked, lifting an eyebrow. "No, not many do. Discretion's our motto. Open-and-shut collusion job. Husband and this bint followed me down to Brighton as prearranged, lost me on the front. He was phoning up all over, forgotten the rendezvous. Then the silly blighter goes and ogles the chambermaid. Keen, see, making sure she'll know him again. Fell for him, she did. Got her into Court, said she'd never seen him before in her life. What a mess!"

The lift stopped a foot below the fifth floor, Carstairs pressed the button for the sixth floor and the Emergency Stop simultaneously. The lift dropped a foot, then rose two. Rex snatched open the gate and sprang on to the concrete. Paul followed him. "Well, Abyssinia," mumbled Carstairs as the lift shot out of sight.

Paul led the way down the long, dark corridor. There were green-painted doors set alternately on either side and livid strip lighting at intervals in the ceiling.

Rex said, "I've changed my mind."

"No, you haven't. Come on."

Paul hurried on past a door behind which a telephone was ringing unanswered, past a row of fire extinguishers, past the passage which led to the model kitchens. He opened a door upon which was painted *Editor-in-Chief, You*, and bundled Rex into the room before he had time to protest.

Egon was marching round and round his desk clutching his hair and making faces at one of the telephones. "Listen, you hound!" he was shouting into the receiver. "Nothing, nix, not one peep! I'm not even going to say 'No Comment,' get it?" He disconnected the line with a crashing fumble and saw Rex. "Who the hell are you?" he snarled. "What do you want? Go away!"

"Doon's brother," explained Paul. "Rex, Sam Egon."

"Oh *God*!" said Egon. He pushed a crumpled pile of morning newspapers across his desk to Paul. "Get a load of them," he ordered, grabbing up the second telephone and barking out a number.

"Good morning," said Rex, at a loss.

Paul glanced quickly through the papers.

It had been an eventful night. Most of the front page headlines concerned either the flood in Essex or the third Bush killing. The victim had been identified as Sven K. Paullsson, a company director of no fixed abode. There had also been an earthquake on a Pacific island, and a tornado had snatched up a house in South America, dropping it half a mile away. A film star had alienated her fifth husband by pushing him into an empty swimming pool. A dog had saved three people from a burning building in Wandsworth, and somebody had again thrown a bucket of pig blood over the French Minister of War.

The Marley story was featured in only one paper, a half inch paragraph on page 5. Either a careless journalist or a misprint had renamed her Enid Marler.

Egon was roaring into the telephone, "I said *no*! I said no last Thursday and I still say no! Now *you* tell me! What was it I said? Exactly. How do you spell it? Correct." He replaced the receiver and clapped Paul on the back.

"Respite," he said, rubbing his hands. "And the evenings, please God, will be too busy with this Bush stuff." He seized the first telephone and told it "Hey, find out what the tide's doing in Essex." He eyed Rex. "Any previous experience?"

Rex cleared his throat. "Well, I once wrote a thing for *Ballet*."

"They published it?"

"No, not exactly."

"What's wrong with the following sentence? A young anaconda was found in a bunch of bananas at Bristol on Friday?"

"I don't know."

"Make a sentence using the word cursory."

"I feel cursory."

"Can you type?"

"No."

"How's your spelling?"

"Medium."

"What do you think of Enid Marley?"

"I think she's marvelous."

"Oh, you do, do you?"

"No. I think she's poison."

"What do you think about this business yesterday?"

"I entirely agree with you."

"What do *I* think?"

"I don't know."

"You're hired." Egon lit a cigarette, puffed at it then dropped it on to the floor, and trod on it. "Coming in?" he asked the telephone. "Fine, fine! Okay, beat it, will you, kids? Show him the drill, Paul, mm? Luck, Roger! You'll need it!"

"Rex," said Paul.

"Sure, sure. See you later. If anybody pushes you out of a window, let me know at once."

Paul steered Rex out of the room. Ellie's office was next door. The door was open and a pair of long green gloves lay on the desk, but Ellie was not in.

In Enid Marley's office, the desk, the chairs, the filing cabinets, and the floor were covered with hundreds of letters, all unopened. There were envelopes of every shape, size, and color. There were parcels and telegrams. There was a large cardboard box and two bunches of dead flowers. The chaos and charts on the walls gave the room the air of some ransacked wartime headquarters.

"Fascinating," said Rex faintly. "Now I'm going home."

Paul laughed reassuringly, as his blind hero was in the habit of doing. "Courage, friend," he said. "Remember the darkest hour comes . . ."

"Oh be quiet! Where shall I *start*?"

Paul picked up a letter and tore open the envelope. "What could be simpler?" he asked, reading. "A Miss Doris Williams. She wants to be a nurse."

"So do I."

"Well," said Paul, retreating. "Buy you lunch in the Indian joint."

"Where are you going?"

"Proofs. Ellie'll be in any moment now."

"Oh, you monster! You come right back here!"

But Paul had gone. After a moment of indecision, Rex ran after him into the corridor, but he had disappeared. He went back into Enid Marley's room and sat down at the desk. Gradually, his panic gave way to extreme curiosity. He opened two of the parcels. One contained a hand-knitted bed jacket and the other a small jar labeled FISH PASTE. He opened a telegram. WHAT A SCARE EXCLAMATION MARK, he read. SO GLAD YOU ARE OKAY, MAGS, CORNWALL.

Rex began to enjoy himself. He had always been frankly interested in other people's letters. It occurred to him that he might never again have a chance to read them on such a scale.

He threw the fish paste out of the window and used the bed jacket to dust the room. Then he began to open the mail.

It took him only half an hour to discover that Enid Marley's job was not so simple as Doon, Paul, and Ellie had claimed. Apart from all else, they had forgotten to return the charts which they had borrowed the previous evening. The entire section on *Difficult Relations: (A) Blood, (B) Erotic* was missing, leaving a yawning chasm of doubt.

He started to shake again. He waited for Ellie, but she did not appear. Wishing he was at home mending his *Igor* costume, he ran to the charts and consulted them about his problem. *My dear*, he was advised. *Many a square peg has eventually fitted into a round hole, you know! Have patience, give this new venture a chance. By this time next week, you will probably be laughing heartily at your present doubts!*

He placed his thumbs in his ears and wiggled his fingers at this message. He made a disgusting, bubbly noise with his lips and tongue, and ran into the corridor with the intention of finding Ellie. He found himself face to face with a near-dwarf.

"So," said Doctor Feltz, beaming. "You are Reggs?"

"Yes."

"Delighded, a bleasure! When you huff sorded the Dreams, you will send to me?"

The little man nodded and hurried away. Rex went back into Enid Marley's room and sat down.

Dreams?

He rang up Paul's office and got no answer. He rang up the cosmetic factory where Doon was arranging a Free Offer. He was informed, after some delay, that she had selected an eyeshadow named Mystery and a blue-green mascara; that she had now left, with a volunteer fat girl, to test the reducing properties of a Swedish Bath in North Hampstead.

He searched feverishly in the telephone directory for the number of the Swedish Bath, and failed to find it. He told the girl at the switchboard to connect him with the photographic studio. Jimmie greeted him boisterously, then said could he hang on a tick because there was a model frying under the arc lights, went away, and forgot to come back. Rex rang up the model kitchens. A harassed, girlish voice advised him that Mrs. Ryder was trying to make a cake on a primus stove, because of the gas strike, and was in no mood for human consumption.

Rex laid down the receiver with great care. He had lifted one foot off the ground and was about to take a flying kick at a heap of mail when one letter caught his eye. Intrigued, he picked it up and opened it. It was written in a hand which suggested that some tiny creature had fallen repeatedly into an inkwell, sprung out on to the paper, and made off sideways at speed.

The opening sentence fascinated him. Was it, *I am rude?* Or, *I had rope? I am ripe? 'E's a rube?* Or, *I'm an ape?* For the first time, he realized that his new job might have its own weird attraction.

An hour later, he had laboriously answered two letters and found one Dream. *I dremp I was walking up a steep hill. My dead wife was sitting in the snow on top throwing rocks which killed my Tabby. What can this mean? I am about to remarry.* He was considering this when the door burst open and a plump girl with a scarlet mouth hurried into the room and sat down.

"Sylvia," she announced. "Dictation."

Rex swallowed. He seized a handful of letters and began to move from chart to chart, to dictate the formulas in a clear, false voice. He realized with terror that she was writing in shorthand, that his haphazard deductions were passing into a state beyond coherence or control.

He stretched the strings with shaking hands. One had somehow become knotted with another which belonged to a different chart. He stood in front of the tangle, wrestling with it, blocking it from her view with his shoulders.

When, some minutes later, she looked up and said, "*Hullo?*", he smiled and said, "Hu*llo!*" Nobody had yet told him that Enid Marley was also responsible for the page of readers' letters entitled *Hullo, Hullo!*

"Patterns?" she asked, yawning.

With desperate calm, Rex searched his desk for the envelopes which had, for no apparent reason, contained postal orders. Other readers had sent no money, but had filled in unexplained little coupons. He blew his nose in order to gain a few seconds, then dictated the names and addresses of the former group.

She said, "Knitting, dress, embroidery, crochet, or transfer?"

For an instant, Rex stopped breathing. He stared at her, mesmerized by the lipstick on her teeth. "Knitting, naturally," he said with a reasonably successful laugh.

"Dress?"

He dictated the other list.

"Crochet?"

He told her the address of the ink creature.

"Embroidery? Transfer?"

"No," he said, avoiding her eyes.

"That's unusual. Free pencil?"

He told her the names of eight friends who he could ring up later and bribe or jolly into cooperation. She rose, pulled down her skirt, nodded, and left the room.

Rex sat down and mopped his forehead. He was about to start ringing up his free pencil people when Ellie came in and pulled up a chair. She wore green silk and a strange white hat. "Having fun, dear?" she asked.

"Where have you been, you swamp thing?"

"Dress show. Tea flowing like champagne. Like my hat?"

"Not much."

Egon, without noticeably passing through the door, was suddenly in the middle of the room. "Look, kids," he said, managing to give the impression that he had been reasoning with them for hours, and was now proving his point. "There's an element creeping in I don't like." He struck the proofs of a coming issue of *You* with the back of his hand. He had no real idea of what he was going to say, but he had been driven hurriedly out of his own office by the news that Kidder, the most dogged crime reporter in London, was on the way up to interview him. "Take Paul's *Hannibal* caper," he said. "What's all this 'silken tent, dot-dot-dot' stuff? I tell you that girl's got to reach the top of the Alps absolutely . . ."

Mrs. Ryder pushed open the door with her foot and held out an elaborately iced cake for his inspection.

"No, no, *no!*" said Egon. "Not in my present state of health. Take it away."

"Full color page," said Mrs. Ryder. She held her head backwards and sideways to prevent the smoke of the cigarette clamped between her lips from getting into her eyes. "Bowl of roses, Wedgewood teapot just out of focus, called *Sweet Tooth, query*. Anyone want it when we're through?"

Jimmie put his head around the door. "Ready when you are, Mrs. Ryder," he announced. He looked critically at the cake. "No sheen, have to spray it." He grinned broadly at Egon. "The lift's bust again," he said. "Between the third and fourth. Kidder's in it roaring for out."

Egon hugged himself and performed a curious shuffling little dance. "What a break!" he cried happily. "How long will it take?"

"The janitor implied that it may take several weeks."

"Splendid fellow!" said Egon. "Give him ten bob." He stood for a moment trying to remember why he was in Enid Marley's office, then vanished from the room as suddenly as he had appeared.

Jimmie hastened after him. Mrs. Ryder flicked her cigarette out of the window and followed Jimmie. She was determined to be present when he photographed her cake. She had never forgotten the time when he had produced a picture of her carpetbagger steak reflected in a large copper urn. He could resist neither flashy props, nor later adding wisps of steam with an airbrush.

As the door closed behind the small procession, Ellie sighed. She divided the nearest pile of envelopes on Rex's desk and pulled half towards her. About a third of the letters were aimed at the *Hullo, Hullo!* page and were marked with an H in the top left-hand corner of the envelope. As these needed no answer, she dealt with them rapidly, cutting them open in handfuls with a huge pair of scissors.

Rex watched her for a moment, then followed her example. "A clever canary," he paraphrased, reading. "When she plays the piano, it hops about."

"Out," said Ellie crisply.

"Why?"

"It'd touch off five hundred likewise."

"But it can whistle its telephone number."

"No, dear. No *said*, no *meant*."

Rex took up another letter. He read aloud, " 'When we go to sad films, my wife shames me by crying. When I reprove her, she says Westerns make me behave like a cowboy! Mr. P., Devon.' "

"Good." Ellie took the letter and wrote across the top in red chalk, *Caption: Stick 'em up, Mrs. P!* "Get the sketch? Now *you* try. Caption this. 'Gran is 97 mum is 79 i have 4 uncles and 3 aunts all over 70 i am 61 my youngest gronchild is 16 our combint ages add up to over 1000 years is this a record? W. O. Moore (Mrs.).' "

Rex thought for a moment. "*The Moore the Merrier!*" he suggested tentatively.

"Exactly. Try this. 'We had a duck sent but it was alive and looked so sad. Our Xmas dinner has now become our favorite pet!' "

"*Lor-love-a-duck!*" Rex offered.

"Correct," said Ellie. "And again! 'I am deeply in love with three boys. They fight all the time but I cannot make up my mind.' "

Rex went over to the charts, stretched the strings and took a bearing. "M2/xs + 3," he announced.

"Translate."

" 'My dear, I suspect that you are very young. Obviously, you are in love with none of these boys. When the Real Thing comes along, it will leave no room for doubt in your mind. Why not join a youth club where you can make more friends of both sexes?' "

"All right. One more! 'Dear *You*, Yesterday morning I entered Enid Marley's office and saw her standing on the window ledge. I knew at once that I would never again have so excellent an opportunity to murder her. I sprang across the room and gave her a savage push, an action which I shall never regret . . .' " Ellie's voice trailed away. She dropped the letter as if it had been red-hot.

"*No!*" said Rex.

"But *yes*, dear!"

"My God!"

"Agree, agree!"

"Is it signed?"

"Yes. 'Friend.' "

"*Well!*"

Ellie picked up the envelope "Posted in Kensington," she remarked. As always in moments of stress, she produced her compact and powdered her nose. "Egon will be wild! He's still plugging away at Misadventure."

Rex said, "You ought not to touch it. It's a *clue*. Fingerprints."

Ellie looked at him. "You're not going to have an attack of Public Spirit, are you, dear? If you are, you'll never make the grade in this outfit."

"What are you going to do with it?"

"Give it to Sa . . . Egon, of course! It'll come in very, very handy when he changes his mind again and puts his shirt on Murder." She rose, patted Rex on the head, and hurried towards the door.

Rex protested. "You'll be an accessory after the fact."

"No, I won't. There isn't any fact."

"Then it's Contempt of Court."

"*What* Court?"

"All right, it's Perjury."

"No, it's not."

"Well, it's *something*."

"Not to fuss, dear," said Ellie, leaving. "See you in jug."

Rex forced himself to work on. His mind was not on his task and the pile of letters in his OUT tray grew slowly. Some while later, when he was wondering what to do with a drawing in lipstick from an obviously dangerous lunatic, Sylvia returned with a handful of typed letters. He forged Enid Marley's signature twenty-four times without a qualm.

"Where are the addresses?" she asked.

He indicated a scrapheap of small pieces of paper.

"Oh," she said with an ill-concealed sneer. "In that order?"

"I agree it's not a wonderful system. I'll think of something else at lunch."

She gathered up the contents of his OUT tray. "Will you give two bob towards Jean's wedding present?"

"No, absolutely not. To hell with her!"

She looked at him for the first time with a glimmer of respect. "Yes, sir," she said.

To hell with the lot of them! thought Enid Marley three miles away. *To hell with you, and you, and you, and particularly You!*

"Was complications what took Mae, poor thing," remarked Mrs. Pickett, the charwoman, wheeling the Hoover into the sitting room. "Never showed up in the X-ray, see. You just can't tell. Never know which way they'll jump next. Once they get to your . . ."

Enid Marley ignored her. She lay on the couch absently rattling a bottle of aspirins and staring out of the window. The police had left half an hour before. It had been their third visit. She was no longer certain that they were even partially satisfied with her story.

Inspector Woodman had said formally, "Mrs. Marley, do you realize that you're making a very serious accusation?" Then the younger detective had burst into the room and said, his voice slightly breathless with excitement, "They've pulled in Kayes, sir!"

Woodman had looked suddenly much younger. "Fine!" he had said. "Fine, fine, splendid!"

Enid Marley picked at the stitching on a cushion. Why had her story been featured in only one morning newspaper? Why had there been no hint of foul play? Why had the police issued no statement? Could it be that they were too intrigued with this Kayes, this Bush murderer? Did they regard her case as, so to speak, a hyphen between matters of more importance? Or did they know, with their vast capacity for suspicion, exactly what had happened? Did they know in some secret manner that she was a liar and a fraud and a fool? Should she, somehow, perhaps weeping softly into her pillow, have paved the way to Accident?

Had she heard a faint sigh as Woodman, impatient to be away now, to question this Bush brute, had said, "Now about this wounded bird, Mrs. Marley. You had climbed on to the window ledge with the intention of rescuing it *before* or *after* you felt this malign something behind you?"

Damn that blasted bird! Yet how else, with Suicide out of the running, could she have explained her presence on a sill seventy feet above the ground?

"Did you *get* the bird?" he had asked. She had looked at him sharply, suspecting impertinence. But his face had been bland, official.

She had been waiting, her story prepared, her stare of astonishment rehearsed, for him to question her about the farewell note in her OUT tray. But he had not even mentioned it. Why? Clearly, because he had not found it. Then who had it now? The owner of those snatching, desperate hands, that anonymous voice which had gasped. *It's all right! I've got you!*

"Mrs. Pickett," she said, reaching for her handbag. "I do not wish you to answer any questions put to you by either the police or the Press."

Mrs. Pickett's thin red claw closed over the proffered note. She was puzzled. Being unable to attach any importance whatever to anything which did not immediately affect the routine of her daily life, she had long ago completely forgotten the episode of the gas oven. She had other and more pressing problems on her mind. Her favorite grandson had been arrested in Tottenham Court Road for felling a Negro with a bicycle chain. Her daughter had fallen for the wiles of an old man mixed up with horses. Her husband, a member of the Gas Workers' Union, was on strike and had a boil in his nose. She herself, if she did the step, would not have time for a snack before Mae's funeral . . .

"Orright, dear," she said. "Ta."

Enid Marley relaxed against her cushions.

"Do you intend to make a charge?" Inspector Woodman had asked her. "Surely you must suspect somebody?"

She had said faintly, "My husband? I suppose he . . ."

"Was playing golf? We've checked. He was."

She had wanted to say something dramatic, to woo his interest away from that Kayes killer, to enlist him on her side. She would have accused any one member of the staff of *You* with pleasure. But she had to be careful. Which of the seven had had the opportunity? How many of them had cast-iron alibis?

For only one of them was her accusation tailor-made! The owner of those frantic hands, the one who had tried so strenuously to save her!

All right! she thought viciously. *It's all right! Whoever you are, I'll get you!*

Rex met Doon, Paul, and Ellie for lunch in the Indian restaurant. "That crime reporter's still caged in the lift," he remarked, sitting down. "He's in such a *rage*!"

"Kidder was born snarling," said Paul, studying the menu. "I shall have *Briane Mahee, Dahl*, and *poppadums.*"

"Wronk," said the Singhalese waiter. "Is no gingly oil."

The proprietor appeared, fanning himself with a menu. "During the war, she screams for rice," he stated angrily, continuing a conversation he had had with Inspector Woodman the previous day, "knowing full well I could obtain only pitiful old barley and thankful for it. She was daily shouting and raving like all-get-out!" He threw the menu recklessly over his shoulder. "Had I known she was to altogether bust up my new canvas . . ."

"Ellie," said Rex in a low voice. "What did you do with it?" She looked at him vaguely, clearly thinking of other things.

"That letter," he insisted. "That anonymous confessing letter?"

"Not now, dear. Later."

"No. *Now.*"

"Not to nag, love."

Rex pinched her. He said in a fierce undertone, "*Yield!*"

She sighed. "I gave it to Egon."

"What did he say?"

"A mouthful. That it was a practical joke, that it had been written by some madman, that Madam had written it, that *I'*d written it, that he'd written it himself, that we weren't to tell Paul, and that he loved me." She turned away, thanking God that she could no longer blush. *I love you*, Egon had said. Seeing her out, he had thrown an arm around her shoulders and given her a propelling pencil. She would not be able to eat for a fortnight. She was doomed.

Rex tapped her on the wrist with a spoon. "Then what?"

"Then he filed it. I knew he would."

"You think he'll switch back to Murder?"

"It was still Misadventure five minutes ago. Who knows, dear? *Who knows?*"

Chapter 6

By the time that Rex, Doon, Ellie, and Paul returned from their lunch, Inspector Woodman had returned to Egon's office. He was questioning the charwoman whom Enid Marley had passed in the corridor on the morning of the whatever-it-was. She was proving to be a difficult witness.

"Had you or had you not been polishing the linoleum since eight o'clock in the morning?" he asked patiently for the fifth time.

She sat massively, scowling at him. "Young whippersnapper," she growled into her shapeless bosom.

"Is it or is it not a fact that anybody who had access to Mrs. Marley's office between the hours in question would have had to pass you in the corridor?"

"I know your sort," she mumbled. "Straight into the pocket o' the Government."

"I beg your pardon?"

"Granted."

Woodman considered her, reflecting that he would have enjoyed bouncing a billiard ball off her lumpy forehead. He said, "Did, for instance, Doctor Feltz pass you?"

"Foreigners!" she spat. "When they flock in, there's war up."

He drew a land mine in his notebook. The policeman in him forced him to add a notice announcing *Danger!* "And the photographer? Jimmie Simmons?"

"Art once give Gwen a Brownie," she exclaimed with sudden vivacity. "Just before we left, '23 it was. No, I'm a liar. Was when . . ."

"And Paul East?"

"One drag an' 'e flung it down," she said. "There's good money in fag ends, I always say. Waste not, want not, pick it up an' eat it."

The billiard ball and the land mine were too merciful for her, he decided. He would have liked to soak her hair in gin and set fire to it.

"I propose to read your statement to you," he said, his face expressionless. "Please listen carefully. 'I, Romaine Carlotta Barker, of 46M, Bogota Crescent, SE 23, have been employed by *You* since March 1956. On the morning of the 8th, I was occupied with my duties from 8 a.m. until 10 a.m. During the hours in question seven people passed me in the corridor, to wit, Mr. Egon, Doctor Feltz, Mr. Paul East, Mr. Jimmie Simmons, Mrs. Ryder, Miss Ellie Sansome, and Miss Doon Travers. I did not observe anybody actually entering Mrs. Marley's office for the reason that I was then engaged in the passage leading to the model kitchens. But having an uninterrupted view of the main corridor, and being by nature curious, I am prepared to swear on oath that any person or persons who gained access to the aforesaid office can only have been one or more of the above mentioned.' "

He looked up at her. "Is that correct?" he asked gently.

She wagged her head approvingly. "Dead on," she agreed. "Certainly catch on quick, you monkeys!"

An hour later, Woodman sat in another office very much like Egon's. It was his own. He and two colleagues had been re-interviewing the forty-eight witnesses who had seen, or claimed to have seen, Enid Marley's fall. To each, the same questions had been put.

Was there anybody in the window behind Mrs. Marley? Was it a man or a woman? And *Can you describe him or her?*

Without surprise or even resentment, he reviewed the list of answers assembled from the stenographers' notebooks. *Oh, it was a man, sir: medium height, dark hair, gray suit. Oh, it was a girl, mister: very like a friend of mine, really, only fair. Oh, man, inspector: couldn't see his face but he had a mustache. Oh, a peacherissimo, old chap: young, blonde, strictly yum-yum! Oh, definitely one of the weaker sex, constable: elderly, graying hair, false teeth. Oh, it was a gentleman, officer: white as a sheet, he was, sort of sad-looking like in that book where he had a mad wife.*

Woodman looked at his last witness, the only one in whom he had instinctive trust, and suppressed a sigh. He disliked children and never knew how old they were. This one he reckoned to be about fourteen. Uncertain how to approach such an age group, he decided in favor of perching nonchalantly on the corner of his desk.

"Hi, pardner!" he said robustly, despising himself. "Have you a license for that deadly weapon?"

The boy stood slightly turned away, head down, glowering from beneath white eyebrows. He jerked his hand off the butt of the multicolored plastic space-gun tucked into his belt. "'S just a crummy toy," he growled. "Got to be eighteen to have a real gun."

"How old are you?" Woodman felt as presumptuous as he would have done had he been asking the same question of the Commissioner's wife.

"Seven and three-quarters."

"That's great," said Woodman unhappily. How was he to win this creature's confidence? Was it too old to be shown the inside of a watch? Too young to be promised a visit to the Black Museum? Would food help? "What are you going to be when you grow up?" he tried. "Space pilot?"

"Coshboy."

"Do you know what happens to kids who tell lies to the police?"

"They get clobbered, if they're caught."

"Exactly." Woodman realized that this might be interpreted as a threat and added with shameful fervor, "You bet your boots!" He surprised the mild eye of the stenographer on him and said sharply, "On the morning of the 8th, did you or did you not observe any person or persons in the window behind Mrs. Marley?"

The boy pulled up his left sock with the toe of his right shoe. "No," he said. "Just those hands."

"A man's hands? Or a woman's?"

The boy raised his shoulders to the level of his ears, then let them fall.

"You didn't see?"

"The old cow's skirt was waving around. *Course* I didn't see. *Nobody* could of."

"You're absolutely certain of that?"

"Course."

"You'd swear to it on oath?"

The boy pointed the space gun at the center of his forehead, raised one hand in a fascist salute, and stood on one foot. He said rapidly, "Ari-ari, jaggeri-jaggeri, oogly-oogly, alabala-booshi, Chinese king!"

Ten minutes later, Woodman sat alone cracking his knuckles. He had feared the worst immediately he had been assigned to the Marley case. She reminded him of his mother-in-law, the most slippery liar in Clacton. He had hoped that the affair would prove to be a straightforward Attempted Suicide. He still hoped so, and he believed it to be so. But if it *were* so, then there were two points which had to be cleared up. There had been no farewell note, and there *had* been somebody in the window behind the silly woman. If he or she had been there for any candid reason, then why on earth had he or she not come forward at once and said so?

He chewed a splinter off his pencil, spat it out, and reminded himself that he was, of course, dealing with a bunch of lunatics. Just look at their alibis! Breathing hard through his nose, he pulled his notebook towards him and looked at them.

Samuel Egon, Editor-in-Chief: The vital ten minutes? Me? On the blower, old chap. Some fool laying eggs because his perfume ad shared a page with an onion soup. Then I shaved. I always shave in the office. If she'd had her throat cut, I could understand it. Look, you're wild-goosing, old fruit. Take it from papa, this is Misadventure.

Paul East, Fiction Editor: I was looking up some stuff about Hannibal. I'm writing this serial. I'd got the dates mixed and it was printed. I was wondering how to get around it.

Doctor Feltz, Medical Editor: You will not believe this. There is a spiderweb in one corner of my office. Each morning, I look at once to see whether there are flies in it. This morning, there were two. I was trying to free them with a compass. I cannot work with this spider eating flies, yet I cannot destroy the spider.

Jimmie Simmons, Photographic Editor: I don't know, moseying around. Some of the time, I was nattering with the kids in the typing pool.

No, I didn't look at my watch. How could I? It's being de-coked.

Mrs. Ryder, Cookery Editor: I had a recipe for red herrings. Cochineal, you know, but it sounded amusing. Useless, of course, unless I got a color page. I went along to see the Art Editor, but he wasn't there.

Doon Travers, Beauty Editor: Well, I was coping with mail and stuff. Some pig had sent a pot of homemade hand cream. I tried it and honestly, ducky, straight away I was scratching like a dog. So I went to wash. Then I went and sewed a button on to Doctor Feltz.

Doctor Feltz (recalled): Yar. I remember. Very kind. I was forgetting.

Ellie Sansome, Fashion Editor: Not to nag, dear. I was doing my nails. They take hours to dry and one's just not in the *mood* for Murder.

Woodman slammed his notebook shut and drew a wigwam on his blotter. Adding a tree and two tufts of grass, he clenched his teeth. If he decided, as he had, that every witness – why were they *all* Editors? – in the case – if it *were* a case – was either lying or had something to conceal, including the victim – if she *were* a victim – *then where the hell did he go from here*?

His stenographer came into the room and stood watching him sympathetically. "Rum do, sir," he remarked. "Think it was Attempted, sir?"

"Attempted what?"

"I was thinking of Homicide, sir."

"Why?"

"I take your point, sir. But whatever it was, sir, I know who *I*'d put the zing on."

Woodman drew a red Indian lying on his back with an arrow sticking out of his left shoulder. "Who?"

The stenographer did not hesitate. "Oh, that Mr. Egon, sir. Mean to say, seeing there's no proof either way, why's he keep harping on Misadventure unless he knows it was Murder? And if he knows it was Murder, then he done it. And if he knew it was Misadventure, than he'd of said so, because he *wouldn't* of done it, although he had, if you follow me. And if it was Suicide . . . well, he wouldn't want that on account of he probably drove her to it by overwork. He'd of done it in theory, see, but not in practice. Seems to me he's an all-rounder, sir."

In Enid Marley's office, Ellie sat down and began to revolve her feet twelve times clockwise, twelve times anti-clockwise. When she had first joined the staff of *You*, she had been a smiling, buxom girl with thick ankles. Maddened by the taunts of Mrs. Marley, she had forsworn all starches, sugars, and fats. Daily, she had performed fourteen different exercises on rising in the morning. Now, three stones lighter, gaunt as a rail, her smile reduced to an enigmatic curl of the lips, the old habits persisted. But she had decided, in the absence of Madam, to spend half an hour longer in bed and to do all but her rolling routine in the office.

"It's all rather embarrassing," she said, reversing her feet. "There was nobody here except *You*. Doesn't it occur to you, hoof-brain, that one of us seven gave her the heave?"

It had occurred to Rex. The possibility had been nagging him since the previous evening. "No, no," he said stoutly, attempting to comfort her as he had already partially comforted himself. "Some smelly old tramp."

"No dice, dear! Tramps, *Me*, Sylvia, mysterious strangers, and passing maniacs are *persona grata*. It's been proved by that animal who polishes the corridors. It was one of us."

Rex paled. "Is that official?"

"Absolutely."

He bit off a piece of his left thumbnail. "Well, isn't that just *minky*."

"You're all right. You've got an alibi."

"Haven't you?"

"Not terribly."

"What about Doon?"

"She said she was scratching."

"And the others?"

"There were some fancy tries, but Woodman wasn't exactly wowed by any of them." She patted his cheek. "With you alone, dear, can the innocent parties feel entirely safe."

"How do I know I'm safe alone with you?"

"You don't. Hop on to the window ledge and try me."

Rex stared at her. Her head was sunk on to her breast, her mouth wide open. As he watched, she threw back her head and closed her mouth against some colossal invisible pressure to a count of ten. Against his will, he found himself considering her as a possible murderess. Surely anybody sufficiently fanatical to behave in such a manner in public would stop at nothing?

He rallied. Of course Ellie – she was one of the *chums*! – would have stopped at Murder. *Well, wouldn't she?*

Jimmie burst into the room and tossed a heap of doilies on to the desk. "Crochet competition," he said. "Don't miss the set of Buckingham Palace in Spring, Summer, Autumn, and – you've *guessed*!"

As he hurried away, Rex studied his departing back thoughtfully. He considered the faulty crew cut, the large red ears, the somehow endearing pimple on the back of the neck.

No, no, not Jimmie! Whatever next?

He picked up the telephone and said, "Doctor Feltz, please."

"Dark tar fair ellts," sang the girl at the switchboard.

"Yar?" said Doctor Feltz.

"It's me," said Rex. "Will you do the Dreams now?"

As always when this question was put to him, Doctor Feltz was silent for a moment. He contributed the psychiatric column very unwillingly. He lived in fear from issue to issue that somebody in the medical profession would recognize his photograph, that some forgotten and embittered colleague would revive the old scandal. The name Feltz, the removal of the distinctive beard, the rejection of Adler, might confuse many . . . but not Kurt, nor Liesel, nor Ali. Nor, above all, the crazy, homicidal Mangoyian.

He forced himself to speak. "You saw?" he asked. "Is drouble?"

Rex said apologetically, "Offhand, I'd say three nymphomaniacs and one paranoiac."

"Vine, vine!" Doctor Feltz blew his nose and rang off.

Rex sat stabbing a pencil at an ink stain on his desk. He tried and failed to think of the small foreigner as a murderer. He thought of the noble head, of the tiny womanlike hands, of the diminutive feet which did not reach the ground when their owner sat on a chair.

Doctor Feltz? What nonsense! The mere suspicion seemed shameful, bullying, somehow politically caddish . . .

The door swung open and Paul East looked in. His hat was on the back of his head and he was clearly in a rage. "Where's Egon?" he demanded. "Some illiterate lout's cut five hundred words from my Hannibal piece! It's gibberish! It's printed! Who *did* it?"

"Madam," said Ellie. "She said you knew."

Paul struck himself in the forehead with a clenched fist. "My God," he croaked, "if I'd pushed that bitch, I'd confess and be hanged laughing." He rushed out of the room, slamming the door behind him.

"Not Paul," said Rex.

Ellie raised her eyebrows. "What?"

"Nothing."

The phone rang. Rex lifted the receiver.

"Ducky?" said Doon's voice at the far end of the wire. "I'm sweating it out with this repulsive fat girl. I won't have time to get the bread. Will you tell Egon that this Natural Beauty lark won't do? All the vegetables are out of season. How are you?"

"Windy."

"Why?"

"Charlieboy has proved that one of *You* pushed the Marley."

She said, "I knew he was a troublemaker the moment I set eyes on him."

After a slight, anxious pause, he asked, "Angel, if you'd . . . well, you know what I mean . . . I mean, even if you *had* and I somehow didn't know which I would have done, of course . . . but just suppose I *hadn't* . . . I mean, you would *tell* me, wouldn't you?"

"*Darling!*"

"Sorry. Snatched back as soon as said."

"Well, *really!*"

"Bang my head on the ground, eat slime."

"All right. Don't forget the bread." She rang off.

Ellie was lying on the floor. Her feet were wedged under the handle of the bottom drawer of a filing cabinet, her arms crossed behind her head. Slowly, she raised her rigid trunk into a sitting position. Rex stepped over her and hastened along the corridor to Egon's office. He tapped nervously on the door, advanced three feet into the room, and cleared his throat.

Egon was clutching a tuft of his hair with one hand and gripping a telephone with the other. His face was gray and he had apparently lost his voice. "Listen, you literary hunchback," he was whispering. " 'Please turn to page 53,' it says. Okay, I spit on my thumb and turn. And what do I get? *A page of ads!* Where the hell's the carryover, you professional maniac?" He tugged at the tuft, nodding in an exaggerated fashion with his eyes closed. He said softly, "Yes. Yes. No. Why not? Listen, I don't give a damn about your dog-faced wife . . ."

Mrs. Ryder stood in the middle of the room. She still wore her food-stained overall. A cigarette drooped out of her mouth. She was balanced on one foot, scratching her calf with the toe of the other. She squinted at Rex through the smoke of her cigarette. "I'm a cooperative woman," she said, "but I have my limitations. There is this gas strike. Tell me, could *you* cook a photogenic *souffle* on a Primus?"

Rex considered her. Doon had known her for years. She said that the Cookery Editor was kindhearted, reliable, forthright; that she was worthy, patient, and tremendously efficient. She was the brawn behind the brain of many committees. She had decorated many big halls with strings of tiny flags, made and dispensed thousands of sausage rolls, and later raised her gruff baritone to encourage the community singing. She was an excellent citizen. There was no possible reason to dislike her.

"No," he said shortly, hating her, wondering for a giddy moment whether she were a man. Would she, he asked himself hopefully, have attempted to murder Enid Marley?

He looked sideways at her blunt, capable hands, at her untidy gray hair, at the smear of flour on her plain, kind face. She wore no powder, no lipstick. Her nose gleamed. Zeal shone from her like a beacon. She was above suspicion.

As Egon crashed the receiver on to its rest and reached for another, Rex seized his opportunity. "Mr. Egon," he said quickly. "Doon says no Natural Beauty. No veg."

"It has to be *souffles*," said Mrs. Ryder simultaneously. "The page is made up. They're just waiting for the picture."

Jimmie put his head round the door and said, "Doc wants the green light on that Insomnia thing."

Egon, to whom a single catastrophe was as a red rag to a bull, could deal with a holocaust like an experienced matador. In his heyday, a journalist had once called him The Emperor of the Snap Decision, and he had never forgotten it.

He rapidly assessed the problems of Rex, Mrs. Ryder, and Jimmie, smeared a sandwich with mustard, calculated the possible profits from the free eyeshadow offer, and examined a hole in the heel of his right sock.

To Rex, he said curtly, "Fruit." To Mrs. Ryder, "Use eighty candles. Use marsh gas. Use your initiative." And to Jimmie, "Tell Doc I won't have it, now, or next week, or ever. Insomnia's dated."

He bit into the sandwich, realized that it was not ham but beef at the same time that he realized that he would have to charge one and three-pence for the packaging of the free eyeshadow. He dismissed the hole in his sock as just one more defeat in the constant war of attrition between himself and all his clothes, planned to buy fifty new pairs on the way home, and dialed a number on the telephone.

"And Chloe Carlisle rang up," said Rex. "She's going to Australia and she won't have time to finish *Kiss Me Goodnight!*"

"But, Sam, it was *color*," protested Mrs. Ryder.

"How about Rheumatism?" asked Jimmie.

Egon said into the telephone, "Claxton? Well, go and find him, you ruddy ape!" He turned to his staff. "Get Paul on to it. Another six thousand. Tell him to okay it in with Chloe before it's printed. We'll switch pages 11 and 13. *Souffles* in black-and-white, Rheumatism in color."

Jimmie left with Mrs. Ryder.

Rex asked desperately, "What about the end? Jolly or pathetic?"

Egon ejected a piece of half-masticated sandwich into his wastepaper basket. "Hate beef," he remarked. "Bump her off on her wedding day."

"Fatal disease or shot by lover?"

"Shoot her, *shoot* her!" Confronted with only one problem, Egon at once began to lose his temper. "Shoot the whole bloody boiling! Beat it, Reg. Beat it!"

"*Rex.*"

"All right, all right."

Rex backed out of the room and turned down the corridor towards his own office. Hating and fearing him, he suddenly knew beyond a shadow of a doubt that it had been Egon who had pushed Enid Marley to what appeared to be a certain death. All at once, it was so obvious, so logical, that he could not understand why he had ever doubted the other suspects.

All of them had loathed the woman and therefore had a motive. All of them had had the opportunity. In theory, all of them were under suspicion. In practice, only Egon had that little extra something which the others hadn't got. His alone was the type of face which lowered from beneath screaming headlines in the Sunday press. He alone had no scruples whatever, and an ungovernable temper. He alone was psychologically capable of Murder.

Egon!

Egon who wore dirty collars and bit his nails, who drank gin out of a teacup and cut his own hair. Egon who lived in some private world, maddened by his own doubts. Of course! Egon had tried his hand at Murder and failed, as he had failed at everything all his life. If any of the six remaining suspects had attempted to kill Enid Marley in so foolproof a manner, he or she would have succeeded. But not old Jonah Egon! The very bungling of the crime stamped it with his signature.

In the Marley office, Rex stood undecided. Ellie had disappeared. Where she had sat, there was a half-empty cup of milkless tea with two cigarette stubs disintegrating in it, a kirbigrip stuck into an indiarubber, a spicy hint of scent.

Rex closed the door and leaned against it. He had no idea what to do about his new knowledge. Should he alert the police? No. They would listen patiently, smother their yawns, and disbelieve him, for he had no proof. Should he face Egon in his den, accuse him point blank? No. Egon would simply grab him and throw him out of the window. Should he ring up Enid Marley, appeal to her? *I know who murdered you. What shall I do? Please help me!* No. It seemed somehow unethical.

What then?

Obviously, the charts!

He ran to them and fumbled with the strings. He made a note of the formula, moved on to the files. UR G8/4. He scrabbled among the carefully typed sheets. URP, URQ, URR, URS . . . The wrong cabinet? No, the wrong drawer. He dragged open the one above and found URG immediately. He seized the entire section and dropped half of it. He was on his hands and knees when he found the relevant reference.

My dear, it read. *The tone of your letter suggests that you may be "run down." It could do no harm to consult your medical advisor. Could you not get away for a short holiday? Nobody is indispensable, you know! I'm sure that a change would make you see things in a different perspective . . .*

Enid Marley closed her sitting-room window with a bang. She knew well that Mrs. Pickett had opened it solely in order to provoke her. There existed between her and her charwoman a constant state of cold war.

She sat down at her pretty little desk, sighed, and drew a piece of notepaper towards her. She picked up her pen.

MY MURDER, she wrote and underlined it.

I. *Must play for time yet retain hold on waning Woodman interest. Drugs? Fainting? Amnesia? Too late for further bruises?*

II. *Must either (a) pump Woodman or (b) visit* You *to discover which suspects have unshakable alibis. Must NOT accuse anybody until then. In the case of (b), if challenged by police on premises, imply that have come to remonstrate with murderer. ("Inspector, if I can make him/her/them see the error of his/her/their misguided ways, I shall make no charge, etc.")*

III. *Remember risked life to save sparrow. Love birds. Buy one? If so, large, humane cage, coconut, ants, eggs, etc. HATE CATS?*

IV. *Anonymous communications to Chairman, all senior partners Helseth and Marley, Lord Soderman, Mr. Haskin, all clubs, all influential clients. ("Are you aware that Harold Wentworth Marley, having abandoned his loyal and loving wife, is living in flagrant sin with a woman whose family is in service? His wife trusted him. DO YOU?")*

V. *Letter to Harold, forgiving all, sweetness and light, disposing of motive for Suicide. Three copies.*

VI. *Place daily order for flowers for broken arm. St. German's Hospital. Apology note no.* 2a/85 + 4cb.

She sat back and looked the list over carefully. It seemed to cover her immediate plan of campaign. Provided that she stuck to her story, that she told it always more in sorrow than anger, that she allowed no new development to fluster her, then she had only to name her attacker to be safe forever from a charge of Attempted Suicide.

She took a fresh piece of paper and headed it *SUSPECTS, YOU.*

Let X = Unknown, she wrote.
All seven suspects dislike me heartily. Therefore X, in attempting to save my life, has proved himself/herself/themselves to be quixotic/ mad/drunk.
Q: To which can one/any/all of these descriptions be applied?
A: The lot.
Conclusion: Am mystified.

She tapped the end of her pen thoughtfully against her teeth. She decided to review each suspect individually, to award marks for Motive. Clearly, the one with the greatest desire to see her plunge to her death would have been the least likely to have tried so desperately to save her. Therefore he or she who scored the highest would automatically be the lowest on her list. Only those who had little or no motive for Murder deserved her further consideration. The favorite suspect of the police would be the one whom she herself least favored.

She thought immediately of . . .

Doctor Feltz, she wrote.

For he alone had a classic motive for murdering her. Some years before, she had, at considerable expense, discovered the grim secret of his past. She knew all about Kurt and Liesel and Ali. She knew the whole terrible truth about Mangoyian.

She had never – oh, ugly word! – actually blackmailed him, but the little doctor had apparently thought it necessary to send her a large, expensive present on the last day of every month. She knew, and he knew, that she could ruin him. She therefore accepted his offerings as tokens of gratitude that she had not yet done so.

He would, of course, never have overcome his prejudice against violence. He had the heart of a trembling blancmange. It was rumored in the office that he regularly shared his supper with the huge, tame rats which lolled around his bed-sitting room. He would have turned pale at the mere thought of shooting, strangling, poisoning, or even lifting a finger against her, anybody or anything else.

But had he seen her, a perennial threat which he could ill afford, swaying and about to fall into an abyss, would he have lifted a finger to help her?

No.

He would have turned away and closed his eyes. In due course, he would have bought a neat little wreath and fainted at her funeral. She awarded him ten out of ten marks and crossed him off her list.

Paul East.

Poor Paul! He too had, if not exactly a motive for Murder, at least a deep grudge against her. How many years ago was it that he had burst into her office, strident with ambition and hunger, to demand her opinion of his first novel? She had realized immediately that he had unusual fire and promise. She had decided to corral him, to persuade him to join the staff of *You*. She had told him that his book was terrible. Week by week, month by month, year by year, she had tactfully tamed him, persuaded him through the hoops, taught him every trick.

Now, he could write twenty thousand words a day in any one of at least eight entirely different styles. In a single evening, he could write a short story of exactly the desired wordage around an illustration rejected by *Me*. He could dash off a series of twelve captions, each of forty-eight ems, without turning a hair. He invented puzzles and quizzes. He was responsible for the Children's Crossword Corner. He was a first-class hack.

Occasionally, the old fire would erupt. Only recently he had told her, almost incoherent with rage, that she had ruined him, that she had deliberately dragged him down to her own level. He had added that, had she been a man, he would even have attended her funeral. Nine marks.

No, he would not have tried to save her. He would not have attended her funeral. Nine marks.

Ellie Sansome.

Ah, yes, Ellie! Eight years ago, she had been a jolly lout from a country town. Eagerly, she had turned to Enid Marley for advice upon her slightest problem. Gratefully, she had allowed herself to be bullied from her chrysalis of fat. Obediently, she had broadened her mind. Gradually, she had outpaced her retinue of rustic followers. Now, men were alarmed by her elegance, frightened by her conversation, terrified by her hipbones.

Enid Marley, satisfied with the metamorphosis, content that Ellie was now a confirmed career girl, an integral part of the machinery of *You*, had only a week before been deeply shocked to overhear a conversation so ungracious that it had remained etched on her memory.

"Oh, yes indeed, dear," Ellie had been saying. "If it hadn't been for Madam, mum would have hooked the most scrummy gent. He hadn't actually *asked*, but it was touch-and-go, if you see what I mean. Like a clunk, I asked Her advice. My dear, she went holy on me quick as a milkmaid. Take a tip from mum, dear. If ever Madam starts dishing out the milk of H.K., race away and climb a tree. She asked me to dinner. 'Come all al fresco!' she cried. 'We'll have a boiled egg and lay our plans.' Well, mum hurries trustingly around with a melon and, my dear, *what?* Twelve assorted, full evening dress, six courses, and some swine with a violin. And guess who was present in his little white tie? Correct. He took one look at my slacks and my shimmering office face and decided never to do it again. I swear I'd have bundled Madam out of the window then and there if she hadn't lived on the ground floor!"

The girl had actually said that! She had, of course, been exaggerating as usual. She would not push anyone even off a pavement. But nor, quite definitely, would she have made a frantic attempt to drag Enid Marley to safety. Eight marks.

Jimmie Simmons.

Jimmie, too, had, or thought he had, an old score to settle. Silly boy! Just because she had once advised his ailing guardian to change his will! Finding himself a pauper, Jimmie had slouched into her office and said with bitterness appalling in one so young, "You did this for my own good, naturally. One of these days, I may be able to do something for *you.*"

No, he would not have saved her. Indeed, noting her plight, he would probably have cried "Hold it!" and darted from the room to fetch his camera. Seven marks.

Mrs. Ryder.

Enid Marley frowned. There had been an occasion some six years before, when Mrs. Ryder had been invited to make six thousand Cornish pasties for a charity whist drive. She had considered this a great honor and had bragged about it at length in the office.

On the eve of the affair, the committee had received three anonymous letters. The first had stated that Mrs. Ryder had obtained her mutton from a horse butcher; the second, that she had caused five hundred extra tickets to be printed and had sold them for her own benefit; the third, that although she had produced four children, there was not, and never had been, a Mr. Ryder.

The worthy woman had the next day stalked into Enid Marley's office, flung down twenty-four paper carriers full of Cornish pasties, and accused her of being responsible for these communications.

Not deigning to defend herself, Enid Marley had given her a serene and pitying smile. Since then, the two women had not spoken.

Mrs. Ryder's dogged principles would certainly have driven her to the assistance of anybody in danger. Seeing an enemy teetering on a high sill, she would have done her utmost to effect a rescue. But those same principles, in this case, would have forbidden her to break the silence of six long years.

She would have been quite incapable of saying, "It's all right! I've got you!" She would have struggled grimly, but mutely. She would not have uttered a word. Five marks.

Doon . . .

. . . on the other hand, would have chattered. Enid Marley's lip curled as she pictured the child's eyes huge with fear, the sun flashing on her unbecoming spectacles. "Oh, corks!" she would have cried. "It's going to be all right, I think, but you *must* stop kicking! Let go of that thing and grab me! I may be small, but, honestly, I'm terrifically wiry. Coo, you are an ass! This is jolly dangerous! I'm scared absolutely green!"

For Doon would certainly have tried to save her. Also, she had no real motive for Murder. It was true that she made no secret of her dislike of Enid Marley. Once, invited to a coffee party, she had said, outspoken as usual, "No, thank you. It's very kind of you, but I don't like you, so I wouldn't enjoy it."

But dislike was not hatred and even hatred was rarely sufficient motive for Homicide. Yet, Doon was a possibility. In fact, if one accepted that her first taste of drama might, for once, have stilled her tongue, she was a first-class suspect. One mark.

And there was nobody left except . . .

Egon.

Wild, wilful Egon, who loathed and respected her. Egon, who fifty times a day said, "I love you," with warmth and charm, yet who loved nobody and nothing except *You*. Egon, who knew that she was the life and breath of his sickly brainchild, that without her, it must waste and die.

Egon would have fought, wrestled, sweated to save her. He would have seen her, not as a woman whom he hated in danger, but as the mainstay of his beloved publication swaying towards bankruptcy. Without her, he too was finished.

He had no motive for Murder, every motive for rescue. Unless she had, with her wide experience, misjudged somebody, unless the years of petty problems had warped her reason, then it had been Egon's hands which had strained to save her. It had been Egon's voice which had said with such breathless desperation, "It's all right! I've got you!" It was impossible to award him even a fraction of a mark.

It was Egon whom – provided, of course, that he had no alibi – she must accuse of Attempted Murder.

Samuel Wildman Egon!

Sam Egon!

Egon!

Chapter 7

By half past five, the last girl had gossiped her way out of the typing pool. At six, the first strict tempo record announced the beginning of the evening session in the dancing school on the fourth floor. By half past six, only Egon, Rex, and Inspector Woodman remained in the offices of *You*. Together, they left Egon's room and walked along the corridor in silence.

Going down the stairs, Rex hurried past the windows on each half-landing. Since he had decided that Egon was a murderer, he had cautiously refused to be left alone with him. Now, he was safe, for surely Egon would not try anything homicidal in the presence of the police?

He glanced sideways at Woodman, hated his tie, wondered how the man would react if he were to say, "My dear, I've solved this caper for you. All I need is a drop of proof."

The detective was sucking in his cheeks. It had been a horrible day. He hated cases where there was nothing for him to get his claws into, no clues, no leads, nothing for the laboratories. While his friend Willis assembled his case against the killer Kayes – ah, what a splendid business! Sixty-eight prosecution witnesses, hair, blood, dust, shreds of cloth, four sorts of mud – *he* was forced to play Chase-me-Charlie with a couple of bruises and a lot of argey-bargey. Charlie! He darted a look at Rex, despised his waistcoat. The man had had the effrontery that afternoon to announce Woodman to Ellie Sansome by crying, "Clap hands, dear! Here comes Charlie!"

Woodman bit his lip. While Willis gloated among his exhibits – his slides, his pieces of skin and fingernail parings, the tiny piece of green fluff upon which the case stood or fell – *he* was obliged to deal with these maddening people who, amongst themselves, obviously called him Charlie.

And why did they keep contradicting themselves?

Why had Ellie Sansome, asked whether Enid Marley had any enemies, said, "You could have counted them on the fingers of every right-handed woman in Europe, dear. No, sorry. Cancel that. I meant no, of course she hadn't. Not one." And Jimmie Simmons, the photographer chap, asked whether Enid Marley normally kept her office window open or shut, had said, "Oh, yes, invariably. By which, of course, I mean never. Hang on a tick will you? I'll go and ask." And Doon Travers, the Beauty Editor, had been heard to whisper quickly to Egon, "How long do you *get* for perjury? Do they let you knit?"

What was Egon up to? Would Willis see the significance of that tiny piece of fluff?

Egon, gray with weariness, was two steps behind the detective, staring sightlessly at the back of his neck. He was deeply troubled. Less than an hour before, a news agent had telephoned him and said, "Look, if this is going to be Attempted Murder, I'll take another hundred copies." Egon had said thoughtfully, "Mm? I'll see what I can do."

Well, what *was* he going to do? He had finally persuaded his staff to accept Misadventure. Had he been wise? Was he missing a great opportunity? How would the provinces feel about Murder?

Will Murder make it without a corpse? he wondered. From the provincial point of view, was it not preferable that way? Was it not in the best traditions of *You*, a story with wide family appeal? The ballyhoo without the blood. The thrill without the chill. The doom without the gloom. A killing for the kiddies. *Mm?*

With some foreboding, he realized that he was about to change his mind again. Yet surely he was justified? Surely, the Murder way, he had, in the phrase of his tailor, the warmth without the weight?

Between the third and fourth floors, Kidder, the most dogged crime reporter in London, sat in the broken lift drinking whisky and soda and arguing with the janitor. The electricians who had attempted to free him some hours before had departed, saying that a certain part of the mechanism was missing and could not be replaced until the morning.

"I *told* you She wasn't Herself, sir," the janitor was saying. "Yet you slammed the gate and jumped about. I said to meself at the time, 'Oh, she won't like that.' An' I also 'ave to tell you as this missin' part was 'andmade by a gentleman in Germany 'oo is now dead . . ."

The reporter saw Egon and Woodman. "Hi," he said. "What's new?"

"No comment," said Woodman.

Egon hesitated, then plunged. "She says she was pushed."

Kidder raised his eyebrows. "So? Fall Victim Claims Murder, eh? From Our Special Correspondent trapped in death building."

"Nobody's dead," said Woodman coldly.

"A technicality, old chap. Know who dunnit? Husband? Disillusioned fan? Sex angle?"

"No."

"Arrest expected hourly? Anybody helping you with your inquiries yet?"

"No."

"How many suspects?"

"No comment," said Woodman.

"Seven," said Egon.

"One," said Rex before he could stop himself.

Kidder stared at him. "No, Winsome," he said. "Not at this stage! Wait for it, *wait* for it! Seven, eh? Yes, I like seven. Sounds kind of mystic. Strange rites and stuff . . ."

"Now look here, Kidder," said Woodman. "I've had trouble with you before."

Kidder grinned. "Sure, 1952, the Kayes acquittal. I surely did give you the razzamatazz, eh? How's it feel, having Willis on the case now? That might make a couple of paras."

"No comment," said Woodman.

Kidder rattled the gates of the lift. "Ah, come across, you old terror of the underworld," he pleaded. "Give me irony, give me pity, shoot me in the stomach, but don't give me 'no comment.' Look at me! Trapped, helpless, stuck with this damnfool story that just doesn't exist. Normally, I wouldn't touch it with the leaning tower of Pisa. Last night, some broad was dredged out of the Channel wearing a lot of hot rocks about which I know a thing or three. Now that's a *story*! Come on, come on! Do I have to watch this page until next week? *Give!*"

"Good night," said Woodman stolidly. "And you can quote me." He pushed Egon ahead of him down the stairs.

"YARD MAN ASSAULTS WITNESS," remarked Kidder.

Egon looked back over his shoulder. "See you later, pal," he murmured, closing one eye in a conspiratorial manner.

Kidder raised his glass. "Keep it exclusive and I'll play ball."

On the half-landing, Woodman said, "Mr. Egon, if you give that bird enough straw, he's going to start dropping ruddy great bricks."

Egon dropped his cigarette and trod on it. "Mm," he said noncommittally.

On the second floor, Carstairs, the private detective, lunged around the corner. "See the spic?" he asked, pointing his large head upwards towards the Hungarian photographer's studio. "Gave me the slip again, blast him! Don't know how he does it." Although he had not once looked directly at the Scotland Yard man, he told himself aloud, "There's poor old Woody. Demoted two o'clock, 12 April 1952, after the Kayes boob."

I remember that soggy face, thought Woodman. *Had his pocket picked on the beat 1942. Lost the ashes in the Bogotez Case, 1943. Found tied up in a train, 1944* . . . He nodded distantly and continued on his way downstairs.

Rex and Egon followed him. Egon nudged Rex with his shoulder. "Look, Reg," he said in a low voice. "Will you do me a nondescript little favor? Will you please keep clammed up until I get the hang of this thing? What's all this about *one* suspect? Hell, you aren't even a witness!"

Rex held tightly to the banisters. "Rex," he said. "My name's *Rex*."

"Okay, okay."

On the pavement outside the building, there was a small crowd. A constable stood by the archway. A squad car waited across the street. A child in white socks asked, "Mummy, is that the murderer?" The woman whose hand she was holding said, "Ss-ssh, dear! The lady's still alive."

"Look at 'is 'orrible great eyes," said a woman wearing a man's cap. "You can always tell by their eyes."

"Boo," said a spotty youth tentatively.

"I absolutely agree," said his girl friend. "*Boo!*"

"Hang the lot, *I* say," said the youth, encouraged.

"*Boo!*"

"Boo!"

"Boo-oooo-oooo!"

"Now move along, now," said the constable.

Woodman said to Egon, "Good night. I'll probably see you tomorrow."

"Afraid so."

"Afraid?"

"Figure of speech, cock. Figure of speech. Good night."

"Good night."

"Bye-bye," said Rex.

Woodman crossed the road and got into the squad car. The constable moved forward with gentle menace. The crowd shuffled back. A well-dressed woman pushed an autograph album into Rex's hand.

"Mate A?" she asked in an ultra-refined voice.

Taken aback, Rex scrawled *With best wishes, Rex Travers.*

"Think your," she said, and hastened away.

Pushing through the crowd, hurrying towards the corner, Egon put his hand on Rex's elbow. Rex jumped, trying to edge away. Nervously, he glanced at Egon. Would the man suddenly foam at the mouth and push him under a car?

Egon was chewing his thumbnail, his head bent, staring at his feet. "They want Murder," he said. "You felt it? But that's *here*. How about Cornwall? How about Wales? How about the Fells?"

"Gas Talks!" roared the news vendor on the corner "Wicked flood swindle! Kayes latest! Exclusive interview with fallen woman! 'Orrible disaster everywhere! The lot!"

Egon bought three papers The flood in Essex was still rising. An official of the Gas Workers' Union had said, "We mean business." The murdered woman in the Channel had been identified as the mistress of a man whom the police were anxious to interview. The killer Kayes had appeared before a West London magistrates' court, pleaded Guilty, and been removed to Wandsworth. The French Minister of War had resigned.

The fallen woman proved to be not, as Egon had anticipated, Enid Marley, but another who had been arrested for the twenty-third time for soliciting. There was no mention of the Marley story.

"That's great," said Egon, wondering whether he meant it or whether he was being sarcastic. Still gripping Rex's elbow, he walked on to where his tiny, moody car was parked. Some sixth sense told him that it was not going to start without being pushed. Without getting in, he turned on the ignition and pressed the self-starter. It made a shrill yet drowsy noise like a dog hunting in its sleep.

"Look, Ron," he said. "How do *you* feel about Murder?"

Rex took an involuntary step backwards. "You mean *now?*"

"Mmm."

"No. *Not.*"

"Why?"

"I've got a date."

"Give you a lift?"

"*No!* I mean, no. Thank you very much."

Egon kicked his car absently. "Maybe I'll go and parley with our lift captive," he said. "I need a twenty-second opinion."

Rex backed away. He paused in the door of the Indian restaurant and looked back. Egon had not noticed his absence. He was punching his right palm with his left fist and saying in a confidential manner to nobody, "Murder's all very well, old boy. But I must *not* forget the overseas circulation . . ."

Rex pushed open the door of the restaurant. There was a notice stuck to it with adhesive tape reading *Seen of Calamity! Inquire within!*

Except for the proprietor, the restaurant was deserted. The Indian sat at a table reading the *Times of Bombay* and cleaning his nails with a toothpick.

He looked up and saw Rex. "So there you blow, man," he said listlessly. "Such a day, ho? Regard me, I say. Am I ruined? My cookhouse stocked with vittles for hundreds, expecting the jolly notoriety. My stables full of gates, yet the horses gone. My awning fouled, my bay trees removed as evidence, my insurance johnnies in a stew . . ." He eased the tines of a fork inside his pink turban and scratched his head.

Suddenly, his brown finger stabbed furiously, repeatedly, at a photograph on the printed page before him. It showed a handsome Sikh flashing white teeth from the back of a horse. "See him, man, *see* him!" keened the proprietor. "My brother! While *I* am in ruins, *he* plays polo!"

"The shops are shut," said Rex. "Can I borrow some bread?"

The Indian screamed towards the kitchen in Tamil, "Bring bread, you rat of hell!" Then his shoulders slumped. "What to do? Thirty pounds of mutton, twenty chickens, this weather, no icebox. Already the flies are intrigued. *Polo!* Inform me kindly, from whence did he obtain this immense animal?" He glared out of the window. "If I had not that morning raised my perishing awning, the joint would be jammed and overflowing."

Hoping to comfort him, Rex said, "I think Mr. Egon's beginning to want Murder again, too."

"Give me the suckers, I will shake down the shekels. But now, what next? Vultures are embarrassed by perfect health."

"You'll be all right," said Rex gloomily. "I'll be bumped off any day now. I know too much."

The Indian sprang to his feet. "You promise so on your word of oath?" he cried. "Fine man, I say! Place it there!"

Twenty-five minutes later, Rex sat at home peeling potatoes in his kitchen. Doon sat on the draining-board wearing her reading spectacles and shelling peas. Rex told her about the anonymous confession note of the morning.

"Egon wrote that," he said impressively. "He's a wicked murderer, that's what."

"No, no, ducky," Doon protested. "You don't know him like I do. He might do for Misadventure or Suicide, but not Murder. Anyway not Madam's Murder."

"Prove it."

"Prove the opposite."

"Explain to me why he didn't declare that letter to Charlie-boy."

"Explain to *me* why he wrote it if he didn't want to declare it. And particularly when he was grouting away at Misadventure."

Rex was silent for a moment. He picked up another potato and said hopefully, "Perhaps it was a forgery."

"There's no such thing as an anonymous forgery."

"True, true."

Fifteen minutes later, Doon carried a laden tray through into the dining-room. Rex followed her with the mustard.

"How many potatoes?" she asked. "If it *was* Murder, I rather fancy Jimmie."

"Two, please. Why?"

"Well, he more or less accused *me*."

"*No!*"

"Yes." She added fairly, "I admit he was in a rage at the time. Something to do with a camera, but even so I've distinctly gone off him."

"My God, he's got a nerve!"

"Just what you need for Murder, Q.E.D."

"What about me? I rather accused you as well."

"You're *family*. And anyway you've got an alibi."

"Isn't he rather *young*?"

"People kill people when they're still at school these days."

"A fact, a fact. These chops are tough as Madam."

"How would you cook *her*?"

"I wouldn't. She's cooked already."

"Shall we talk about Misadventure?"

"All right."

"More peas?"

Doing the washing-up, they agreed that Misadventure was unlikely but not absolutely impossible, that Murder was impossible but in no way unlikely, that Inspector Woodman was about forty-eight, probably had blood pressure, and should go on to a strict diet, nothing fried and no salt.

Making coffee Rex said uneasily, "You know, angel, I may have made rather a nonsense this morning. I mean what with patterns and all those coupons, and the *Difficult Relations* not being there, and not knowing about *Hullo, Hullo!* until it was too late, and the lipstick on that vile girl's teeth . . ."

Doon dropped a fork. "It's the addresses that matter," she said anxiously. "You did get them in the right order, didn't you, darling?"

He avoided her eyes. "Well, I made this neat little pile of bits of paper," he said. "Everything was more or less under control until it fell over. Does it matter terribly?"

"It does rather, darling. I mean, *You*'s always in a jam of some sort. And these days, what with Madam grumbling away about Murder, and Egon dead set on Misadventure . . ."

"Not any more."

"No?"

"Bet you fourpence it's Murder again tomorrow."

"Well, whichever. And Kidder in the lift just wanting to make front page trouble, and the police being so bossy and difficult . . ."

"Well? Go on."

"Well, if on top of that you've got a whole lot of readers righteously narked . . ."

"You keep stopping."

"I can't go on, darling," she said helplessly. "I just don't know what comes next. I suppose almost anything might happen."

Chapter 8

You, like most publications with small and inefficient staffs, was always in trouble of one sort or another. That night, quite apart from the old familiar troubles and the new troubles caused by the Marley affair, there were also a number of totally unexpected ones looming in several different quarters. The largest category, the Old Troubles, included the Board, the Chairman, the printers, the advertisers, the contributors, the artists, and all the readers who had been irritated, angered, or incensed by *You* for lengths of time ranging from six months to ten years. In the last group most of the staff boasted of at least one hardy enemy.

A notorious vexatious litigant had at various times attempted to sue Egon for Fraud, Defamation, Battery, Trespass, False Imprisonment, Alienation of Wife's Affections, Seduction of Minors, Breach of Contract, and Libel.

A woman in Kent had for five years been convinced that Doctor Feltz, as Viennese Psychiatrist, was deliberately misinterpreting her dreams because he desired her and was too bashful to diagnose his own inhibitions.

Planter's Wife, Sarawak, had been writing with growing impatience to Mrs. Ryder for four and a half years. The main text of her letters was unchanging. *I am expecting the Governor to a small, informal supper. What should I serve?* But as she never supplied her address, her letters were never answered.

A grocer's wife in Southampton still threatened Paul East. Her two daughters, aged twelve and fourteen, had so inflamed by a travel story written under the name of *Lamek* that they had stowed away on a cargo boat flying the Panama flag and whose destination was Marrakesh. They had never been seen again, but a shocking postcard from Montevideo had reported that they were well and rich and very happy.

Doon had once advised a girl in Hyderabad to treat a gumboil in a manner which had not proved successful. Since then, she had received twenty-three letters informing her of the loss of yet another tooth and adding, *Bet you feel awful!*

Ellie, advocating a tweed burnoose sewn with beads, had won the lasting displeasure of a certain *Miss Wisley, Ealing*, whose fiancé, upon seeing this creation, had rocked with laughter and turned his attentions else-where. The jilted woman wrote regularly, always in verse, reminding Ellie of the tragedy. Her latest communication had read,

Tho' Fashion is a foible, Fashion is a Jade,
Your wanton tip has plunged my life in shade!
He told me I was marvelous, swearing to be true.
I was in Seventh Heaven till I bought that fateful You!
How I'll live without him, I simply cannot tell!
One thing I am convinced of is You *should go to hell!*

All these letters, and there were many of them, were known affection-ately in the *You* offices as the Old Beefs. They were tactfully answered and placed in a large file labeled *Complaints, Regular*. Every member of the staff was resigned to the fact that each issue might, and usually did, bring a new crop. Doon swore that some sixth sense informed her when she had made a new enemy.

"Now this," she would say, plucking one letter from a heap of several hundred, "has O.B. written all over it. Feel it, it's still warm."

The previous week's number had been no exception.

The short story, written by Paul under the name of Lotta d'Arcy, had persuaded an already disillusioned girl to marry a confirmed drunk in the belief that the wedding ceremony would instantly reform him. A misprint on the news page had stated that a certain destroyer weighed six tons, enraging one *Colonel Quincey* and two *V. Angrys*. The cookery spread had sponsored fourteen rough letters about Frog Cooking, one telegram ordering enigmatically *TAKE A CARROT*. The book reviews, written by Egon, had earned a furious telephone call from a woman novelist whose latest work he had described as ideal reading for a television breakdown.

But of all the potential troublemakers in this group – although all said firmly that they intended to do something soon – not one was planning any immediate action.

In the second category, the New Troubles, three people at nine o'clock that night were wondering singlemindedly how the present spark could be fanned into a blaze . . .

In the *You* and *Me* building, Kidder, the trapped reporter, sat in the broken lift and sharpened a pencil. He had had a long discussion with Egon, who had returned with an ingratiating smile, a bottle of gin, a tea-cup, and the anonymous confession note of the morning. Having consumed half the man's liquor, Kidder became mildly fired by his enthusiasm.

"*Murder!*" Egon had said in a ghoulish whisper, pacing up and down in front of the lift, slapping the gates with an open hand. "Lovely, lovely Murder! Gorgeous grub!"

Kidder had passed the empty cup through the bars. "It's conventional to have a body, buddy."

Egon had crouched by the lift gates, in his excitement pouring a little gin into the cup and a lot down the shaft. "To hell with convention!" he hissed. "The Murder That Wasn't! The Living Corpse! The Killer With The Jinx! How does he feel, sweating it out? Does his victim know, does she *know*? Will she expose him? Will he have another bash? Murder with a body's *old-fashioned*. This is new! It's revolutionary! Don't you *get* it?"

"No. They want blood."

Egon had clawed at his hair, exasperated. "They've got bloody blood, chum, every man, woman, and child!" he had shouted. "They've all *got* blood. Blood's old stuff. It's *dated*!"

"Gin's not."

Egon had refilled the cup, held it just out of Kidder's reach. "No Murder, no hooch," he had growled.

"Okay, I'll give it a whirl."

"Front page?"

"Maybe."

Some while later, after Egon had left, Kidder had begun to wonder whether the Marley story might rate a small paragraph on page 3. Later still, he had remembered how he had once, in a crimeless week, plastered the *Echo* with the story of a stolen greyhound which had never existed. He had bet himself ten pounds that he could do it. He had done it, triumphantly, then sallied forth and squandered ten pounds in a single, happy hour.

Was he now getting old? Could he no longer accept a challenge? Of course he could! The cost of living had gone up since the greyhound, so he bet himself twenty-five pounds.

When, five minutes later, the old janitor shuffled up the stairs and stated flatly that the missing part of the lift was immediately obtainable for the sum of five guineas, Kidder shook his head. He no longer wished to be freed. His plight enormously enhanced his story. Five guineas changed hands, but on the understanding that the lift remained out of action, anyway during the daytime.

This arrangement suited the janitor very well. While She was not working, nobody could ill-treat Her. Moreover, the reporter had promised to send for a photographer to take a photograph of Her. Tomorrow morning, millions of people all over England would be able to admire her frail beauty. The janitor smiled for the first time in nine years.

"Built by Jenson, Matthews & Werndorfer, 1868," he offered. "Brass by Blackstone & Cutler . . ."

Kidder was not listening. He was already considering the rival merits of various possible headlines. PLUNGE VICTIM ALLEGES FOUL PLAY? OR, DEATH PLOT CLAIMS SAGE? Or simply, MURDERED WOMAN LIVES?

As he pondered, scribbled, pondered again, a bicycle-clipped messenger lounged against the wall and waited for his copy.

Three miles away, Enid Marley lay in bed and waited for the morning. For then she would accuse Sam Egon of Attempted Murder.

Ah, rewarding moment! She anticipated it with a glow of pleasure. She would wear her black suit, her gray toque, a single rope of pearls. She already saw herself standing on the threshold of Egon's office, saw the surprised circle of faces turning towards her.

What was she going to say?

Perhaps she would ask him brokenly, "Sammy, Sammy, why did you *do* it?" Or, if he were as usual speaking into two or more telephones, then she might cry in a voice clearly audible to his callers, "You tried to kill me, Egon! Why, *why!*" Or, should he be eating one of the many sandwiches always cached in his desk, then perhaps she would say sternly, "Enjoy the last crumb, you rat! You won't get cheese in *jail!*"

Whatever her approach, he would be forced to show his hand. If it had been he, as she was convinced, who had tried to save her life, then he would either have to produce some spurious alibi or insist that he had done his damnedest to rescue her. In either case, she had him cold.

In the first, she would face him and plead, "Think, Sammy, *think!* You have no alibi, and you and I know it! You are forcing innocent, if misguided, people to commit Perjury."

In the second, she would appeal to the police, to the brisket-faced Woodman. "Inspector," she would say with an obvious effort. "Mr. Egon and I have worked harmoniously together for many years. Had he apologized for trying to kill me, I should have let bygones be bygones. But his present attitude forces me to . . . *et cetera.*"

Perhaps at this stage, Egon would produce her farewell letter. But she was prepared for that, too. She would take it from him in a wondering manner, frowning, puzzled, read it through at least twice. Then she would raise her head slowly, gaze at him. Her eyes would flash with scorn.

She lay in bed in the darkness and practised flashing her eyes several times, with and without a slight frown.

"I could perhaps have understood and forgiven an impulsive crime," she would say, tossing the note aside, brushing her fingertips together fastidiously. "But not this, not a deed which obviously was coldly premeditated. Inspector Woodman, in the interests of justice I am obliged to declare that this . . . this document is a *wicked forgery*!"

She punched her pillows cozily around her head, pulled up her eiderdown, and composed herself for sleep.

Ah, sad, mad Sam! Prison bars would not become him.

Or *would* they?

Mmm?

In the Casualty Ward in St German's Hospital, Mrs. Fred Turner lay stroking the cast on her broken arm with deep complacency. Her husband sat beside her in angry silence. He had been obliged to cook his own breakfast, to cut his own sandwiches for lunch. He had not made the bed. He had no clean shirt for tomorrow. He could not find anything at home. There was nothing to eat there and the boiler had gone out. Presently, he would leave. It would cost him two-and-five-pence to return to pandemonium. He had not been in such a rage since his daughter was born.

He glowered at a huge vase of red roses. Red roses, was it? They stood for something shifty all right! And attached to them was an unsigned card reading 2a/85 + 4cb.

He curled his toes inside his boots. Who would have sent his wife so expensive a present? Who, with nothing to hide, would have written to her in code? Had she been playing fast-and-loose all these years? If so, who with? Jed Loomas? Mister mow-'em-down Bartlett? Or creepy old Friggett?

His wife said, "Stop kickin' the bed, Fred, do! Know 'oo it was what jumped on me? Enid *Mar*ley! I wrote to 'er once, I did. 'Adn't been for 'er, I'd of gone off with Tim Crick."

"I'm goin' to take out a Case," he said, breathing heavily through the unlit cigarette stuck to his upper lip.

"You'd never," she smiled, knowing him well.

"I will that," he argued, hunching his narrow shoulders. "I'm wild, I am." He did not look at her. He knew, and he knew that she too knew, that he always had been and always would be incapable of doing anything at all unless he was bullied into it. His family and his few friends deeply distrusted the Law; he would get no encouragement from that quarter. No, on this occasion he badly needed an ally, but he must be a stranger.

And how, he asked himself helplessly, was he to win friends and be influenced by people with his Beer Money in bed with a broken arm?

His wife understood his predicament. She eased her fingers into the top of her cast and withdrew a small roll of notes. "'Ere," she said simply, giving him a pound.

The third group of troublemakers, the New and Totally Unexpected ones, might never have amalgamated with the other two had not the deserted bridegroom of Enid Marley's most devoted fan, Browneyes Jackson, marched into the bar of the ninth best hotel in Bournemouth with the firm intention of getting fighting drunk.

"Enid whahaha Marley!" he sneered, accepting his fifth double whisky from the barman. "Look at me! Where am I?"

"Exactly," said the barman, eating a nut.

"You know what I'm going to do?" asked Mr. Jackson. "I'm going to beat up *You*."

The barman tossed a small biscuit into his mouth. "Quite," he said, turning on the radio.

Mr. Jackson's bleary eye panned around the room. He scowled at the green wicker chairs, at the poster announcing a show on the pier, at the enormous Irishman drinking rough cider at the far end of the bar. "*You!*" he shouted. "Just wait till I've finished with *You!*"

"Might you be talking to me?" inquired the Irishman.

Mr. Jackson curled his lip. He swayed on his stool and saved himself clumsily. "I'm going to take *You* apart and enjoy it!" he announced proudly.

The Irishman put his drink carefully on to the counter. He stood up and took off his coat. Walking on the balls of his feet with the dreadful grace which only huge and very angry men can achieve, he advanced upon Mr. Jackson.

The barman knew the Irishman of old. He knew exactly what was going to happen. He therefore telephoned for the police, placed his signed picture of Marilyn Monroe under the counter, leaned his forearms on a barrel of bitter, and watched with interest.

The fight was one of the best he had seen. The two men were surprisingly well matched. Whereas the Irishman had the brawn and the reach, the Englishman had the brain and the verve. It was the former who struck the first foul blow, the latter who started the kicking. The former wielded the first broken bottle, the latter countered with the first smashed chair. The Irishman began the throwing of siphons. The Englishman hurled the first potted palm . . .

By mutual agreement, the two men continued to fight during the ride to the police station in the Black Maria. Still fighting, they were locked into a cell.

It was not until an hour later that both began to tire. The battle became sporadic, dwindled into a series of feeble pushes. Eventually, both men sat down. They kicked out at each other at intervals, but without real anger.

At some time during the long night, they reached an unspoken armistice. As the first light streaked the sky, the Irishman remarked that Mr. Jackson certainly was a terrible scrapper. Mr. Jackson took this in the spirit meant, as a compliment, and admitted that the other's left might alarm some people.

"O'Leary," said the Irishman. "My friends call me Trouble."

"Jackson."

They shook hands.

At nine o'clock, hung over and unshaven, they entered the Magistrates' Court arm in arm, pleaded Guilty, and insisted upon paying each other's fines.

As they stood on the pavement, freed, blinking in the sunshine, O'Leary glanced at his watch. The public houses would not be open for another two hours.

"I have an unholy thirst," he complained. "This ozone can kill a man in my condition."

"Your eye looks bad," said Mr. Jackson sympathetically.

"And I fear that your ear will thicken."

"Your wrist?"

"A trifle stiff. Your knee?"

"A bruise, no more."

O'Leary smiled reminiscently. "And where was it you found that thing with the castors? I missed it entirely."

They walked towards the center of the town. As they passed each closed salon, O'Leary frowned and Mr. Jackson sighed. They were staring moodily into an ironmonger's shop when a train wailed in the distance.

O'Leary stiffened like a pointer. "On such conveyances," he murmured, "healing beverages are served at civilized hours."

They crossed the road and turned towards the station.

"Two," said Mr. Jackson, spilling change on to the brass counter.

"Where to, sir?" asked the booking clerk.

"I do declare he wants a fight!" marveled O'Leary. "Will we oblige him, Jack?"

The clerk looked up. The two battered faces glared at him from the far side of the glass pigeonhole. "Just wondering which train you preferred, sirs," he said quickly.

"*That* one," said Mr. Jackson, pointing.

Fifteen minutes later, O'Leary banged his empty glass on to a table in the restaurant car and grabbed a passing waiter by the coat. "Speak up!" he boomed. "Where is this place going to?"

"London, sir," said the waiter with practised calm.

"Strange," brooded Mr. Jackson. "I know a fight in London."

O'Leary let go of the waiter. "Business or pleasure?"

"Both."

"May I assist you, Jack?"

"Thank you, Trouble."

"A pleasure, Jack. You have only to name our fist bait."

"Marley, Enid. She's a magazine."

O'Leary's bloodshot eyes squinted back across the years. "More than twenty years," he mused, "since I smashed my first press. In Bantry, it was, a soft day in June."

"What a team, by God!" Mr. Jackson banged his glass on the table. "You there in the monkey suit! Bring the bottle!"

"Can't do that, sir," said the waiter.

"*Bring it!*" yelled O'Leary.

"Yessir."

Neither Mr. Jackson nor O'Leary the Troublemaker could have known that they had a staunch ally in the very heart of the enemy territory. Rex's system of addressing envelopes had already considerably advanced their cause. Most of the results of his first day's work arrived at their destinations with the first delivery of the post . . .

Just outside Maidstone, Farmer Jepson found his wife behind the bungalow feeding the chicken. She was wearing galoshes, leaning against the rain butt. She was holding a letter in one hand, and scattering bread with the other.

"An' 'ow's me old girl?" he asked fondly, slapping her shapeless hip.

"Well, it's odd, Dad," she said. "'Member I wrote to that *You* 'bout Billy's bad arm? Well, they sent me ten shillin's. They say congratulations an' let's 'ave another amusin' letter soon."

In Norwich, Mr. Cream kicked the cat out of the window and picked up the envelope with the smart green lettering. It was addressed to his wife, so he opened it. He read the letter, then stamped through into the kitchen, pointed a fist, and said, "Ho, so you would, would you?"

His wife emerged from a cloud of steam around the sink. "I got porridge an' kippers, Ted," she gabbled, shrill with fear. "You like that. You *said*."

"This 'ere letter," said Mr. Cream. He picked up a colander and glared at her ferociously through the holes. "Want to adopt a nipper, do you?"

Her mouth fell open. "Eh?" she said, backing away from him. She had written to *You* about how she cut the sleeves off her husband's shirts in the summer and sewed them on again in the winter. She had hoped to win ten shillings from the *Hullo, Hullo!* page.

Mr. Cream sprang at her. He gripped her arm and twisted it. "I don't like kids," he said heavily.

"Ted! Oh, *Ted*! Aaaou! *AIEEEOOOUYEEEE!*"

"But I wrote for a *knitting* pattern," said Laura Morehouse in Hampstead. "Enid Marley thinks I ought to be a nurse." She laughed, a single note. "Me! With my delicate stomach and my nerves!"

Her husband had eaten a colossal breakfast and he did not want to talk. He said from behind the *Telegraph*, "Quite, my love."

She threw a lump of sugar into her coffee. "And out at all hours! What *fan*tasy! You wouldn't like *that*, would you?"

"Yes, of course, darling."

"*What?*"

"I said yes, my love."

"Oh, you beast!" she cried. "You're the most callous brute I ever met in all my life!"

"Me?" He looked up, puzzled.

"Yes," she whispered. "You, you, *you*!" She put down her cup with a splash and rose abruptly.

He followed her around the table, over to the window, down the steps and into the garden, over to the pear tree, past the bird bath, back into the house, through the dining room, and into the hall. She was cramming on her hat.

"Where are you going?" he asked, amazed.

"Away!" she snapped. She called to the bearded, colorless spaniel, "Oyster! Oyster!" But it was old and deaf and sluggish and it only watched her. She ran to it, snatched it up, and staggered back towards the front door. Over her shoulder, she panted, "Good bye, swine! I'll send for our luggage tomorrow!"

In Fulham, Madge White slumped on to the sagging bed which she shared with her two younger sisters and gnawed at her thumb. She had tried everything; nothing had been any good. *You* had been her last hope, and *You* too had failed her. What was the use of her joining a tennis club in her condition?

There were, of course, due to Rex's misguided efforts, many other examples of this type of trouble – in all, one hundred and twelve. But only these four people determined to avenge themselves without delay . . .

"They couldn't of saved Billy, Dad," sobbed Mrs. Jepson just outside Maidstone. "Was *meant*."

Her husband was lashing himself into one of his rare furies. "If that *You*," he said, working his lips, "thinks she can push *us* around, she's going to find out ruddy well different! I'm goin' to ruddy well ring 'er up an' go on an' on tellin' 'er so till I've used 'er ruddy ten shillin's ruddy well right up!"

"Ho, so it's faint, is it?" snarled Mr. Cream in Norwich, pushing his unconscious wife with his foot. "Well, let me tell you, I got a word or two to say to *You*. Jump to it! Get me bike!"

In Hampstead, Mr. Morehouse thought for the fifteenth time over the events which had led up to his wife's furious departure. She had mentioned the word MAR-something. If only he had not eaten so much!

Lea!

Lea! That was it! Marlea? Marley? Maarlie?

What was the name of the charwoman who hated Oyster? Of that interfering old poop who dished out advice in some magazine? Of the reef of rocks off Cornwall? Ma Lee? Enid Marley? Or the Marlees? Had not Laura said something about knitting? The Knittins were coming to dinner next Friday. But did they know Enid Marley? No. All right, ordinary knitting with needles. Needles? There was the Cornish motif again! But Laura thought Cornwall was rather twee, in a suffocating sort of way. Cornwall had never made her really angry. No, Cornwall was a red herring.

Sister Susie knitted socks for soldiers!

A clue?

Yes!

Laura was always knitting socks for some Army bloke whom she described as rather a pet. What was his name? Cedric. But Laura, for some reason she would never explain, always called him Toga.

Toga Marr-Leigh!

So that was it! Laura and Oyster had left him for Toga Marr-Leigh! Oh, so they had, had they?

Mr. Morehouse pursed his lips and hurried upstairs to change into his worst suit. He began to rehearse his speech. *Now look here, you damned blackguard! Thought you fooled me, did you? Take that, you oaf! I've known about you and Laura right from the start! Now how do you like THIS, eh? Stung a bit? well, try this, and that, and this and THAT!*

For he intended to hire a taxi, to go to Throgmorton Square, to beat the living daylights out of Toga Marr-Leigh.

In Fulham, after some thought, Madge White filled in the telegraph form and pushed it across the counter.

The girl behind the grille counted the words. *I will do myself in*, she read. *And it's all YOUR fault.* "Two an' four, dear," she said, scratching her knee.

The trouble, in fact, was well under way by the time that Rex anointed a piece of toast with honey and propped up the *Echo* against the coffee pot. For an instant he sat quite still. Then he moved with a jerk, knocking over the milk.

"Oh, crikey!" he said in a stranger's voice. "That's torn it!"

Alarmed by his sudden pallor, Doon dropped her knife and scuttled round the table to him. She looked over his shoulder.

The story shared the front page with the flood in Essex. There was a large picture of Kidder trapped in the lift, a smaller one of the front of the *You* and *Me* building with a perpendicular line of white dashes showing how Enid Marley's fall had been broken by the awning. There was a picture of Egon pointing a finger at the smashed window of the Marley office, and one of the anonymous confession note.

The headline was in heavy type.

PLUNGE SURVIVOR ACCUSES *YOU*!

Chapter 9

IT was nearly nine o'clock by the time that Egon nosed his tiny car through the crowd hovering around the archway in Croissant Street. He had read the *Echo* and was delighted with the results of his efforts. "It had to be *You*!" he sang, idiotically happy. "Murderous *You*, criminal *You*!" He told himself that he had always wanted Murder, right from the start. Why on earth had he ever allowed himself to be talked into silly old Misadventure?

As his motor horn had long ago ceased to function, he normally advertised his presence by leaning out of the window and bawling curses. That morning, he called benevolently, "Move an inch, you lovely piece! Hey, mother, will you marry me? Come on, kid, race you to the moon!" As the crowd moved back, he heard snatches of conversation.

"'Undred an' forty yards, it said! An' not a scratch!"

"Wasn't yards, was feet."

"Then feet then. But when you think Edna copped it just fallin' off 'er bike . . ."

". . . *that* window!"

"No, it wasn't. It was *that* one!"

"You'd have thought he'd have shot her first, or something."

"Never can tell with maniacs 'cos they can't tell theirselves, see."

"Mummy, can they hang them if the person isn't dead?"

"'Ere! Keep yer plates to yerself, can't you?"

"Don't shove, you . . ."

"Watch yer face, you . . ."

"Why, you . . ."

". . . *you!*"

". . . YOU . . .!"

"*YOU!*"

Beaming, Egon turned into the car park. The attendant loped towards him. "Over by the Riley, sir," he said. "Quiet today. Funny, isn't it? Oh, well, mustn't grumble. 'Spose it's 'cos she's not dead."

Ellie arrived a minute later. She wore gray and a pink hat. She looked so alarmingly smart that the crowd moved back silently, staring.

She too had seen Kidder's story in the *Echo*. She had not read it. She had been distracted by the picture of Egon pointing to the broken window. He looked straight into the camera, long, thin, dark, marvelously saturnine, slightly dishevelled, desperately in need of a woman's loving care. She had cut out the photograph, stuck it carefully on to a piece of cardboard, wrapped it in cellophane. It was even now deep in her handbag, a secret talisman. *Oh, Sammy! Ah, Sammy! Let me cook you a nourishing stew, turn your collars, cut your naughty hair . . .!*

"You a suspect miss?" asked a young man with a box camera. "Could I 'ave a sort of sarcastic smile, please?"

Doctor Feltz dismounted from his Hercules Junior bicycle and chained it to the railings with shaking hands. Since he had read the screaming headlines in the *Echo*, he had been unable to stop trembling. So now it was Mörder, Mörder with its inevitable glare of publicity! There would be reporters, photographers, smiling pictures of the seven suspects!

Of *him*, Emmanuel . . .

No, forget the name! Don't even think it!

Now, surely, his secret – the terrible secret known to nobody in the country except Enid Marley – would be discovered? Now, surely, the skeletons in his cupboard would track him down, expose and humiliate him before breaking his neck. Kurt? Liesel? Ali? But first, always first, the madman *Mangoyian!*

Where was he now? *Where?* Was he safe in custody? Was he being watched every second, every fraction of every second, by his guards? Did they realize how bad, how mad, how saturated in evil he was? Had they underestimated his vast cunning? Had they recognized Mangoyian the Pussyfoot, Mangoyian the Uncanny, the Mangoyian who, in half light, could make himself look exactly like a bush or a tree or a lamppost? Did they know that Doctor Feltz, making a precipitous escape, had once left the deadly fellow eating a pie on an airstrip in Bulgaria only to find him, at the end of the flight, eating apparently the same pie in London airport?

At all costs he must avoid photographers, or, if he were unable to do so without attracting suspicion, at least try to make himself unrecognizable. For a mad moment, he had considered coming to the office in his Romany Nemo outfit. The headscarf with the gilded dinars would have concealed his eyes and eyebrows. The bronze makeup and the ring in the false nose were convincingly oriental. The gaudy satin shirt would have disguised his cringing heart . . .

A small girl in long white socks approached him. "Are you one of the murderers?" she asked diffidently. "Could I have your autograph, please?"

Doctor Feltz was so startled that he dropped his briefcase. His eyes wide with panic, he backed away from her as if she had held a ticking bomb in each hand. Who was she? Was she as innocent as she appeared to be? *Had Mangoyian got a daughter?*

Mrs. Ryder bustled out of a taxi carrying a string bag of vegetables and a large, elaborate meat loaf which she had baked at home in her electric oven. Jimmie, whose first duty of the day was to photograph the meat loaf, followed her with his props, a branch of artificial spindle, three paper chrysanthemums, a carefully varnished loaf of French bread, and a decanter full of red ink.

Neither of them had seen Kidder's story in the *Echo*, Jimmie because he seldom read anything except paperbacked American Westerns or magazines devoted to jazz, and Mrs. Ryder because her third child, who had whooping-cough, had been sick all over the front page.

Jimmie frowned at the crowd. "What gives?" he asked, puzzled.

"There was an 'orrible murder," confided a woman whose turban bulged with partially concealed curlers. "Disgusting, I call it."

"Murder? Who?"

"Some poor thing called Marlowe. They say she was blind, too."

"Oh, *her*," said Jimmie, relieved. "Nothing new?"

Doon and Rex met Paul East on the outskirts of the crowd.

"You saw the *Echo*?" Paul asked. "What the hell's Egon up to?"

Doon pinched him. "It's all your fault," she said. "He'd have been perfectly happy with Misadventure if you hadn't gone on and on and on about Murder."

Paul was annoyed. He at once assumed the voice and manner of Spike Raven. "Vamoose, you jerks!" he barked. He laid hold of the man in front of him and jerked him aside. "Beat it, bums, unless you want to cool off in the morgue!" He seized Doon in his arms as Spike Raven had once in similar circumstances seized the treacherous Dolores del Castiglion, and began to elbow, threaten, and jostle his way towards the archway.

Carstairs, the private detective, lounged against a lamppost surveying the scene through small, half-closed eyes and thoughtfully picking his teeth with a sharpened match. As he saw the Hungarian photographer turn the corner, he straightened up and shifted the match to the corner of his mouth.

"Here he comes," he announced quietly to the man on his left. "That's him. I don't like Murder, never did. Let's let him have it!"

The man stared. He looked from Carstairs to the Hungarian and back. Then he turned to his neighbor.

The word spread quickly, whispered behind hands, muttered between heads close together, finally broadcast by an excitable barrowboy selling oranges. "*There 'e is! 'E's the one what killed 'em! 'Oo's for wipin' the grin off that wicked face?*"

The crowd turned, murmuring, elbow to elbow. All were unwilling to make the first or second move, all were eager to make the third or fourth. All gazed unwinkingly at the Hungarian photographer.

The Hungarian hesitated for only a second. He then walked nonchalantly up to Carstairs and gripped his arm in such a manner that it appeared that the detective was molesting him.

"My old woman pays you to trail me, shamus," he said softly. "Okay, trail me."

Carstairs rubbed his back against the lamppost and shook his large, misshapen head. "*Oh*, no!" he said equally softly. "Protection is extra."

Mr. Jackson and O'Leary the Troublemaker did not arrive until nearly two hours later. They had consumed a large quantity of whisky on the train and a slight coolness had developed between them. O'Leary had wished to gather reinforcements, to start conscripting for the cause immediately; Mr. Jackson was against it. O'Leary was keen to contact a certain professional wrecker named Skidder Murphy whom he knew in Pimlico; Mr. Jackson insisted upon a preliminary reconnaissance of the *You* and *Me* building. O'Leary wanted to walk to Croissant Street and pick a few fights on the way for practice; Mr. Jackson contended that they must save their strength and hired a taxi.

The crowd outside the archway had swollen considerably. Two policemen were trying to persuade it to disperse. The café on the far side of the road was doing a brisk trade in ice creams and minerals. The door of the Indian restaurant now sported a notice reading, SEEN OF MURDER! *Eggs-and-ships 2/-, Bacon, Sorsage, Ships 3/-*, MURDER SPECIAL, *Esteak, shop, bacon, sorsage, ships, 7/6d. All inquiries personally answered.*

A man with a bundle of pamphlets slapped one into Mr. Jackson's hand as he got out of the taxi. "Grow your own tobacco," he said dully. "Save 'undreds a year like millions of others."

O'Leary glared at the crowd. "And what might *they* be after wanting?"

"Seems there was a terrible murder, sir. Some madman went barmy an' threw two girls off the roof. You got a garden, sir? If not, millions grow it indoors. They say one of them was deaf an' dumb an' 'e 'acked 'er up before 'e 'urled 'er down. Frustration's what does it, sir. If 'e'd 'ad a nice cool smoke without 'avin' to fret about the cost . . ."

O'Leary, eyeing the crowd, nudged Mr. Jackson. "Conscripts," he murmured. "Now if I were to overturn that car and climb upon the roof . . ."

"No," said Mr. Jackson.

"And why not? I have a remarkable gift of oratory and if that fails, my fists are persuasive."

"Reconnaissance," said Mr. Jackson. "Intelligence, Conscription, Established Lines of Communication, Briefing and Coordination, *then* Attack!"

"General!" cried O'Leary, saluting.

"General!"

"Then who might be Commanding Officer?"

"Both. I'm Admin., you're Ops."

"General!"

"General!"

Mr. Jackson paid off the taxi and hurried after O'Leary through the archway. The Irishman pranced ahead, his huge hands curled into the shape of boiled lobsters, weaving and feinting. The crowd stepped back respectfully.

"That'd be the blind one's husband," remarked a fat-faced woman in a piercing whisper. "Going to knock the murderer down, I suppose."

Mr. Jackson caught up with O'Leary at the lift shaft. He pressed the bell. An anxious voice from above called, "Hey, don't monkey with that thing! You want to kill me?"

Mr. Jackson peered upwards. The guts of the lift, two looped black cables, and a frayed piece of steel rope hung creaking in the void. "Shut the gates!" he shouted.

"Out of order," came the voice. "Get walking, brother."

"Now that," remarked O'Leary, shooting his cuffs, "is fighting talk."

"No fighting," said Mr. Jackson.

"Just one could do no harm, Jack."

"Wait for it, *wait!*"

"Just a slap, Jack, a quick backhander . . ."

"No." Mr. Jackson peered upwards through the bars. "I want *You*," he roared.

"Come and get me, Kitchener!"

Mr. Jackson and O'Leary started up the dark stairs which circled the shaft. Mr. Jackson glanced sideways at his new friend. The Irishman had clearly lost immediate interest in the project. He was sulking. He trailed behind, scowling heavily.

"In my condition," he grumbled, "such wanton muscular effort can make a man cry like a little child."

Mr. Jackson hurried on. On the third floor he saw the lower half of the lift and the lower half of a man sitting on a rug inside it. On the floor were a thermos, two bottles of whisky, three paper bags, and an untidy heap of morning newspapers. Mr. Jackson ran up to the fourth floor.

The man's head was now at knee level. "Don't ask me," he advised. "I like it here." He began to tinker with the aerial of a walkie-talkie transmitter set balanced on his knees.

"Where's *You*?" demanded Mr. Jackson.

Kidder looked at him suspiciously. "Press?"

"No."

"Police?"

"No."

"Nosey parker?"

"What's it to you?"

Kidder hesitated. He badly needed an ally, somebody who would bring him news from *You* which he could relay to his paper. Egon was more than willing to cooperate, but he was busy. Inspector Woodman and the police were stolidly admitting nothing. Carstairs, the private detective, had been interested in the proffered fee but had finally refused it, saying that Murder gave him the willies, always had, and always would. Two char-women had volunteered details of the offices and the dirty habits of the staff, but were unable to help further.

Kidder stood up and stretched. He smiled at Mr. Jackson. "Ever give a bun to a polar bear?" he asked. "Ever sling a herring at a sea lion?"

"What?"

"Will you do me a small favor like you would for any wild creature in captivity?"

"No."

"Amazing, isn't it?" said Kidder, sitting down again. "That's exactly what the gypsy told me."

"Where's *You*?"

"Up one, turn right."

O'Leary appeared. His fists were deep in his pockets and he looked disgruntled. Kidder studied him, then offered a bottle through the bars.

"Hiya, pal," he said. "Could you use a drop from the village fountain?"

O'Leary brightened. He said gratefully, "Now you are a man I would never kick without provocation."

"Come on, Trouble," said Mr. Jackson.

"See you later, Jack," said O'Leary. "Up there is Admin. Here is Ops." He closed his eyes and tilted the bottle to his lips. His Adam's apple rose and fell rhythmically. He wiped his mouth on the back of his hand, sat down, and offered Kidder a cigar.

Mr. Jackson ran a palm over his prickly chin, jerked angrily at his hat, and started up the last flight of stairs . . .

In Enid Marley's office, Ellie sat on the desk helping Rex with the morning mail and nibbling her lunch. This consisted of a bunch of water-cress, two carrots, and a vitamin pill. Rex, unsure what people ate on such occasions, had provided himself with four sausage rolls, three hardboiled eggs, a flask of tomato soup, a bag of prawns, a jar of pickled walnuts, and a coffee cake.

Ellie eyed this strange feast with some resentment. She knew that until she fell out of love with Egon, she would be unable to taste anything at all. She therefore had a tendency to dislike anybody whom she saw eating a square meal.

"By the time you're forty," she remarked, "you'll be the size of a block of flats."

"Whereas you, dear," said Rex comfortably, "will much resemble an antler. Have a sausage roll?"

"Six hundred calories? No, pig."

"Sausage rolls are eighty per cent water. Have a prawn. Prawns *are* water." Rex selected a letter at random and began to peel an egg on to it. " 'In my considered opinion,' " he read, " 'your publication is prominent among those which deliberately and flagrantly encourage juvenile delinquency. I am therefore obliged . . .' "

"Signed Holmes?"

"How did you know?"

"She's an Old Beef. Stuff her into *Complaints, Regular.*"

"I wonder whether she's got a silver-haired old mum called Stately and a jammy little boy called Flat."

"You're not earning your lolly, dear. Read on."

" 'Feeling extravagant? Chop an avocado pear, mix with diced smoked salmon and French dressing, pile back into halved shells. Serve on a bed of shrimps soaked overnight in a dry hock and surrounded by a border of cracked ice. Result, delicious!' Well, *really*! Clock me down with a cast-iron lawn dog!"

"File it. Sa . . . Egon says to lay off anything controversial until we see which way this Murder's going to work out."

"Done."

"More?"

" 'My boyfriend punched a man with a beard and broke his wrist. This man walked off laughing. Naturally, I was interested and realized my former mistake. I now wear a lovely zircon on the fourth finger of my left hand. It was given to me by the man with the beard!' "

"*Hullo, Hullo!* Caption?"

"*Close shave*?"

"I'm afraid so. Next?"

" 'I will get Enid Marley yet, and then all of *You*. It's the moon makes me feel queer. *Beware!*' "

"Oh, God! Not *another*!"

"That's the fifth."

"Sixth."

"Postmarked Leeds."

"I'll give it to Egon. He collects them these days."

YOU, read the large notice at the top of the stairs. *The Weekly Which*

Has Everything! Under this, somebody had scrawled, *Except the circu-lation!* An arrow pointed to the right.

Mr. Jackson turned down the long corridor. The first eight of the doors on either side had *Me* painted on them. From a right-angled passage marked *Model Kitchen* came an alarming smell of burning. Mr. Jackson followed the smell, pushed open a swing door.

The kitchen was painted blue and yellow. It was dirty and extremely untidy. Somebody had dropped a bag of flour in the middle of the floor and somebody else had skidded on a tomato. On the two gas cookers were notices declaring that they were OUT OF ORDER. A girl in a pair of jeans was scouring a saucepan over which hung a small pall of smoke. Another was cooking something red on a primus stove. Another was kicking a broken bottle of nail varnish under the dresser. Another was touching up a lobster from a pot of crimson paint. A gray-haired woman in a food-stained overall, a cigarette stuck between her lips at an aggressive angle, was carefully icing a large upturned biscuit tin.

Mr. Jackson coughed loudly. "Where's Enid Marley?" he asked, nar-rowing his eyes, bunching his hands.

"No visitors today!" said Mrs. Ryder sharply. "Out, my man! *Out!*"

Mr. Jackson retired. He turned right into the main corridor and found himself face to face with a frightening girl in a pink hat. "Enid Marley?" he asked.

"You insult me, dear," said Ellie, and passed on.

Mr. Jackson moved two yards forward and looked around an open door. In the office beyond, a tiny man with a large head sat watching him wide-eyed.

"Who are you?" he asked hoarsely. "Wad do you wand?"

"I want Enid Marley," said Mr. Jackson.

Doctor Feltz passed a shaking hand over his eyes. "Ah, yar," he murmured. "Vorgive me. This Mörder. You musd go blease. I am un-well." He rose, pushed Mr. Jackson gently out into the passage, and closed the door.

Mr. Jackson hovered. From where he stood, he could partially see into the room on the opposite side of the corridor. A small girl with unbecoming spectacles was kneeling on the floor forcing a fat woman into a stern white corset.

"Oh, stop it, *do*!" the fat woman was saying angrily. "I tell you it's not any *use*. Look at me! I'm all comin' out 'ere!"

Mr. Jackson stared at the corset, mesmerized. There were two fierce-looking buckles on it and about eight suspenders. It was crisscrossed with strings like the keyboard of a zither. The girl with the spectacles looked up and saw him. She jumped to her feet, marched across the room, and slammed the door.

Mr. Jackson walked on. He heard raised voices in the next room on the right. The door was marked *Editor-in-Chief, You*. It was ajar. Mr. Jackson pushed it open with his foot.

A thin, dark man with untidy hair sat on the desk eating a sandwich, smoking a cigarette, and talking into a telephone. "Yes, yes, terrible," he was saying. "Twenty-five hundred more? Sure. How about some back numbers?"

Another man was pacing up and down the room with his hands plunged into the pockets of a shabby trenchcoat. He waited impatiently until the first had replaced the receiver, then said angrily, "I ought to pull you in, Egon. Why the hell didn't you show it to me yesterday? How much more evidence are you suppressing?"

"My dear old gopher," Egon began patiently.

"The name's Woodman, Egon."

Egon bit into another sandwich and sighed loudly. He said reasonably, "Now look, cock, if you'd told me that you'd set your heart on a confession note, I'd have done my damnedest for you. You're my pal. I love you. I want you to be promoted. I want you to be rich and famous and happy. You want a confession, okay, ask papa and you *get* a confession. You get *six*. To save you trouble, you get them in alphabetical order. Here's one from Battersea, one from Bristol, one from Cardiff, one from Hull, one from Leeds, and one from Portsmouth. There! All for you! And if you'll nip in Friday, you shall have all the overseas crackpots too. Now dry your eyes and let's have a great big smile, mm?"

Mr. Jackson cleared his throat.

Egon looked at him, at the swollen, blackened eye, the bruised, unshaven chin, the torn lapel. Then he crossed the room and wrung Mr. Jackson's hand. "*Bonjour*," he said heartily. Then, enunciating each syllable with great care, "Me no French." And over Mr. Jackson's shoulder, "Paul! Hey, Paul! Here's your Resistance joker!" He patted Mr. Jackson's arm, nodding and beaming, and told Woodman, "Amazing character. Supposed to have captured a whole German company, shot the lot. Only five of them, these guerrilla birds. He was the kingpin. Lived in hollow trees, ate dogs, writing his memoirs."

Woodman inclined his head. "Good morning," he said.

"You're wasting your time, old son," said Egon. "Doesn't understand a word of English."

Mr. Jackson was about to protest when he was seized gently but firmly by the elbow. He turned to face a young man wearing a battered hat on the back of his head and an ingratiating smile.

"*Ah, ici vous-êtes, êtes-vous?*" said the young man briskly. "*J'ai peur que ma Français n'est pas si chaud. Voulez-vous venir avec moi?*"

Confused, Mr. Jackson tried to shake off the detaining hand.

The young man gripped him harder. "*Pas de flics ici!*" he said with a reassuring laugh. "*J'ai écrit trois milles mots partout votre bêtises horribles. J'ai vous appelé Le Marquis de Sade. Bon, eh?*"

Mr. Jackson reminded himself that time spent on reconnaissance was seldom wasted. He allowed himself to be hustled down the corridor, led into a darkened room.

"I got him, Jimmie!" called the young man with the hat. "Make it snappy, will you? He looks capable of anything."

A single naked light burned over an upturned orange box at the far end of the room. Dark arc lamps stood about, three huge cameras, and one small one on a tripod. Behind the orange box, a sandy-haired youth was arranging a piece of black material over a screen. He gave Mr. Jackson a sharp, appraising look. "Gawd!" he said. "Is he armed?"

The young man with the hat said, "*Ça, c'est Jimmie, notre – peut-être il serait mieux de dire VOTRE, ha, ha! – photographeur. Il ne parle pas un mot de Français.* Come on. Jimmie! Get weaving! He gives me the yelling habdabs."

"Thanks, Paul," said Jimmie. "Who tried to rip off his left ear? Parlez him up there and tell him to look friendly. That ought to bring our public out in a muck sweat. I wish his nose was bleeding."

Mr. Jackson allowed himself to be led to the orange box. He sat down. A battery of lights blazed suddenly, blinding him. He raised an arm to shield his eyes.

"Swell!" said Jimmie. "Blimey, isn't he gruesome! Okay, switch off Two, turn him around. Muss him up a bit. Push Three forward a foot. I'm going to shoot from down under. I want that Oh, hell-I've-been-shot-in-the-back look. Fine! Now horrify him! Offer him a glass of milk."

Mr. Jackson's gorge rose.

"Wizzo!" cried Jimmie. "God, if I dared to get him alone for an hour with a red filter, I could do something really *Grand Guignol!*"

Paul said, "Let's get him out of here while we live to tell the chums." To Mr. Jackson, he smiled. "*Ça c'est tout, monsieur. Merci beaucoup.*"

"What'll he eat for lunch?" asked Jimmie. "Spaniel?"

Mr. Jackson found himself back in the corridor.

Paul patted him on the back. He said, "*Jimmie dit que nous avons deux tableaux tout à fait féroces et dégoutants,*" bowed, went back into the studio and locked the door.

Mr. Jackson frowned after him for a moment. He wished he had not drunk so much whisky on the train with O'Leary. He rasped a thumbnail over his jaw and moved on. He was beginning to wonder whether to go downstairs and pick another fight with O'Leary when he found Enid Marley's name painted on the last door in the passage. He squared his shoulders and kicked open the door with a crash.

A bright-haired young man wearing a green brocade waistcoat sat at a littered desk filing his nails. He sprang up and said anxiously, "What do you want? Whatever happened to your eye?"

"Who are you?"

"You ought to get a bit of steak."

"I demand to see Enid Marley."

"Are you one of Charlie's boys?"

"What?"

"Are you a rozzer?"

"I intend to know why Enid Marley deliberately wrecked my marriage."

"Oh. Well, I should sit down if I were you. Push everything off something, I'm past caring. I'll go and find somebody who can cope."

The young man in the brocade waistcoat scuttled out of the room.

Mr. Jackson looked around curiously. So this was her lair, this wrecker of homes! How should he greet her? Curt and distant? Reasonable yet menacing? Or should he – as he felt inclined to do – knock her down at once and spit in her eye? No, he must control himself. All he wanted at this stage was to declare war, to decide upon the most punishing weapons with which to attack not only Enid Marley but *You* too.

He sat down at the desk and carefully snarled up the nib of her fountain pen. He took a handful of letters from her IN tray and placed them in the OUT. He ripped a large piece off the blotter, chewed it, and forced it into the inkwell. Gazing around, wondering what further small disappointments he could arrange to undermine her morale, his eye fell upon the topmost letter of a large pile. It came from somebody called Holmes, and accused *You* of aiding and abetting juvenile delinquency

Mr. Jackson smiled. Amazed at his own cleverness, he pulled the typewriter towards him and answered the letter. *Dear Mrs. Holmes*, he rattled out. *If you will send me a stamped addressed envelope and a bottle of gin, I will answer you personally. Yours sincerely, Enid Marley*. He addressed the envelope and hid the whole in the OUT tray.

Temporarily satisfied, he studied the furniture. It was light, cheap stuff. Later, perhaps, it would smash well. A match applied to the hessian curtains would start a nice little blaze. There were two telephones, one for him, one for O'Leary, a real pleasure to uproot. One of the windows was already broken, but the others were asking for trouble. The desk itself, presumably the nerve center of the room, was large but rickety. It should respond to organized kicking . . .

He found himself reading a telegram. *I will do myself in*, it announced. *And it's all YOUr fault, Madge White, Fulham.* So! The diabolical old witch was not content merely to sabotage marriages! She also drove her readers to suicide! Mr. Jackson was pocketing the telegram when the telephone rang.

He looked at it sideways. Should he answer it? Why not? He picked up the receiver. "Yus?" he said roughly.

". . . an' what's more," a furious voice was bawling at the far end of the wire, "you've upset my old girl proper chronic. *Ten shillin's!* I'd like you to ruddy well know that Billy was took Wednesday. Jepson, my name is. I was 'is Dad an' I'm wild. If you didn't ruddy well *know*, why didn't you ruddy well . . ."

Mr. Jackson thought fast. Here, obviously, was a sympathizer with the cause. O'Leary was confident that he could corral a large number of supporters within a few hours, but surely one man with a genuine grievance was worth any ten conscripts?

"*Shut up!*"

"Eh?"

"Now you listen to me," said Mr. Jackson.

Mr. Jepson listened. The story of Mr. Jackson's ill-treatment at the hands of Enid Marley made him even angrier than his own. "A bride, too!" he kept saying. "Mean, Billy was only one of ten, but a *bride*! No, that's not right. It's wrong."

Four and a half minutes later, he had agreed to board a train and to meet Mr. Jackson under the clock at Victoria Station in two hours' time.

Mr. Jackson laid down the receiver and drummed his fingers thoughtfully on the desk. Idly, he began to pull out and look through the drawers. In the first two, he found nothing more interesting than stationary and a sponge bag. In the third, he discovered a powder compact, a pair of galoshes, and a huge bottle of aspirins. In the fourth, he came upon a large file marked *Complaints, Regular, Staff Only*.

He lifted it out and with growing excitement began to thumb through the thick pile of letters inside it. Isolated phrases and sentences caught his eye.

Upon my life, there fell a blight: now it's You *I'd like to slight! . . . I wish to draw your attention, not for the first time, to . . . Madam, In my considered opinion, you are an unmitigated donkey! . . . to a*

*small, informal supper. Why don't you ever answer? . . . What I'd like
to know is where you was educated. . . . read anything so coarse, so
calculated to drive innocent young people to . . .*

Mr. Jackson whistled silently. Hundreds of them! And each with a
name and address! A whole Corps of loyal allies – and no conscripts, but
regulars!

He tapped the side of his nose with his forefinger and shot a quick look
at the open door. He seized the file and slipped it under his coat.

Except for a girl in a pink smock who was scratching her ankle at the
far end of the corridor, there was nobody in sight. Mr. Jackson jerked his
hat over his eyes and stepped forth nonchalantly.

The door of the photographic studio was open. Inside, the young man
called Jimmie was scattering artificial snow over the head and shoulders
of a girl wearing a knitted cap, a lumber jacket, a silk skirt, and a pair of
high-heeled sandals. The one called Paul was standing by with a pair of
skis and a bare branch with a stuffed robin sitting on it.

Mr. Jackson strolled past unnoticed. A man in dungarees came down
the passage towards him carrying a large sheet of glass. "Broken window," he said. "Marley office."

Mr. Jackson pointed. He eyed the glass in a proprietary manner. The
man hurried on. As Mr. Jackson turned, he met the amiable gaze of the
tall, untidy man whose name was apparently Egon. The other was standing in his office door drinking something out of a cup. He was smiling
broadly, humming, making unnecessary movements with his feet.

"Ah!" he said. "My dear old pal from the black lagoon! *Comment ça
va, monsieur? Au revoir*, chum. *Au revoir!*" He pranced back into his
office.

Mr. Jackson frowned after him. From inside the open door came the
voice of the gray-haired woman whom he had last seen in the Model
Kitchen. "Sam," it said. "You're either mad or drunk."

Mr. Jackson heard a scuffle and a loud, smacking kiss.

"Madge," said Egon. "I love you. They're buying up the back numbers! Ah, this marvelous Murder! It's gone to my head like old, old wine!"

Mr. Jackson pulled at the lobe of his ear. In his glee at finding the
Complaints, Regular file, he had forgotten about the murder.

Could it have been Egon who had pushed the deaf mutes off the roof?
Surely not? If the man were in hourly danger of arrest, would he be so
wildly happy? Or was he already rehearsing for an Insanity plea?

Troubled, Mr. Jackson slid past the door. If the *You* premises had indeed been the scene of the murder, would it help or hinder his own cause?
The presence of the police would obviously be an obstacle. One could not

expect an officer of the Law to stand by while one smashed windows and wrecked furniture and cuffed people . . .

The alarming girl in the pink hat hastened out of the corridor leading to the Model Kitchen. She was carrying a frilled petticoat in one hand and a blue satin dress in the other.

"No, dear," she said before Mr. Jackson could speak. "I am *not* Enid Marley and nor have I ever been murdered. Pick on someone else, will you? A girl gets bored."

Mr. Jackson ran after her. "Did *he* do it?" he demanded. "That editor, that Egon?"

"Do what?"

"Hack them up and sling them off the roof?"

"Who?"

"The mutes."

She stopped and looked at him. "Sammy?" she asked. "Did he say that?"

"Not exactly. His behavior implied it."

"Oh." Her eyes softened. For an instant, she looked almost human. "He is naughty. He's just like a little boy sometimes."

"But *did* he? I've got to know."

She said, "Let him have his fun, bless him." She walked on, a secret smile on her lips and disappeared into an office across the passage.

Mr. Jackson was about to follow her when a voice behind him called "Oh, there you are! Frankly, I was praying you'd gone. Do you still want to see Enid Marley?" It was the young man with the brocade waistcoat.

Mr. Jackson pressed the *Complaints, Regular* file to his side with his elbow. "No," he said. "Not today."

"I *am* glad. I mean, one feels such a fool saying she's not dead. Well, I must hop off and cope with my illegits. 'Bye!"

Mr. Jackson strode away as fast as he could without actually running. He found O'Leary on the third floor, sitting on the concrete and talking to the man trapped in the lift. Both of them were smoking cigars. O'Leary was deep in a description of the closing scenes of the earlier trial of the killer Kayes, which he had witnessed some years before, when he noticed Mr. Jackson.

"General!" he cried. "Fine news! This is Mr. Kidder from the *Echo*. He has volunteered to run our propaganda department. I have made him a colonel."

"Hi, general!" said Kidder. "What cooks up there?"

Mr. Jackson sat down. He said simply, "I swiped this," and offered the *Complaints, Regular* file.

Kidder reached for it. It would not go through the bars so he was obliged to read it outside them. "Might make an inflammatory little article," he said thoughtfully. "But it's not front page."

Mr. Jackson offered the telegram from Madge White of Fulham.

"Better," said Kidder. "Dead?"

"I don't know."

Kidder rolled over and reached for his transmitter set. He tapped out a signal, then said into the mouthpiece, "Kidder calling, Kidder calling! Stan? Over. Tell Bert to get a couple of legmen out to Fulham. Broad called Madge White, possible stiff. Repeat, please. Over. Right, get cracking, snatch pix if. Let me know pronto if anything breaks. Kidder off, Kidder off."

"Suppose she's still alive?" asked Mr. Jackson.

"WRONGED WOMAN ACCUSES MURDER VICTIM."

"And if she's dead?"

"MURDER VICTIM ACCUSES WRONGED WOMAN." Kidder sat up. "Now get this," he said, throwing his cigar butt down the lift shaft. "With a spot of staff work at this stage, we should be able to arrange a real honey of a fight. Are you on?"

"Yes," said Mr. Jackson and O'Leary simultaneously.

"Right. Here's what we're going to do. You two soldiers are going to round up these Regular Complainers. We're going to hire a hall. We're going to get 'em beefing, get 'em good and steamed up, get 'em hopping mad. *But we're going to keep 'em united . . .*"

A red-faced man in a straw hat stamped up the stairs from the floor below, stopped, and stood glowering. "Where's *You?*" he snarled, his prominent eyes snapping with rage. Behind him was an undernourished little man in a shiny blue suit.

"Press, police, or ghouls?" asked Kidder.

"Them as asks damnfool questions," grated the red-faced man, "is liable to get their heads broke."

"I like his attitude," O'Leary murmured.

"What do you want?" said Mr. Jackson.

"My name's Cream," growled the red man. "I want to see Enid Marley. I want to twist 'er arm."

Kidder pointed. "Who's he?"

"*I* dunno." Mr. Cream turned on the man in the blue suit. "'Oo are you?"

"I'm Fred Turner," said the little man aggressively. "An' I want to *break* 'er arm, like she did my old girl's."

"That's nothin'," said Mr. Cream. "Know what she did to *me?*" His fury overcame him. For a moment, he looked as if he were about to drown. Then he clawed at his collar and said in a stifled voice, "Tried to get me to adopt a nipper! I 'ate kids, '*ate* 'em. *I*'m numbers one to ten in my 'ome an' anyone 'oo thinks different 'as flamin' well got another think comin'." He clicked huge, hairy fingers. "Come on, come on! Where is she?"

"Yes, where is she?" echoed Fred Turner. "Jumpin' on innocent people, breakin' their bones! An' some chap down there said she just shot an old blind man on the roof. Oo does she think she is?"

"Wasn't a blind man," argued Mr. Cream. "Was three girls, an' she knifed 'em, only they can't prove it. So don't talk daft."

"No one calls me daft," said Fred Turner. He clenched his small hands and turned pale.

"*I* do," said Mr. Cream. "I say you're daft."

O'Leary and Kidder exchanged glances. Kidder raised his eyebrows at Mr. Jackson. Mr. Jackson looked at O'Leary. O'Leary winked.

"Gents, gents!" said Kidder, offering a bottle through the bars. "I propose and second that we thrash this Murder out first, and then . . . won't you sit down, Major Cream, Captain Turner?"

Chapter 10

Enid Marley had not read Kidder's story in the *Echo*, nor indeed any other part of that journal. In her opinion, it was, like tobacco, an evil best ignored. She knew that occasionally her husband had smoked a furtive cigar behind the locked doors of the garage; she knew that her butcher occasionally delivered the *Echo* wrapped around a piece of meat. If she discovered evidence of either occurrence – a hidden stub or a crumpled, bloody sheet of newsprint – she would lift it at arm's length, carry it between finger and thumb to the boiler, and there discard it with an eloquent shudder. To Enid Marley, tobacco and the *Echo* headed a long list of things utterly taboo.

To Mrs. Pickett, her charwoman, the *Echo* and a cigarette were breakfast. She consumed both avidly on the bus every day on her way to work. That morning, she had prodded a crony and announced with quiet pride, "My old cow certainly copped a packet yesterday."

Her friend had read the story, handed the paper back, and said scornfully, "That's nothin'. Not as if she's dead. You 'ear 'bout Lil's eldest, poor thing? Well, see, there was this mad 'orse what caught on fire . . ."

Mrs. Pickett had countered with the tale of her grandson and the Negro in Tottenham Court Road and the affair of her employer had paled into insignificance. Nevertheless, on her arrival at Enid Marley's flat, she had thought it only nice to mention the matter.

"See you took a tumble, dear," she had murmured noncommittally, splashing about in the sink.

Enid Marley had gazed at her for a long moment and then said frigidly, "I was murdered, Mrs. Pickett, and kindly don't forget it." She had given Mrs. Pickett ten shillings without explanation, disappeared into her bedroom, and closed the door.

Some hours later she emerged wearing a black suit, a gray toque, and a single rope of pearls. Talking, to Mrs. Pickett, was as necessary as food or air. She talked all day long, even in her sleep. She therefore followed her employer through into the hall and plunged at once into the story of a searing, inexplicable pain which had attacked her right thigh during the early hours of the morning.

Enid Marley was not listening. Drawing on her gloves, she said, "Mrs. Pickett, suppose for a moment that you were obliged to accuse somebody of Murder. How would you do it?"

The charwoman pursed her lips thoughtfully. "Well, I'd get Tom," she offered.

"And then?"

"An' then Mick – 'e's a treat in a brawl! – an' then Fred an' Dora's boys an' . . ."

"And if you had no supporters?"

"Wot, not *one*?"

"No."

"*Well*." Mrs. Pickett drew a deep breath. "I'd think meself, 'Now *why* 'aven't I got no supporters? Is it 'cos I'm some'ow 'orrible? 'Ave I *wronged* 'im? Did I drive 'im to it with me nasty, lashin' tongue?' An' if, after I really searched meself, I was forced to answer meself in the infirmative, I'd go off an' see 'im. An' you know what I'd say?"

Enid Marley did not want to know what Mrs. Pickett would say. She wound up her watch, nodded distantly, and left the house.

At the top of Croissant Street, a constable was waving on the traffic. He told the taxi driver, "Left and left. Can't get through here. Obstruction."

Enid Marley got out and paid.

"'Orrible Murder!" roared the news vendor on the corner. "You stand on the scene of an 'ideous crime! Cost you twopence 'alfpenny to know the worst!"

Enid Marley tapped him peremptorily on the shoulder. "Murder?" she said. "Who was killed?"

He looked at her briefly, recognized her, spat on to the pavement, and turned away. "Terrible Misadventure!" he bellowed. "Victim defies Death! Police Baffled!"

A woman with a bulging string bag touched Enid Marley's arm. "The paper didn't dare say," she said. "They 'ad to put 'alleged,' but 'e killed these three girls with acid, then shot 'imself an' fell off the roof."

"Who did?"

"They don't know yet."

Enid Marley pushed through the crowd. She collided with a man selling jumping toy dogs made of rabbit fur.

"Widower," he croaked. "Wife killed under similar circumstances."

Enid Marley forced her way through to the archway. A young constable blocked her way. "*You*," she said. "Staff. Good afternoon. Tell me, officer, who murdered whom?"

He shuffled. People kept on and on asking him this question and he did not know the answer. "Haven't got the full facts yet, madam," he said. "I understand some gentleman called Marley went off his rocker."

Frowning, she moved on to the lift shaft. A notice printed in violet ink hung on the gate. It read, OUT OF ORDER. DO NOT TOUCH. BY ORDER, JANITOR. She began to stalk up the stairs.

On the first floor, she came upon Carstairs, the private detective. He was lounging against the wall gnawing an orange, bending over so that the juice fell on to the concrete.

"Afternoon," he said, raising his hat a millimeter off his forehead. Having handled her first divorce for her, he knew many of her secrets and treated her with a certain leery *bonhomie*. "What can I do for you? Auntie playing up? Granny missing? Hubby up to his old tricks?" He opened the door behind him, upon which was painted *da Gongas Bros et Cie, Ltd*, threw in the wreck of the orange, closed the door, and wiped his hands on a gray handkerchief.

She asked coldly "Who was murdered here?"

Carstairs winked, but his eyes were so small that only the keenest observer would have noticed. "I don't know, somebody said you. I never went for Murder. Mention the word and I just switch off."

The door behind him was snatched open. A small brown-faced man appeared trembling with anger, and threw the remains of Carstairs's orange at him. He raised both fists above his head and shook them. "*Schittinarangitumpiekharnakatchurkabatcha!*" he screamed.

Carstairs yawned. "No spikka," he said, unmoved. "Whatever you spikking, me non spik, latch on?"

Enid Marley hurried on upstairs. On the second floor, she heard lowered voices from the third and, she thought, the mention of her name. She moved closer to the lift shaft. The veteran eavesdropper in her made her stoop to fumble with a shoelace. She crouched, straining her ears . . .

". . . vote of confidence in Colonel Kidder. Good old Colonel! Have a cigar!"

"Now, look, boys, about this Maidstone character . . . what's his name? Jarrold? Jenkins?"

"Jepson, General. *Jepson*."

"I want him on the front page, on a bloody great horse. I see it in Piccadilly, no, outside the Houses of Parliament. I want to work up a crusading angle. *Farmer Jepson is an angry man. Having spurred his mount through the night* and stuff. Kidder calling, Kidder calling! Stan? Over. Marley case. Tell Frank to be at Victoria in an hour with a large black horse and a photographer. Contact General Jackson, repeat Jackson. Over. Fine. Anything yet on the White stiff? Over. Okay, buzz me when they connect . . ."

Enid Marley stood up and straightened her toque. Who *were* these drunk soldiers? Who was this white corpse? Why specifically white? Had the others been colored? If *You* had been the scene of some flamboyant massacre, was this the moment to accuse Egon of pushing her out of a window? By claiming that he was responsible for her own Attempted Murder, would she cause the police to suspect him of the other genuine ones? She did not want him actually to hang, she merely wanted to visit him in jail, to make several little jokes about files and rope ladders, to take him *Good Housekeeping* and the latest copy of *Me*. This picture so delighted her that, involuntarily, she allowed a small chuckle to escape her.

The voices above stopped abruptly. A hurried murmur reached her. "Go on, cheese it, you guys! I'll handle this. Go on, go *on*!" There was a brief, barely audible, argument, then four pairs of feet tiptoed noisily away.

On the third floor, she saw the lower half of the lift. A man was lying on his stomach in it, his chin on his crossed forearms, watching her.

"Hi," he said. "They just had to lock me up. I bite."

"5AL–B2n," she said automatically, before she could stop herself.

"What?"

"Exactly what is going on in this building?" she asked stiffly. "I hear that there have been some murders."

"*Some?*"

"Three, to be precise."

"Honest, I love my job," he said. "Give 'em an inch and they take a cross-country sprint."

"Who was murdered?"

"Character officially known as Enid Marley and, unofficially, as Sister Toothache. One of those old witches who know all. Bob was her uncle and Charlie was her aunt."

Enid Marley raised her chin. "There has obviously been some mistake. *I* am . . ."

He did not allow her to finish. "You bet there has!" he said morosely. "Somebody forgot she had a built-in broomstick."

She stood for a moment, her knuckles white on her handbag, then she compressed her lips and with rigid calm began to mount the stairs to the fourth floor. The trapped man stood up to watch her pass. He sketched an ironic salute and remarked, grinning, "Too bad I can't give you a lift!"

On the fifth floor, Egon was holding a conference in his office. All his staff were present except one. Mrs. Ryder was in the Model Kitchen, telling Inspector Woodman about the anonymous letters which she suspected Enid Marley had written at the time of the Cornish pasties.

Egon was in high spirits. During the past hour, he had been rung up by no less than twenty-three news agents, all of whom wished to double their orders for the coming issue of *You*. The current issue, for the first time, was sold out. Pale with elation, unable to keep his feet still, Egon scooped up a telephone and rang up B.F., the Chairman of the Board.

B.F., with the fetching insolence of the very rich, was at the time also trying to hold a conversation with his wife in the next room. "*Don't know offhand, old girl,*" he shouted. "*Ask Benson.*" And to Egon, "Well, done, my boy! Knew you had it in you!"

Egon said, "I didn't actually push her, sir."

"*Was in the garage Thursday, saw it myself!* Sorry, son! You didn't, eh? Why not? Ha ha! Terrible woman. *What?*"

"I thought we might substantially increase the next print order, sir. J.L. agrees, so do C.G. and A.B."

"Do, do they? Dreadful fellows! *Oh, God, woman, I don't know! By the hose. Ask Palmer!* You go ahead, my boy. I'll back you to the hilt."

"Thank you, sir. I'm absolutely confident that this is the psychological moment to . . ."

"Quite, quite. I absolutely agree. *I tell you I saw it myself on Thursday.* Last *Thursday, you blithering idiot!* Use your own discretion, son. Tell the old fools I said so . . ."

Egon rang up J.L., C.G., and A.B. and informed them shortly of the Chairman's decision to increase the next print order by seventy thousand copies. They said, respectively, "Yes, yes, shrewd move, I'm sure of it," and, "Well, it's a risk, but if B.F. says so . . ." and, "Oh *no*! Has the old gaffer gone round the bend?"

Glowing with excitement, Egon paced up and down his office waving a sandwich which several times he raised half way to his mouth only to be overcome by another onslaught of speech.

"I want," he said, narrowing his eyes and staring into the middle distance, "a slight change of policy. I want a touch of horror. I want the hair to rise on a hundred thousand heads. I want a challenging editorial. *Have you ever wondered how it feels to share a room with a secret, homicidal maniac? Are you absolutely certain that you are not doing so AT THIS MOMENT? Pause, ponder, draw a deep breath! Look . . . if you dare! . . . at the familiar faces around you . . .*"

His staff looked at each other uneasily. There was a long pause.

Ellie, eager to help, suggested, "Why not photograph the knitting supplement models being held up by masked men?"

Egon seized her by the ears and kissed her on the forehead. "I love you," he told her. He did not notice her turn pale. He rushed on, "Now how can we spook up the cookery spread? Maybe everything black, mm? A great black cake . . ."

Doctor Feltz asked dubiously, "Would you gare vor a biece on Glebdomania?"

"Sure, sure, sure," said Egon. "And re-angle that Insomnia stuff. *Are YOU afraid of the dark? If not, why not? YOU too can have insomnia!*"

Paul offered, "I could dash off a grisly little serial. Nice normal family till they find the parrot hanged . . ."

Jimmie said helpfully, "Then this wild laughter starts up in the cupboard under the stairs . . ."

Doon could never resist such a challenge. "Drip, drip, derip!" she said in a ghoulish whisper. "Who tampered with Buster's tricycle? Who is it that sobs at night in the old well? Nanny's found hacked up, the dog goes mad. Who branded baby? Who cut off Mummy's hand?"

"Daddipops," said Rex promptly. "Not dear, funny old Daddipops of the baggy tweeds and the smelly pipe, but a strange, new Daddipops flecked with foam . . ."

It was at this moment that Enid Marley appeared in the doorway. She hesitated for only a second, only long enough to swallow her disappointment that Inspector Woodman was not present. Then she said quietly but clearly, "Samuel Egon, I demand to know why you attempted to . . ."

Egon spun around. For an instant, his mouth sagged open, then he struck himself on the back of the head with one hand and slapped his desk with the other. "My God!" he breathed. "What a story! Victim Returns to Scene of Crime! Corpse Confronts Killer!" He leapt across the room and gripped Enid Marley by the arm. "Oh, is Kidder going to love this!"

She stiffened. "Kidder?" she asked sharply. "Kidder of the *Echo*?" She attempted to disengage herself but Egon dragged her forward, forced her into a chair.

"Come on, you assassins!" he cried. "I want a Murder group! Jimmie, you too! Make with a time exposure!"

She tried to stand up, but he pressed her down. "This is absurd," she said angrily, pushing at his hands. She was confused. The staff were gathering about her, all talking at once. There was no time to think. Egon apparently *wanted* Murder! *Why*? WHY?

"Ready?" called Jimmie. "I'm coming in on Paul's right. Twenty-fifth exposure. Quite still, please!"

"Okay, kids!" cried Egon. "Let's smell carrion! Watch the pretty vulture!"

The delayed action mechanism on the camera began to tick. Jimmie raced to join the group. As Enid Marley tried again to rise, she remembered with sudden, ghastly clarity a photograph in a newspaper which her butcher had delivered wrapped around a shoulder of lamb. A photograph of the man trapped in the lift! Of Kidder! Of Kidder of the *Echo*! Her mind boggled.

The shutter clicked.

Jimmie said, "Wizzo! Thanks, all! That ought to be a killeroo!" And the group broke up.

Enid Marley sat forgotten, outraged, floundering in doubt. What was Kidder to Egon? What was Egon to Kidder? They were clearly in cahoots, and they wanted Murder! Three minutes ago, she had been eager to give it to them. But now . . .

She saw herself in Court. She saw Egon's counsel darting about, waving an enormous enlargement of the photograph which Jimmie had just taken. She heard him boom, "Your Lordship, Your Honour, Your Whatever, I propose to call no witnesses, nor shall I waste time in cross-examination. I shall ask one question only. *Ladies and gentlemen of the jury, does a woman in mortal terror, a woman confronting her murderer, pose for a portrait with him?*" And then, mildly, "Shall we all have a jolly good laugh, and let the Court proceed with more pressing matters?"

Had she forever stymied her chance of a successful Attempted Murder verdict? Would she be obliged to summon Inspector Woodman, to retract most of her story, to steer the way gracefully back to Misadventure?

Wait!

There was one perfectly good suspect who would not appear in the Murder group photograph. Mrs. Ryder! How rewarding to toss a spanner into that efficient machine! But had the woman got an alibi? Also, it would be difficult to accuse somebody to whom one had no intention whatever of speaking.

Mrs. Ryder? Or Misadventure?

Enid Marley glanced around quickly. Egon and his staff had obviously lost all interest in her. Nobody was looking in her direction. She rose, and quietly left the room.

Mr. Jackson stood under the clock at Victoria Station, waiting for his new recruit. He wondered how he would recognize the man. Mr. Jepson was a farmer, but surely it was too much to hope, as Kidder did, that he would appear in corduroy trousers, brimless hat, and dung-encrusted gaiters, carrying a shotgun and attended by several large, lean dogs?

He caught the choleric eye of a thin, spectacled man beside him, who had also been waiting for nearly twenty minutes. As he turned away, scowling, he knew a moment of doubt. He said, very softly, as if to himself, "Jepson, Jepson?" and waited. An equally diffident murmur reached him. "Jackson, Jackson?"

"Mr. Jepson?"

"General Jackson?"

The two men, avoiding each other's eyes, shook hands. Both were disgruntled by the long, unnecessary wait.

"Don't look like a ruddy general," grumbled Mr. Jepson.

"You don't look like a farmer."

"'Oo said I was? I got an 'en, that's all."

Outside on the pavement, a spotty young man in a duffle coat, one of the *Echo's* large team of photographers, stood holding a small black horse by the bridle. A woman in a musquash coat was trying to force it to eat a carrot.

Enid Marley paused outside the half-open door of the Model Kitchen, then pushed it open.

Inspector Woodman was leaning against the stove stirring a saucerless cup of tea. Mrs. Ryder, flushed and untidy, and spattered with cochineal, was sticking candles into a white cake decorated in red with the words *Happy Xmas*! and a china gnome sitting on a toboggan. She was saying gruffly, ". . . haven't spoken to her since, and I don't intend to. I would have strangled her then and there, but I was worried about my Yorkshire pudding."

Enid Marley said with cool dignity, "Inspector Woodman, will you kindly ask that woman what she was doing between half past nine and twenty minutes to ten on the morning of my murder?"

Woodman jumped. Before he could speak, Mrs. Ryder had snapped, "Inspector, ask that creature to leave my kitchen immediately."

Enid Marley said icily, "Inspector, inform that person that I do not intend to move an inch until I know what spurious alibi she has offered you."

Mrs. Ryder's lips tightened. She growled, "Inspector, tell that hypocrite that if, on the morning she mentioned, I had known she was climbing around the building like a . . . like an *ape*, I should have pelted her with rotten eggs. And then tell her that if she doesn't make herself scarce, I shall take pleasure in doing so now." She plunged her hand into a basket.

Enid Marley began to shake with anger. Before she could control her tongue, she heard herself say, "Inspector, tell that cook that unless she instantly puts down that egg, I shall accuse her of Attempted Murder."

"Inspector," said Mrs. Ryder. "Inform that writer-of-anonymous-letters that unless she leaves within the next two seconds, I shall not only let fly with this old foreign egg, but I shall also formally accuse her of Libel."

Woodman asserted himself. He produced his notebook, which he knew on such occasions to be far more effective than a truncheon. He asked mildly, "Can either of you two ladies offer one iota of proof to substantiate your accusations?"

Both turned to glare at him and he felt a spurt of apprehension. He knew from horrid experience that maddened women would frequently abandon an argument in order to join forces against some new enemy. Would they leap at him, stalwarts both, pinch him, jump on him, pull his hair? Women were unpredictable. Look at his wife, look at his mother-in-law, look at that pretty little thing in the Kayes Case . . .

They stood there, glowering. Neither spoke.

Woodman put away his notebook with a tiny shrug. "In that case," he said with the courtesy which he had found so useful in street brawls, "I won't waste your valuable time. Good afternoon, ladies." He bowed and made his escape.

"Slacker!" growled Mrs. Ryder.

"Lout!" muttered Enid Marley.

"In the old days, one could rely on a peeler."

"These degenerate university types!"

"Think only of promotion."

"Or their pensions."

"Huh!"

"Precisely."

It occurred to both women simultaneously that they had, almost without realizing it, at last broken the silence of six long years.

Outside the Houses of Parliament, Farmer Jepson grappled his way up on to the small, black horse. He was grim but determined. He had never before ridden anything except a bicycle, but the idea of seeing himself doing so on the front page of the *Echo* delighted him. His old woman would be proud as anything, and wouldn't it make Mrs. Gordon wild?

Enid Marley went downstairs frowning heavily, furious with herself. Her childish loss of temper had spoilt everything. Murder was now unattainable, undesirable, absolutely *out*. The only comfort was that Egon would now have to accept Misadventure, which for some weird reason – what? *what?* – he clearly did not want.

The drunken conspirators on the third floor lapsed into an abrupt silence as they heard the click of her heels on the concrete. They watched her closely as she descended the last flight of steps and stopped on the outskirts of the group.

They formed an unlikely gathering. One of them, a red-faced man in a straw hat, was squatting on his heels. Another, a small man in a blue suit, was sitting on a rug. Another, a huge, black-a-vised giant with an unshaven chin and a patch of dried blood on his right cheek, was leaning against the wall eating fish and chips from a greasy newspaper. The man in the lift had attached a mirror to the gates and, one side of his jaw covered with lather, was on his knees, shaving.

Enid Marley said shortly, "I understand that you are Mr. Kidder of the *Echo*."

He began to shave under his chin. "Call me Colonel," he said, watching his reflection in the mirror.

"I believe that you are working on the mistaken assumption that this unfortunate *You* affair was Attempted Homicide."

"Sister," he said, "delete the word *mistaken*. My circulation says so, so does Egon's. Brother Kidder, during this period of enforced rustication, has proved again that if you tell it loud and clear, *anything's* news. Regard me what I've done for this heap of nothing, and I'm only just getting warmed up. I'll get Man Eats Egg on to the front page in 144 point Bodoni yet. You know what the Old Man tells the new boys? He says, 'If you've got a sentence, Anson's got a para. If Anson's got a para, Fowler's got an editorial. If Fowler's got an editorial, Kidder's got a twelve part serial.' Okay, take this hunk of crumb. I don't have a stiff. So what? It's Murder. Give me a stiff, just one, and, Madam, I'll give you a massacre. You want my autograph?"

Enid Marley said slowly, "No, Mr. Kidder. You want mine. Do you know who I am?"

Kidder swilled his razor in a mug of water and began to shave his right cheek. "Sure," he said kindly. "You're an exiled royal nanny. You're Garbo's trusted confidante. You're Hitler's army socks. Go on down to the *Echo* and try it out on Features."

Enid Marley closed her eyes, forced herself to start counting up to ten. She got as far as four, then rage swamped her. She swallowed and said in a controlled voice, "I am Enid Marley, you damned fool! *I* am your precious Murder Victim!"

Kidder cut himself.

The man in the straw hat sprang to his feet. The one in the blue suit rose simultaneously. The unshaven giant started forward. They all began to speak at once.

"Why, my friend General Jackson would grab her head off!"

"Adopt me a nipper, would you, you 'orrible old busybody?"

"Jumped on my old girl, you did! Bust 'er arm an' never a word! Got us in a proper mess, you 'ave! Never thought 'oo'd stay with Tinker, did you?"

Enid Marley gripped her handbag tightly. She had expected common decency from even these disgusting people. She had expected them to be impressed, to welcome her, so to speak, back to life. But they were all, obviously, very angry. She did not understand what was going on, so she lifted one eyebrow and said bleakly, "Tinker?"

"Yes, '*im*!" shouted the little man in the blue suit. "Never thought 'oo'd get the tank down to the Studios, did you?"

"Tank?"

The giant with the Irish accent exploded, "Married only a day and all! And furthermore, she took his wallet, the sinful little piece!"

"Animals an' kids, I 'ate 'em all, *'ate* 'em, see!"

"An' if once Tinker gets moody, 'e won't clash an' we get 'undreds o' letters complainin'."

"*Quiet!*" bawled Kidder. "Let me think, let me get the angle. *Exclusive interview with murdered woman!*" He attached a small tuft of cotton wool to his bleeding cheek and darted a sudden, suspicious glance at Enid Marley. He said, "You wouldn't be about to *accuse* anybody, would you? I couldn't print that. Hell, after this confinement, I'm not going to kill my story at birth."

Enid Marley returned his gaze. She said clearly, "I accuse nobody."

Kidder got up and began to prowl restlessly around his small prison. He spoke softly to himself. "I ACCUSE NOBODY, SAYS MURDEREE. The police believe that nobody can help them in their inquiries. Nobody was detained yesterday for questioning. After a light lunch, nobody, having been cautioned, made a statement. As a result of this, nobody was formally charged and held without bail . . . How's that? Or maybe An Open Letter to Nobody. Dear Nobody, You must by now be keenly aware that your identity is no secret to me. You've had it, nobody! Kidder is on your trail. If there is one spark of decency in your dark, mad heart . . ."

Enid Marley reached through the bars of the lift gate, seized him by the shoulder, and dug her nails into him. "*I was not murdered,*" she said, shaking.

He looked at her for a long moment. Then he said with dangerous calm, "No?"

"*No.* I was at the time, as my doctor will confirm, undergoing a period of considerable emotional tension. Upon his advice, I had been obliged to recourse to drugs . . ."

Kidder stopped listening. As usual, when a story appeared about to slip through his fingers, he was concerned only with what little of it he could salvage. *Dope?* Maybe, How Many People Have You Killed, G.P.? *Last night, under cover of darkness, a mysterious vessel dropped anchor off sleeping Seaford. On board, an evil cargo boding repercussions in murky quarters. Later, two small, hooded figures were observed swimming ashore . . .*

"I fell, Mr. Kidder," said Enid Marley. "*Fell.*"

"Oh no, you didn't!"

"I insist that I did. It was an accident."

He said rudely, "Baloney! Forty-eight witnesses saw somebody in the window behind you."

She had not thought of that. It was a shock, but she rallied fast. She held tightly on to her handbag and drew a long, careful breath. "That is perfectly possible," she said and managed to give him a tiny smile. "You see, Mr. Kidder, upon further consideration, I have reason to believe that somebody may well have tried to save my life."

Chapter 11

At half past seven that night, Egon was the only member of the staff of *You* left in the building. He sorted a heap of new confession notes to offer to Inspector Woodman in the morning, tamped out a small, smoldering fire in his ashtray, flung his coat about his shoulders, and left. On the fourth floor, he stopped to speak to Kidder and learned for the first time that Enid Marley had switched to Misadventure.

He at once flew into a rage. He turned gray, shut his eyes, and clutched at the lift gate for support.

"Relax," said Kidder confidently. "I have a brand new slant."

By eight o'clock, the crowd around the archway in Croissant Street had dispersed. The suspects had gone home; there was no more to see. Only a small boy remained, picking his nose and staring unwinkingly at the constable on duty.

In his small, dark room beneath the pavement, the janitor of the *You and Me* building gazed, mesmerized, at the photograph of Her which had appeared on the front page of the *Echo* that morning. It was already installed in a red plush frame with stout gilt cherubs in the corners.

On the third floor, Kidder, Mr. Jackson, O'Leary the Troublemaker, Mr. Cream of Norwich, and Farmer Jepson of just outside Maidstone sat on folding chairs eating steak sandwiches provided by the *Echo* and drinking large quantities of whisky provided, Kidder explained, by *Expenses*. Mr. Fred Turner, whose wife lay crooning to her broken arm in St German's Hospital, had departed some time before, insisting that he had to go home and feed Tinker.

The five remaining conspirators, between mouthfuls and snatches of song, squabbled amiably over the *Complaints, Regular* file which Mr. Jackson had stolen from Enid Marley's office.

They were engaged upon dividing the names and addresses therein into two groups – Telegrams and Telephone Calls. O'Leary and Mr. Cream were to handle the Telegrams, Mr. Jackson and Farmer Jepson the Telephone Calls. All were to be paid for by the *Echo*, on the understanding that Kidder was organizing something which might prove to be really *something*.

At 8:10, Enid Marley rang up Carstairs, the private investigator, and told him that she wished him to trail Egon until further notice, reporting his every movement to her.

Carstairs agreed with an alacrity which surprised her. He was, in fact, for the first time since she had known him, polite and affable.

She could not have known that, some fifteen minutes previously, he had made a similar arrangement with Egon, agreeing to shadow her and to submit regular bulletins upon her whereabouts. Nor could she have known that Carstairs therefore planned to lounge around at home, eating, and making a rug for his mother's Christmas present, waiting for calls from either Egon or herself, waiting to inquire where each could be contacted in order to report to the other.

At 9:02, O'Leary and Mr. Cream of Norwich propped themselves upon the counter of an all-night post office. "Good evening, you little beauty," O'Leary greeted the homely girl on the far side of the grille. "I wish to send one hundred and seventy-three telegrams."

At 9:14, Carstairs unwillingly laid aside the chop bone he had been savaging, wiped his hands on his mother's unfinished rug, and rang up Egon.

"She's *chez* her," he confided. "If she scarpers, where'll you be?"

"Pub on the corner. The Eight Bells."

"Rightyoh!"

At 9:17, in a telephone box at the top of Croissant Street, Mr. Jackson handed the receiver and the small sack of change donated by the *Echo* over to Farmer Jepson, and mopped his brow.

"I've done twenty," he said. "Take over, Captain."

"'Ow do we stand, general?"

"Fifteen resounding victories, two total defeats, one skirmish, two sectors undefended."

"'Oo's next?"

"A Miss Wisley, Ealing. Note from Kidder: Lost fiancé due to poncho pattern. Though she knows it is perverse, she always speaks in verse."

"*Eh?*"

Mr. Jackson sighed. He suspected that, sober, he would heartily dislike Farmer Jepson. "All right, all right! I'll have a bash." Dialing, he thought hard. As the receiver was removed at the far end of the wire, he pressed Button A and said smoothly, "As birds of a feather, let's get together . . ."

A voice said, "What you want?"

"Jackson is my name, General is my rank. Like you, I have been framed, so come, let us be frank! All expenses I will pay, if you'll but step my way . . ."

"You mad?"

"Are you Miss Wisley?"

"No."

"Oh."

At 9:28, Inspector Woodman stood his friend Inspector Willis a pint of bitter in the Stoat and Stag. Beetling over the rim of his tankard, he asked, carefully casual, "How's the Kayes indictment coming?"

Willis mopped his mouth on his handkerchief. "I've got him cold," he said. "It's the assorted muds that clinch it. The nail parings were hers, the skin was his. He sent his regards to you. Blasted cheek, I thought. How's your finangle?"

"Mind if we don't discuss it?"

At 10.02, Carstairs sucked the remains of a chocolate-covered bar of nougat from his teeth and rang up Enid Marley.

"He's in the pub on the corner," he announced. "The Eight Bells. Where'll you be when he blows?"

"Report in the morning. I'm going to bed."

"Rightyoh!"

At the same time, in her smart, impersonal little flat in Chelsea, Ellie Sansome sat trying to concentrate on the captions for next month's fashion spread. Jimmie, on Egon's orders, had photographed two of the models crouching terror-stricken, menaced by a looming man with a shotgun, one lying prettily unconscious on the ground with a garrotte around her neck.

Your money or your life! she wrote. *Yet surely any one of these crummy little numbers would soften the hardest masculine heart? Sammy's? He once said my charcoal tweed was nifty. Did he . . .*

She tore up the page and started again. She rewrote the first two sentences, substituting the word *delicious* for *crummy*. After some thought, she added, *(Left) A real flatterer, this! It's destined for many a romantic evening, at £5 15s. 6d., most stores, in mist, sapphire, Egon, and topaz . . .*

At 11:29, in the sitting room of Rex's tall, ungainly house in Kensington, Doon, Paul East, and Rex sat in weary silence. The argument had been a long one, yet nothing was settled.

Paul roused himself. "I wish we had the charts."

"We have." Doon yawned. "You're sitting on them."

"Shall we give them a whirl?"

"Why not?"

"All right. What's our problem?"

Rex thought for a moment, then offered, "We believe that there may be a murderer (X) in our office, even though the victim (E.M.) is unharmed and claiming that X tried to save her life. She cannot prove this, nor can we prove the opposite. At one time, she was all for Murder, but now insists upon Misadventure. We prefer Misadventure, though we suspect Murder, because X has proved to be one of our friends. Our Boss (S.E.) at first favored Misadventure, but now wants Murder. We all like, respect, and sympathize with X and S.E., but hate E.M. Allowing that our evidence is vital to either case, although we know nothing, to whose side should we be loyal?"

"Nicely put, ducky," Doon admired. "You are clever."

Paul stretched the strings across the charts. "Well," he said, "we've asked for it, and we've got it. Our old chum URG8/4. 'My dear, The tone of your letter suggests that you may be *run down*. It could do no harm . . .' "

"Oh, shut up!" said Rex.

"Hang on! There's an asterisk. 7Q."

"Decode it."

" 'N.B.: Victim poss. Suicide (?) Murder fancier obv. unbal. Writer(s) prep. commit Perjury. Delay answer 3 days, rep. imm. police.' "

"Corks!" said Doon. "You've got to hand it to her!"

Rex sniffed. "I wouldn't hand her a sucked orange."

Paul said grudgingly, "You have to admit that she's way ahead of us. What's more, she's taken her own advice, if you turn the whole thing inside out and upside down and then stand on your head." He stared at his feet for a moment, then said thoughtfully, "Of course, Suicide . . ."

Rex and Doon looked at each other. Rex pursed his lips.

Doon rose. "Good night, Paul dear," she said firmly. "We're so glad you can't stay."

At 12:04, Kidder returned to the third floor from his bath in the janitor's basement quarters. He climbed into the broken lift, shut the gate, and locked himself in as the old man had shown him. He hung up his dressing gown, made himself comfortable on his nest of rugs and cushions, and switched on his transmitter set.

"Kidder calling, Kidder calling! Stan? Over. Sure, everything cooking up nicely. Eighty-three Regular Complainers arriving tomorrow for sure, mostly train. How's the Old Man taking it? Kidder for Dream Boy, eh? Tell Bert to have me woken at eight, ham and eggs and coffee. Well, old cock, it's good night now from Kidder the Kaptive. As the sun sinks into the smoggy west, Kidder, who has aged and coarsened, faces another night of creaking peril in . . . Hey, Stan! What gives with the White cadaver? Did they comb the morgue? Over. Why *not*? Damn you, can't you get it through their hats that I need some cooperation? I've got to have drama! I've got to have dignity, tragedy. For God's sake, man, don't you realize that *I've got to have a ruddy stiff?*"

At 12:08, the killer Kayes was hurried, handcuffed, into a police car with drawn blinds. The inmates of Wandsworth had been rhythmically kicking their cell doors since his arrival, and the decision had been made to remove him to another less fractious prison. At 12:10, the police car was rammed head on by a plain-sided van which swerved across the road and disgorged three men with scarves tied about the lower half of their faces and automatics in their hands.

At 12:27, the killer Kayes bought himself a pie at an Embankment coffee stall, and, eating it, began to walk westward, free.

Chapter 12

EGON'S small, squalid mews flat had once been a stable. The bedroom, clumsily converted, gave the curious impression that the horses had either only just left or that they stood silently inside one of the huge roan-painted cupboards. Egon knew this, but he did not care. Each night, he plunged simultaneously into his rumpled bed and a profound sleep; each morning, at the first neigh of the alarm clock, he found himself, without conscious movement, in his kitchenette, fully dressed and gulping Alka-Seltzer.

That morning, however, he woke up to find himself still in bed. He wasted eleven precious seconds glowering around the room, and two re-marking that his hangover was of the type which he privately described as Houdini. Then he sprang from the snarled nest of blankets and ran bare-footed to his front door.

The newspapers stuck in a thickly folded roll through the rusty letter-box. Egon seized them and prised them free.

The front pages of the first two were mainly concerned with the flood in Essex and the escape of the killer Kayes. Egon tossed them aside and snatched up the *Echo*.

The banner headline announced SLAYER SAVED ME! SAYS SOB SISTER! Scowling, Egon began to read the column beneath it.

Last night, there was a dramatic development in the strangest mur-der case since 1705. Mrs. Enid (Can I Help You?) Marley, who plum-meted three days ago from her lofty office window, revealed in an exclusive interview that the mysterious person behind her at the time of the tragedy may well have been attempting to save her life! "*I intend to reach the bottom of this*," *she declared. "With the help of an* Echo *probe, I shall discover whether I have a staunch and gallant friend, or a mad and homicidal enemy." Questioned by "Kidder" Kidder, ace crime reporter trapped in a treacherous lift on the scene of this baffling enigma, Mrs. Marley, who wore black suit, gray hat, pearls, added, "Can there be an undetected maniac at large on these premises where I have worked happily for over ten years? Will he or she strike again, wildly, blindly?"* Kidder: *You are now again assuming that you were murdered?* Mrs. Marley: *I do not know. It is incredible.* Kidder: *Why were you drawn back to the scene of this amazing puzzle?* Mrs. Marley: *I have always been deeply interested in psychology. The human mind can play strange tricks. My father was a weird man. He was extremely strict and* (contd. p. 3, col. 4)

Egon laid the *Express*, the *Daily Mirror*, the *Daily Mail*, the *Telegraph*, and *The Times* on the linoleum, stood on them because his feet were growing cold, and turned to page 3 of the *Echo*.

There was a small picture of Farmer Jepson sitting on a horse outside the Houses of Parliament. The horse stood placidly, head down, staring at its feet with an air of resignation; on its back, the farmer keeled at an unlikely angle, looking frightened. The caption read, *Mr. Jepson, of just outside Maidstone, will accuse certain alleged plot victim of the death of his son, says, "Negligence! I demand satisfaction!"*

Below this was a large reproduction of Jimmie's group of the staff of *You*. In the center, Enid Marley sat with her mouth slightly ajar. The text beneath demanded, *Does she pose with saint or sinner? Did one of these seven – (L. to R., back row) James Simmonds, Paul East, Rex Travers . . .*

"Ducky!" said Rex, three miles away, eating cornflakes. "I'm a *suspect*, not swanking!"

Doon peered over his shoulder. She said, "Really Kidder is a nonsense!"

"But the *publicity*! I bet Neville turns a funny shade of green!"

. . . Samuel Egon, Editor-in-Chief (L. to R., second row) Miss Doon Travers, Miss Ellie Sansome, Mrs. Enid Marley (victim, seated, arrow), Dr. W. Feltz – push her to what appeared to be a certain death? If not, then the poser . . . a poser surely unique in the annals of crime? . . . remains. WHO DIDN'T DO IT?

Egon raked a hand through his hair. Was Kidder crazy or was he in complete control of the situation? Could even *he* get away with both Murder *and* Misadventure?

Gnawing a thumbnail, Egon began to read column 4. He skipped the paragraph about Enid Marley's father, her weeping listless mother, the long years of cruelty in a house of discord. His eye was caught by his own name below a subheading which asked, *Will Yard Act?*

Samuel Egon, Editor of You, *lifelong friend of the fallen woman, vowed yesterday, "Enid Marley was a fine and generous person, and still is. She has no enemies. Yet surely the dramatic confession notes now in the hands of the police suggest that this was Attempted Murder! Whom is she shielding?" Late last night, indignant crowds thronged Croissant Street. An even greater number are expected today as the controversy rages on. It is understood from reliable sources that police may cordon the area, enforce traffic diversions. East End traffic will not be affected, but motorists who . . .*

The telephone rang. Egon gazed at it for a moment, then sidled towards it. He lifted the receiver and said cautiously, "Mmm?"

"Sammy?" It was Ellie. Her voice wavered, then she cleared her throat and said briskly, "I mean, of course, Mr. Egon, dear. You saw the *Echo*? Well, what to do? Do we lurk at home incognito, or do the girls and boys come out to foul play?"

Egon sat down on the crate of curtains which his grandmother had willed to him seven years before and lifted his feet off the cold floor. "Listen," he said. "Is this absolutely marvelous or is it . . . What do *you* think?"

Flattered and anxious to please, she said enthusiastically, "Oh, definitely *good*, dear, I'd say, no? Did you catch that saucy little map? You note that he's diverted half the West End traffic to our very doorstep? By midday, we should be in a state of siege."

Egon brightened. "Siege," he murmured, tasting the word. "Siege, mm? Yes, I like siege."

She sneezed. "In the meanwhile, we need briefing, dear. Is it still Murder?"

"What's the general feeling?"

"Whatever you say."

"I say we string along with Both until we get the reactions from the provinces. Say, for instance, you, Doc, and Doon plug Murder and Paul, Ma Ryder, and Jimmie yell Misadventure."

"Doc's dead against Murder, and Paul's keen as mustard."

"Okay, switch 'em."

"And you?"

"Me, I vacillate. Right?"

"Right. I'll phone them."

"I love you."

There was a slight pause, then she said, "That's cozy, because I love you too."

He was not listening. "Mmm? Now look, how's this for a gimmick? Suppose we . . ."

"Gimmick yourself!" she snapped, and rang off.

Egon went through into his bedroom and rubbed up his shoes on a corner of the bedspread. Putting them on, taking them off because he had forgotten his socks, putting them on again, he wondered how Inspector Woodman would react to this new development. Would he be too angry to sign a challenging article for the next issue of *You? "Bob" Woodman, who in the course of twenty-four grueling years at Scotland Yard has never once lost his temper nor his fine sense of humor . . .*

"Your little mulligatawny seems to be simmering up," observed Inspector Willis, as he met Woodman at their usual bus stop. "Mum's bet me five bob it's Murder. Is it?"

"Oh, go and catch your bloody Kayes!" snarled Woodman, hailing a taxi. "And tell your damnfool mother to go to hell!"

Struggling into his shirt, wondering briefly how he had managed to get out of it on the previous evening without undoing any of the buttons, Egon paused to consider Enid Marley. If she too could be persuaded to write a fiery yet inconclusive little article . . .

But at all costs, he must somehow prevent her from insisting upon Misadventure. He must try to reach some understanding with her. But how? He hated her, but he had to admit that her principles were of the highest. She would not dream of tampering with the machinations of Justice. She would do her utmost to help the police. She was incorruptible . . .

"Well, I turned round," stated Mrs. Pickett, helping Enid Marley into her black coat, "an' I said to Gwen, '*Course* it's Murder, you silly thing! An' you can tell Stan I 'ad that from the 'orse's mouth!' "

"Mrs. Pickett," said Enid Marley, handing over four half-crowns. "You will kindly tell Gwen, Stan, and all the other members of your family that this is a straightforward case of Misadventure."

Mrs. Pickett dropped the coins into the pocket of her overall. "Orright," she said indifferently, nodding. She pondered for a moment and added,

"Then if I was you, I'd wear me gray, dear, real."

Snatching his belligerent little car around a corner, squealing into Croissant Street, slowing to nose through a large crowd outside the *You* and *Me* building, Egon did not realize that he was talking aloud.

" 'Bob' Woodman," he lisped, wagging his head and simpering, "has for tragic but obvious reasons haunted our offices for some time now. His shy, diffident manner drew the girls from the Typing Pool like a magnet! When we finally managed to prise him loose, he admitted with a faint smile, 'Women no longer baffle me. Why? Well, it's a long story!' You'll find it on page 19 . . . an outspoken article which will make many a girl change her technique! Is he scientific! *Ouch!*"

"Eh?" asked a woman eating a banana. "You all right?"

"Cheese it, madam," said Egon curtly, and turned into the car park.

It was crowded. In one corner, a man sat on the steps of a caravan, plucking a chicken. The attendant shook his head lugubriously.

"Fairly eatin' it up, they are," he mumbled. "Misadventure, aside from the usual lot, we 'ad four bikes. Murder, we 'ad a couple o' police cars an' a 'orse an' cart. But this Both stuff, well, I'm sorry, sir, but you'll 'ave to go over by the nettles."

Egon parked his car and, since it would no longer lock, removed part of the engine and hid it under a rug in the boot. He then set out for the Indian restaurant. Forcing his way through the crowd outside it, he listened, trying to assess the current mood. Which did the London public prefer? Murder? Or Misadventure? Or Both? But the babble around him did little except to underline his own doubts . . .

". . . say crime's crime, an' I don't care what, it's not *nice*."

"I absolutely agree! Mean, look when I found that wallet. Looked inside for the name right away, I did, but all it said was Real Pigskin."

". . . debt to Enid Marley. She wrote my two to leave home and, my dear, I simply could *not* have been more grateful!"

". . . *thrilled!* You know she's built her own kiln at last?"

". . . don't see, Mummy, is if the lady's been killed, then why isn't she an angel?"

"Well, I dunno. All *I* say is if *I*'d been bumped off, I'd of *said*."

Egon pushed his way into the crowded restaurant. Above the service hatch was a large notice attached to the wall with three drawing pins and an air mail stamp. It read, SEEN OF KNOTTY PROBLEM. PROP. GENUINE WITNESS. INFORMATION CUSTOMERS ONLY!

Egon ordered three ham and one cheese sandwich. The proprietor, sawing at a loaf, was droning, "And then behold, as she hurtled down, bolt from blue, and foiled by my canvas, surely a miracle, she did utter short, sharp shriek like animal in jungle. But even as she bit the deck – what a din, heard for miles around! – she was up and on her tootsies . . ." He saw Egon for the first time as he handed over the packet of sandwiches. He closed one eye in a conspiratorial manner. "For you, man," he murmured, "is free. More strength there to your gray matter! All on my house for duration of present conundrum."

"Egg an' chips," ordered a boy in a tartan shirt, elbowing Egon aside. "We can't 'ear at the back. Wasn't there no blood?"

Egon left. Outside the archway leading to the *You* and *Me* building, he saw Paul East, Doon, Rex, Mrs. Ryder, and Ellie being harried by a group of men who were clearly reporters. He broke into a run.

". . . think it was an accident," Doon was saying firmly, earnestly. "I know she was hell, but, honestly, nobody . . ."

"I don't agree," said Mrs. Ryder. "She was, I mean is, an obnoxious woman and I believe that somebody . . ."

"*Shut up!*" shouted Egon. Something had obviously misfired. Doon was supposed to be plugging Murder, Mrs. Ryder was to have advertised Misadventure. He reached the group breathlessly and grabbed Ellie by the arm. "Didn't you brief them?"

"No."

"Why not?"

"Because," she said coldly.

"Well, I'm not actually a *king* suspect," Rex told a man who was taking notes, "because I've got this ridiculous alibi . . ."

Egon pinched him. "Rod," he said with deadly tenderness. "Will you please do a little thing to make an old man happy? Will you please keep out of this? Will all of you nip up to your offices and pay with the ink, mm?"

Rex bridled. "But you distinctly said . . ."

Paul said, "I don't know what you're up to, Egon, but . . ."

"Really, Sam," said Mrs. Ryder. "I wish you'd grow up."

"But, ducky," said Doon. "You told us to . . ."

"I said *shuttup!*" yelled Egon.

One of the reporters said sourly, "Gee, tanks, tosh! May we quote you?"

Another said, "Come clean, chum. I could knock your rag for a loop without removing my hat."

Egon realized that he had begun to dance with anxiety, stood still too abruptly, then fell into a pose of studied nonchalance. "Now, kids, kids," he said reasonably. "You're my buddies, I love you, I love you all. I know, I know, you want the dope. Okay, I'm your boy." He paused as panic swept over him. What was he going to say?

"Cards on the table, brother," said a man with a notebook.

"Or else," said another.

"And no dealing from the bottom of the pack," said a third.

Egon cleared his throat. "Beat it," he ordered his staff tersely. "And traps worn shut, get it?"

He smiled expansively at the reporters, cleared his throat again, and began to speak at dictation speed. "Sam Egon comma cap Editor of caps *You* dash the magazine involved in the most baffling riddle of the century dash admitted this morning comma quote cap We are confused stop. Half of us believe that a dangerous comma fanatical killer is at large in our offices comma waiting dot dot dot italics waiting for the chance to strike again screamer. Others comma aware of the essential integrity of the character of the plot victim dash italics is it a plot query dash . . ."

Moving away, Paul frowned at Ellie. "What the hell's he trying to pull?"

She said hopelessly, "He wants Both."

"Oh, God!"

Doon said, "Honestly, he is a clunk! He might have got away with Murder, but Misadventure, well, it's just not *him*."

Ellie blinked and blew her nose. *Oh, Sammy!* she thought, shaking. *I've failed you, I've deserted you, I've left you to the wolves! I ought not to have lost my temper, I ought to have briefed them, I ought to be at your shoulder, your ally against all comers, levelling my carbine or my muskatoon or whatever they are! But don't you see that in a way it was all your fault? When I tell you that I love you, you really must try to listen.*

She straightened her hat and said fiercely, "That gent ought to be tucked away somewhere safe, making little raffia baskets."

Between the third and fourth floors, Kidder sat in the lift eating ham and eggs and drinking coffee. On the far side of the bars, Mr. Jackson, O'Leary the Troublemaker, Farmer Jepson, Mr. Frederick Turner, and Mr. Cream of Norwich sat on an inflated rubber mattress taking notes. It had been arranged that Mr. Jackson was to meet the first contingent of Regular Complainers to arrive at Victoria Station. Farmer Jepson was to deal with those at Paddington. Mr. Frederick Turner was to operate at King's Cross and Mr. Cream at Waterloo. The recruits traveling by bus, coach, or car were to be handled by a team of volunteers organized by the *Echo*.

"And myself?" inquired O'Leary. "Who am *I* after?"

"You, cock," said Kidder, swallowing toast, "are going to sow the seeds of discontent. You're going to get in among that mob out there and provoke ill-feeling. You're going to alienate lifelong friends, set every man, woman, and child against his neighbor, rend whole families asunder. I don't care how you do it, but I want a demonstration in time for the evening editions and a riot for the Late Night Final."

O'Leary's eyes glinted. "An assignment after my own heart," he said happily. "And if I should be arrested?"

"Ring the *Echo*, ask for MacHabeas Corpus. He'll spring you before you can say, 'This is an outrage!' Okay?"

"I've waited for this," said O'Leary simply.

Kidder finished his breakfast and tried absentmindedly to force the smeared plate through the bars of the lift gates. It would not go. He winked at Mr. Jackson. "I know, I know," he said. "How did it get *in*? *Gulla, gulla! gasps dying witness.*"

"Eh?" said Farmer Jepson.

Kidder ignored him. "Now the way I see this," he said, reaching for a cigar, "is *this*. Our only real danger is that these Old Beefers should pal up with each other or anyone else. We've got to split 'em into rival factions – sheep and goats, and I want the numbers even. Sheep Murder, goats Misadventure, and let's have no Don't-Know stuff. I want 'em fighting among each other before we turn 'em loose on the gang outside."

"Who will also be fighting," murmured O'Leary.

Kidder consulted a piece of paper. "Right, here's the drill. 11:30, Walvis Hall for briefing and major split. 12:30, inadequate and filthy buffet lunch. 1:30, choice of two compulsory tours to plug the six *musts*. The Tower or Harrods. Tower tour to promote class hatred, blood lust, and fear; Harrods, jealousy, greed, and sex. 5:30, the back entrance here for a final pep talk and the distribution of banners. 6:00, the front entrance. No shouting until you hit Croissant Street. Then let 'em rip! All clear?"

Mr. Jepson, of just outside Maidstone, asked, "'Ow about these ruddy photographers?"

"Three in the mob. The fair-haired one's got the camera for smashing, but wait until you're covered by the other two. Manley'll be on the roof opposite with a Long Tom from 5:30 onwards."

"May we break bones?" inquired O'Leary.

"Not indiscriminately. And go easy on the blood, except for this bird." Kidder produced a large photograph and pushed it through the bars. "Name of Solly. He'll be by the hydrant, wearing a yellow scarf. He knows the old capsule trick and he's bringing half a pint. Give him the works, but don't hurt him. He'll be dragged away yelling by a couple of rozzers."

Mr. Jackson asked curiously, "How do you know?"

Kidder lit a cigar. "Proofreaders," he explained. "Get paid in peanuts, poor sods. Glad of the extra." He glanced at his watch. "General Jackson, your bunch is due in eighteen minutes. Blow, the lot of you! Remember, dull sullen rumble by five-fifteen, full-blooded roar and we hope a couple of sirens by six." He sketched a salute. "Gentlemen!"

"General!"

"Captain!"

"Major!"

"General!"

"Watches synchronized? Nine-fourteen . . . *now*!"

The conspirators clattered away down the stairs.

Kidder rolled over on to his stomach and tapped out his call signal on the transmitter set. "Kidder calling, Kidder calling! Stan? Over. Sure, all according to plan. Zero minus nine. Tell Ted to hold the front pages of the last two editions. Over. Kayes? Okay, okay, so he escaped, so *what*? You get anything on this White cadaver? Over. All right, all right, then buzz the hospitals, drag the canals, dig up the parks! I want that stiff by this evening, and no fooling!" He signed off and looked up to see Egon watching him from the far side of the bars.

"Kid," said Egon with a wild smile. "I love you. I've been being grilled by the wolf pack."

"What did you tell 'em?"

"Not a thing, chum, not a single, solitary thing. I talked nonstop for twenty-two minutes flat and I gave them not one item which I didn't immediately contradict, not one. Then I said if they got it wrong, I'd sue them. I got 'em really good and groggy."

"Swell."

"Well, I'll see you. I have to brief the gang. Staff conference."

"Half and half?"

"Sure."

"Tell 'em to lay off even a sniff of Suicide."

Egon stiffened. "Why?" he asked sharply.

"Not even I can make all three stick."

"You wouldn't be rat enough to pull a switch?"

"How do *I* know? I never know what I'm going to do until I see it in print."

Egon shook the gates of the lift. He said hotly, "Suicide'd kill me."

Kidder flicked the ash off his cigar down the lift shaft. "Look, brother," he said impatiently. "At this stage, anything may break, including this cock-eyed lift."

Three and a half floors below, O'Leary climbed on to the running-board of a car and cast an expert eye over the crowd outside the archway. He spotted only three people who looked likely rabblerousers. One of the men wore handicapping spectacles, the other was rather too small, but the woman was a natural. He approached her and touched her arm. "Excuse me, madam," he said courteously. "Will you tell me the joke?"

"'Oo are you?" she growled, instantly aggressive. "Wot joke?"

"That fellow over there keeps pointing at you and laughing fit to split his sides," O'Leary explained. Her nostrils dilated slightly and her ears moved. He knew he had her. "With the green tie," he said helpfully. "By the lamppost . . ."

Enid Marley paid off her taxi and made her way through the crowd towards the *You* and *Me* building. Nobody stopped her or even so much as glanced at her. The photograph in the *Echo* had been unrecognizable; the one which weekly headed her column had been taken ten years before and even then had been so heavily retouched that it looked nothing like her at all.

At the bottom of the lift shaft, the janitor was sitting on a folding canvas stool holding a small, useless-looking cosh. He explained, "Them reporters keep runnin' in an' rattlin' 'Er gates. She 'ates that an' what's more, it's dangerous."

Enid Marley stalked past him. A constable stood on duty at the foot of the stairs. "Sorry, madam," he began. "I have orders . . ."

She said icily, "I am Enid Marley, you lunatic. Step aside immediately."

He stared at her for a long moment, then flattened himself against the wall. She marched up the stairs. She heard him remark to the janitor, "Well, I don't know. What's *she* doing here, if it *was* her, which it didn't look like? Doesn't seem sort of *right*."

On the second floor, she came upon Carstairs, the private detective. He was leaning against a fire extinguisher, trying to force two stubby fingers into a cellophane bag of nuts and raisins.

"Well, well, well," he said heavily, shaking his head at her. "Somebody I know's certainly sticking their neck out, they are, good morning. All very dodgy, this is, *very* dodgy. Like I used to tell your ex . . ."

"Can you explain that crowd outside the building? What do they want? Now that the misunderstanding about my murder has been cleared up . . ."

He coughed untidily and wiped his mouth on a torn gray handkerchief. He said through its folds, "Somebody I know doesn't read their *Echo*."

"I don't understand you."

Carstairs succeeded in extracting a half peanut from the cellophane bag. He laid it carefully on his tongue, then began to chew it. "Well, this Kidder," he mumbled, jerking his head upwards, "says you were creased.

Splat! and that. Only you weren't at all on account of a lot of stuff and stuff and stuff. I don't know, didn't read it. Like your ex used to say, 'Boyo, I couldn't care!' "

As she mounted the next flight of stairs, Enid Marley began to tremble with rage. She stopped on the half-landing, closed her eyes. $H + 2Mn - 4B$, she thought, breathing deeply. Then, comforted, calmed, she walked sedately up to the third floor and eyed the bottom half of the man sitting in the lift.

"Mr. Kidder," she said gently. "Am I to understand that our talk of yesterday was a waste of time? I hear that you have deliberately magnified my unfortunate accident into a vulgar *cause célèbre*."

Kidder was sewing a button onto his pajamas. He looked up and frowned irritably. "Look, sister," he said. "Let's understand each other. Right now, I've got Both jacked up and I'm doing fine. Any truck from you and I switch to Suicide, then we'd have to ask Manley to photograph you up a gum tree, wouldn't we? Because make no mistake, lady, your position is . . . well, let's not use rough talk . . . let's just say *equivocal*."

In Egon's office, his staff watched him morosely. Doon smothered a yawn. Paul tapped his forehead four times with an index finger, implying that Egon was not, and never had been, quite sane. Jimmie shrugged. Mrs. Ryder poured herself another cup of strong, cold tea. Rex sat tapping the ash at intervals off his cigarette in such a manner that it always fell on exactly the same spot on the coconut matting. Doctor Feltz, his head sunk on to his breast, sat tying and untying knots in his handkerchief. Ellie sat staring at Egon.

He was performing one of his graceless little dances before the circulation graph. A spectacular upward sweep showed that the sales figures of *You* had not only drawn level with those of *Me*, but had surpassed them. Egon had already rung up the insufferable Larkin, the editor of the rival magazine, and casually insulted him. He had also rung up J.L., C.G., A.B., and B.F., told them the news, and been granted a further increase in his next print order. Now everything was almost perfect. Except for one small item, life had not been so sweet for him since his Goonatilika scoop fourteen years before.

"Just one tiny detail," he said, happily kicking a filing cabinet. "This stiff. Kidder gives the story only three editions unless . . ."

"*Which* stiff?" asked Doon.

"Egon," said Paul. "I wouldn't put anything past you. You wouldn't be thinking of . . ."

Egon stubbed out his cigarette an inch from the ashtray. "No, no," he said quickly. "Any old stiff. Not to worry. It's in the bag. This Kayes bird's on the loose. He'll bump somebody any time now. Kidder'll tie it up some-how. Now let's get this absolutely clear. Will you stand, murderers?"

For the third time, Doon, Paul, and Ellie stood.

"Grand!" said Egon enthusiastically, and then, as if they had been dogs. "Okay, *sit*! Up, dissenters!"

Mrs. Ryder sighed loudly and stood up. Jimmie half rose from the window ledge. Egon waited. Everybody looked at Doctor Feltz.

"He's asleep" said Doon. "He said he was up all night tiddling up *Are YOU a Schizo?*"

In Victoria Station, Mr. Jackson stood at the ticket barrier and watched the still steaming train disgorge its passengers. He was on the lookout for a certain Colonel Quincey, one of the most regular of the Regular Complainers. The old man, retired from the Indian Army many years before, had volunteered to escort a batch of thirty-two sympathizers from Krunte Abbas in Dorset and points west. Mr. Jackson spotted him immediately.

"Colonel Quincey?"

"Jackson, sir?" asked the Colonel. He was red-faced, white-mustached. He spoke indistinctly, as if there was food concealed in his mouth. "Pleased to. Welcomed opportunity. Spare rod, always say, spoil . . ." He shook Mr. Jackson's hand with a bone-crushing grip. "Terrible journey, terrible. Dog. Dreadful animal. Started barking Salisbury."

"You collected the recruits?"

"Three deserters. No loss."

"Where are the others?"

The Colonel jerked his head backwards. "Poor material," he remarked. "Not an officer among. Sepoys." He added vaguely, "*Bilharzia*, foot rot, worms," then roared over his shoulder, "Fall in there! At the double!"

In Enid Marley's office, Rex and Ellie dealt rapidly with the morning's mail.

"She just loved our last knitting pattern," announced Rex, reading. "But she wears it back to front."

"Who *cares*?"

"And here's some swine who's made a six-decker sandwich."

Ellie did not comment. She said instead, "I'm putting the straightforward illegits under your thermos. Be a love, dear. Look up, 'My mother has fallen for the wiles of a fellow who got my friend in trouble and didn't care, shall I tell her?' "

Rex crossed to the charts and stretched the strings. "B + LM2," he dictated.

"Where are you putting the Misadventure confessions?"

"Under the ink."

"They *can't* of ruddy well gone!" protested Farmer Jepson at the ticket barrier at Paddington. "*Where*'ve they gone?"

"Train was early, sir," said the ticket collector. "They just said to say they'd gone. I did say where, but they said to say you'd know."

"Come on, my lad," said Mrs. Ryder gruffly in the photographic studio, arranging her cake in the middle of a nest of last year's crackers. "Cough it up! Clears the air."

Jimmie trained an arc lamp on to the cake. "Well," he said dubiously, returning to his camera and crouching to focus. "I want a reflector. The off-side looks lifeless." He scratched his crew cut and burst out, "Honestly, I just don't *like* Misadventure! Murder, yes, okay. Quite understandable. But if somebody really tried to save that rancid old fraud, then, personally, I'm jolly windy. There's a madman in the building."

"Come on, get in, can't you?" shouted Mr. Cream, pushing the last of his charges roughly into the charabanc outside Waterloo. "I'm boss 'ere, see, an' don't you forget it! 'Ere! You there! You at the back in the daft 'at! Get that perishin' animal on the floor, an' look slippy!"

"There are two fights going on and we've won a police gent on a horse," reported Doon. She was wearing her spectacles, hanging out of the window of Doctor Feltz's office. "He's talking to an enormous great bruiser with bright red hair."

Behind her, Doctor Feltz drew a shallow breath.

So!

He felt the hair rise behind his ears and the sweat break out on his forehead. And yet at the same time he was conscious of a curious sense of release, a general slackening of all his muscles.

It was all over. The long years of uncertainty were behind him. His future was brief, but no longer unpredictable. Mangoyian had finally tracked him down. Mangoyian would solve all his problems within the hour.

He said steadily. "Yar, I know him. He has nose like ein eagle, bale gomplexion, driangular zgar on levd jeek, und wears ein Norfolk jagged."

Doon took another look at the mounted policeman, then removed her spectacles and peered at Doctor Feltz. "Really, Dock, ducky!" she said. "What *have* you been reading? He's not like that at all. He's rather a dish, actually, and he's being absolutely sweet to that terrifying horse."

"I saw you on the telly," accused an overgrown girl in a round school hat. "You was holdin' that Tinker."

Mr. Frederick Turner ushered her into the coach waiting outside King's Cross. "That's right," he admitted, blushing fierily.

"Mum!" she yelled. "Mum! 'Ere's that man what 'olds Tinker!"

"'Old your 'ush, you 'ulkin' great menace!" boomed her mother from the back of the bus. "An' talk proper, can't you?"

In his office, Egon sat interviewing a woman explorer, making notes for an enigmatic editorial, eating a ham sandwich, surreptitiously signing a pile of rejection slips, and admiring the four billboards which were a rush order from the Art Department. The latter read, respectively, *UP WITH YOU!! DOWN WITH YOU!!! YOU IS YOUR BEST FRIEND!!! and SHUN THE MURDER MAG!!!*

"Of course, the uninitiated think it's revolting," said the woman explorer, coughing horribly. "But if you skin them and roll them up in banyan leaves with a good fid of ghee . . ."

Paul East looked into the room and said briefly, "Kidder's champing."

Egon handed over the bill boards. "Tell him the others'll be down in half an hour," he ordered. "Warn him the paint's wet." And to the woman explorer, with a radiant, intimate smile, "You know, between us, we're going to slay 'em. This is marvelous stuff. I feel we should highlight the episode of the tiger and the dried milk. It's human, pulsing, *real* . . . and yet somehow . . . I know you know what I mean . . . it has that aura of the sinister, the macabre, the . . . and this is entirely between ourselves . . . the *cannibal* . . ."

"*D, Daisy Four,*" intoned the dashboard radio. "*D, Daisy Four. Disturbance, 8 Gibbon Villas. Proceed, stand by. R. Roger Eight, R. Roger . . .*"

Inspector Woodman sat slumped in the back of his car, scowling at the back of his driver's neck, his fingers white around the handle of a brief case bulging with spurious Marley confessions.

Another day! Another long, hard day on this debilitating case which wasn't a case at all! He knew the pattern now. The staff of *You* would lie again, contradict themselves and each other, enjoy giving him the run-around. Egon would perform his maddening little soft shoe shuffle and offer another fistful of crazy confessions. Enid Marley, with her colorless eyes and that depressing collection of long, thin, dead animals about her shoulders, would give him a lot of holier-than-thou stuff and probably again threaten to report him to the Commissioner. And Rex Travers, wearing one of his sickening waistcoats, would certainly call him Charlie . . .

"*M, Maud Two, M, Maud Two. Cat treed Warwick Avenue, Warwick Avenue. Proceed.*"

And then there was Kidder, confident, corny Kidder of the blasted *Echo*! To double damnation with him, for without his fool headlines this non-case would have been dropped into the obscurity where it belonged. And he, Woodman, would be . . .

"*. . . wanted for Murder. Six foot five, red hair, scar left cheek, small hazel eyes, heavy blond brows . . .*"

Kayes!

Killer Kayes, Woodman's own old slippery, implacable enemy! And yet the case had passed into the fumbling hands of poor old Willis! Was Willis – as Woodman would have been – completely preoccupied, even a little infatuated, with his quarry? Did he know – as Woodman did – Kayes's every . . .

"*. . . wearing khaki trenchcoat, black shoes, no hat. Believed to be in Area M2. Last seen Bilton Street. All cars Area M for Mary, all cars . . .*"

. . . mood and habit? Did Willis know with certainty – as Woodman did – where Kayes would *not* be, now or ever? Did he know Kayes's taste in women, in locale, where he was likely to eat? Did he know the fiend's old haunts, his friends, his many foes, the brand of his shaving soap, the name of his dead cat? Did he know that, in 1951, Kayes had been suspected of running a disorderly house and growing hashish in the window boxes in . . .

In Bilton Street!

Bilton Street which ran parallel to Croissant Street, beyond the *You and Me* building, the far side of the car park! Woodman's heart rose like a bird. If Kayes was in this area, then he, Woodman, had a better chance of recognizing and arresting him than any man alive. Poor old Willis hadn't a chance. He knew nothing.

He did not even know that forty-three years, eleven months, two weeks, and one day ago, the killer Kayes had been born in the *souks* of Ankara and, fifteen days later, had been informally christened Gyko Khosrove Melik Mangoyian . . .

Chapter 13

THE Walvis Hall had been bombed twice during the war, but never seriously repaired. Always a hideous old building, it now looked as if some testy giant had first given it a kick and then flung at it, at random, several handfuls of concrete and a tangle of rusty scaffolding. A notice announcing that the premises were for sale had fallen into a leafless hedge and lay rotting while sick yellow grass grew up around it.

By 11:15, three of the four groups of Regular Complainers (Rail) and the supporters (Bus, Road, Underground) being dealt with by the *Echo* team were installed in the main assembly room. An hour and a half later, the gathering was still waiting for the fourth (Rail) group, and was showing signs of restiveness. The wan gloom of the hall, the fact that the hard wooden chairs were nailed together in rows of twenty, the rumor that the paste in the bulky sandwiches was tainted, and an extraordinary display of ill temper on the part of Mr. Cream had all contributed to produce a situation which Kidder had not quite envisaged. Instead of splitting into two or more angry parties amongst themselves, the Complainers, by 1:03, were clearly about to band together in a general revolt against their hosts. At 1:14, a small group started a slow, rhythmic handclap.

Mr. Jackson, sweating freely, hurried up to Mr. Cream. Mopping his forehead, he muttered, "Where the hell are Farmer Jepson's lot?"

Mr. Cream wolfed another sandwich. He did not answer.

Mr. Jackson said angrily, "Start the martial music."

"I don't understand the loudspeakers."

"You said you did."

"These is different."

"*How* are they different?"

"They're not the same."

"Where's Fred Turner?"

"Over there."

"Over where?"

"I dunno."

Mr. Jackson said rashly, "You know what you are? You're a dead loss."

Mr. Cream slapped him with the remains of the sandwich. "Now let's have no lip from you, mate," he said, drooping his eyelids. "I wouldn't want to get nasty now, would I?"

Mr. Jackson gave up and turned away. As he threaded his way through the grumbling groups of Complainers, he heard a dog fight start up away on his left. He was forcing his way through the obstinate swing doors, when Frederick Turner ran towards him shouting, "'Ere! General! 'Alf a mo!"

The doors swung back, striking Mr. Jackson on the hip. He waited, cursing.

Mr. Frederick Turner panted to a standstill. "There's some flamin' geyser over there sayin' as all men is brothers," he said urgently. "An' a lot of 'em are listenin'. We'll never get a row up, not at this rate."

Mr. Jackson cracked his knuckles. "Tell him to go home."

"I did. 'E said 'ome's where the 'eart is an' 'is 'eart's 'ere."

"Then go and separate those dogs."

"Eh?"

"And then start Briefing."

"'Oo, me? You daft?"

"And be persuasive. We've got to woo them."

A stentorian bellow rang from the far side of the hall. Mr. Cream had made a megaphone from a rolled newspaper, and climbed on to a chair. "Now you listen to me, you ugly lot!" he was roaring. "I want complete 'ush an' no muckin' about, see?"

Mr. Jackson gave Mr. Frederick Turner a push. "Go and tell him to lay off," he said desperately. "*Hurry!*"

"No," said Mr. Turner, swallowing. "No. Not me. No."

But Mr. Jackson had gone. He paused to loosen his tie in the seedy foyer. There were dead leaves in the corners and a dusty plait of electric light wires hung from the ceiling. For an instant he wondered whether to abandon the whole project, to contact O'Leary, to suggest that they got drunk all over again and fought their way back to Bournemouth. Then he remembered that Enid Marley had deliberately, with malice aforethought, robbed him of his bride, his helpmeet, his plump, foolish little Browneyes. She had also, indirectly, stolen his wallet. She owed him twenty-seven pounds, a book of stamps, and a photograph of himself taken at Land's End.

He had pulled his wife's farewell note from his pocket and was unfolding it when Farmer Jepson sidled from behind a pillar and cleared his throat nervously. Mr. Jackson sprang at him.

"Where have you been?" he demanded. "Where are your Complainers?"

Farmer Jepson flushed. "They said I'd know," he said, kicking at a leaf, "They just went off."

"Where to?"

"Just said I'd know. Well, I don't."

"Where's the charabanc?"

"They took it."

Mr. Jackson turned back towards the assembly room. As he prised open the swing doors, Farmer Jepson remarked, "Chap out there said he wanted to fix the loudspeakers."

"And about time, too! Where is he?"

"I told 'im to beat it. 'E wasn't 'alf rude, but 'e went, in the end."

"Oh, you damn fool!"

"*What* was that again?"

"I said come on."

Inside the hall, Mr. Cream was still standing on his chair, shouting, but nobody was listening to him. The Complainers were watching the dog-fight. Two men were trying to separate a stout Airedale and an enraged Alsatian. A woman in a gray coat had been bitten. An old-faced young man was telling her that he was her brother and trying to persuade her to put her arm into a sling.

Mr. Jackson found himself face to face with Colonel Quincey. The old man was emptying a flask into his cup of tea. He looked up and shrugged. "*Pukka tamarsha*," he mumbled, turning to stare at Mr. Cream. "Grade A clot, that chap. Never rub a sepoy wrong way. Stuff, mutiny. My day, drove 'em up trees, smoked 'em out, shot 'em evading arrest. No trouble at all."

"What did he say?"

"Lot of guff. Half murderers, half adventurers. Backs up all round. Said Enid Marley, public menace, cahoots with Devil, tried to force him to adopt illegitimate child, black."

"Black?"

"Wog. Other chap said pigment geographical necessity, threw cup. Fellow lost temper, language not fit Sergeants' Mess. All brothers, my foot!"

Mr. Frederick Turner, holding a handkerchief to his left nostril, ran up and snatched Mr. Jackson's arm. "The charas 'ave come for the tours, General," he said breathlessly. "They'll only wait ten minutes on account of they got to be somewhere else for the Gas Workers' Union while our lot's in the Tower or 'Arrods."

Mr. Jackson asked, "What's the matter with your nose?"

"'E punched me," said Mr. Frederick Turner, aggrieved.

"Who did?"

"That everybody's brothers basket. I asked 'im ever so nicely if 'e'd shut up, an' 'e said I was a troublemaker, an' 'e 'it me. 'Ow about the charas?"

Mr. Jackson clenched his hands inside his pockets and tried to think. What had Kidder said? One, that before they separated for the tours, the Complainers must be split into two opposing factions of equal strength. Two, that all must have faith in and respect for their hosts, who were representing the *Echo*. Three, that their hatred of *You* must be maintained, yet canalized, on the one hand, into an enthusiasm for Murder, on the other, into an infatuation for Misadventure.

It was a Herculean task and Mr. Jackson had eight and a half minutes to complete it. Clearly, this was a time for shock tactics. An insane idea dropped into his mind. Before he had time to wonder whether it had even an element of reason, he had hoisted himself on to one of the trestle tables which held the wreck of the refreshments, and banged two large tin teapots together for silence.

Several Complainers turned from the dogfight to look at him. A pockmarked youth in a sky blue suit jeered, "Pass 'im the milk an' sugar!" Another roared, "Do us a dance, mister!" A flower-faced teenager with long blonde hair yelled, "Stow it, you stinkers! Give the poor old gent a flipping chance!"

It took Mr. Jackson four and a half minutes to produce, except for the snarling and heavy breathing of the fighting dogs, complete silence. "Ladies and gentlemen," he began sternly.

"Friends!" called the old-faced young man who claimed to be everybody's brother, climbing on to another table. "Before our comrade here begins to remind us that we peace-loving people are gathered today in the name of trouble, a situation which I'm convinced that every one of you decent citizens deplores . . ."

"'Ear, 'ear!" said a man in a green hat.

"Trouble nothing!" shouted Mr. Jackson. "I want peace too!"

"Ah, familiar, hollow words!" cried the old-young man. "How often have we heard them, particularly before some major war?"

"'Ear, 'ear!" said the man in the green hat.

"I *demand* peace," said Mr. Jackson fiercely. "I insist upon seeing the immediate end of hostilities between these two dogs! Let us split into two parties and work together for this common cause! Will those in favor of the Alsatian move to the right of the hall, those for the Airedale to the left?"

The talk broke out again. The crowd swayed, began to separate into arguing groups. The dogs, left to their own devices, fell into a terrible, snorting deadlock. A woman said, "Well, you got to admit that's different," and marched firmly across the floor. Two men followed her, then five women, then a large posse.

Mr. Jackson watched, speechless and appalled, while, to a man, the Complainers massed to the left side of the hall.

"Ladies and gentlemen!" he pleaded. "Is this *fair*? Come, come! Who owns this noble Alsatian?"

The old-young man bowed his head. He admitted with loud, practiced humility, "I am deeply ashamed to confess that the horrible animal is mine.

I freely allow that this disgusting battle was one hundred percent his fault. For seven long years, I have attempted to train him. For my pains, I have been bitten savagely over fifty times. I have turned the other cheek and been bitten again. Frankly, I hate him. His behavior today is perhaps the thousandth manifestation of his profound love of violence. Believe me when I tell you that that monstrous creature of darkness intends to kill that plucky old Airedale! Friends, believe me when I tell you that that evil, eerie, demented animal has accounted for eleven innocent lives, that he is as surely a murderer as any felon who swung by the neck until he was dead!"

"'Ear, 'ear!" said the man in the green hat.

"Thank you, sir," said the old-young man warmly. "Will you tell our friends here what you personally think of violence?"

The man in the green hat guffawed. "I've 'ad it," he said. "Get enough at 'ome to make me 'air curl."

"Then how, sir," thundered the old-young man, "do you explain your presence here today? Friends, as men and women of the world, let us agree that we have been assembled here by the *Echo* for the sole purpose of furthering trouble. How little that organ cares for our finer feelings has been clearly demonstrated by this choice of neighborhood and the quality of the sandwiches . . ."

The crowd, murmuring sympathetically, began to surge slowly towards him.

"Do we not rate fresh bread? Hot coffee? Are we dupes? Are we pawns?"

"'Ear, 'ear," said the man in the green hat.

Mr. Frederick Turner caught Mr. Jackson's eye. "'E's got 'em," he murmured. "What'll we do, General?"

"Go and stall the charabancs," hissed Mr. Jackson.

"It's too late," said Farmer Jepson.

"What do you mean?"

"They went off. They've gone."

"Oh, God!"

"We been routed, General," said Mr. Frederick Turner. "Might as well pack up, *I* say."

"Oh, shut up!" said Mr. Jackson, climbing off his table.

"Get out o' me way, you!" snarled Mr. Cream, elbowing his way past roughly. "I'll show 'im!" He plunged across the hall, laid hold of the trestle on which the old-young man was standing and gave it a savage jerk.

"SHAME!" shouted twenty-eight people as the old-young man picked himself up off the floor.

"'Ear, 'ear!" bellowed the man in the green hat.

"That's done it," said Farmer Jepson. "That's all we ruddy well wanted!"

"Well, I know just what *I*'m going to do," said Mr. Frederick Turner, squaring his small hands. "It's the only thing."

Mr. Jackson looked at him. He himself had no idea what to do next. Was it possible that this weedy little fellow had struck on some desperate strategy, some maneuver which at this eleventh hour might save the day? "What?" he asked with a flicker of hope.

"I," said Mr. Frederick Turner with an air of finality, "am goin' 'ome to feed Tinker."

Chapter 14

By two o'clock, the crowd outside the *You* and *Me* building had almost doubled in size. Rex, venturing out to buy a bottle of gin for Egon, returned pale and dishevelled, with most of the buttons torn off his jacket, with a long scratch down his left cheek, with a bottle of champagne, a bulging paper bag, and a bunch of roses. Egon, Paul, Jimmie, Doon, Ellie, and Mrs. Ryder sat in Enid Marley's office and gazed at him in silence.

"Mobbed!" he cried, combing his hair. "But *mobbed!* They jumped on me like wild, wild animals!"

Doon asked, "Where did you get that champagne?"

"Some man told me to give it to the murderer."

"What murderer?"

"The one that pushed Madam."

"What's in that bag?"

"Pears. A woman said to give them to the saint."

"What saint?"

"The one that saved Madam. Then the Indian character tore up and offered me ten quid to have lunch in his restaurant. He told me to tell you that he'd give any of you twenty because you were the real Mackenzie. Then O'Leary grabbed me. He said he'd been arrested, but to tell Kidder that he was back on the job. Then a girl gave me these roses and said . . ."

Egon seized the bunch of roses and dropped them out of the window. "Oh, if only Enid were here!" he mourned, wondering whether he was serious or just talking. "She could make a speech from the roof. Heart-warming, stirring, a passionate plea for peace . . . and yet at the same time full of double-take insults that'd start the goons scratching themselves ten minutes later . . ."

"She *is* here," said Rex.

"*What?*" shouted Egon, outraged. "It's not nice, it's not ethical! Either she's dead, or she's resurrected, and whichever is it, why the hell isn't she lying doggo?"

"Because she's bullying Doctor Feltz," said Rex, "and loving every moment of it. She looks about eighty years younger."

"I'm hungry," announced Doon sadly.

"Me too," said Paul, looking up from a sheaf of proofs. "I could eat a missionary."

"You'll get torn to shreds if you go out there," said Rex. "Besieged, that's what you are. Besieged."

Ellie said, "I've got some vitamin pills."

Mrs. Ryder dropped her cigarette on to the coconut matting and ground it out with a sensible flat heel. "I have some Cucumber Toscana," she said briskly, "and a raspberry mousse."

"If it was Misadventure," said Doon hopefully, "then whichever of us tried to save Madam is the saint that person was talking about, and they're quite entitled to eat that bag of pears."

There was a short pause. The staff looked at each other dubiously.

Paul said, "Under the circumstances, I might admit Misadventure for a dozen oysters and a whacking great steak, but a bag of pears . . . no."

"Whereas if it was Murder," said Jimmie, "then the guilty party could open that bottle and give us all a swig of champagne."

Rex, who was nearest to the door, heard the approaching footsteps and looked out into the corridor. "Cavee!" he whispered loudly. "Let's all draw water pistols! Here comes Charlie!"

Inspector Woodman swung into the room and looked about him with a broad smile. His hands were plunged into the pockets of his mackintosh and his hat was at a jaunty angle. His eyes were bright, his shoulders back.

"Afternoon, all," he said. "Just popped in to collect the bumph."

Ellie silently lifted the inkwell and handed over the Misadventure confessions. Doon offered another small pile of letters and explained, "These are the Both ones. You do look well, ducky. Are you in love?"

Woodman frowned briefly. He remarked in a conversational manner, "I'm going to ask you all one question. I intend to have the truth and no jiggery-pokery. Think carefully before you answer. Understood?"

Everybody looked at Egon. Egon looked back at his staff. He propped up his nose with his right thumb and said quietly behind his hand, "Watch it, kids!"

Woodman walked steadily across to the window and turned, forcing his audience to face the light. He raised his left eyebrow one eighth of an inch and looked in silence from face to face until he felt that he had everyone present at a psychological disadvantage.

"*Which of you*," he barked suddenly, "*knows something to the detriment of a tall, red-haired Armenian named Gyko Khosrove Melik Mangoyian?*"

In the silent second that followed, he realized almost immediately that he had made a mistake. The seven were genuinely surprised.

"Who?" asked Jimmie.

"Mango what?" said Rex.

"Never met an Armenian," growled Mrs. Ryder. "What's more, shouldn't trust him if I did."

"Most red-haired men are so *brash*," said Ellie.

"There's a delicatessen called something like that," said Doon. "It looks rather grand. They always have just one smoked eel in the window."

Paul said, "I once had a cousin who went to Armenia by mistake during the war, but he got drowned."

"Mangoyian, Mangoyian," mused Egon, tugging at the lobe of his ear. "Wasn't there that shifty old codger in Calcutta . . . dreadful fellow, used to collect match boxes . . .?" He looked at Woodman curiously. "Why?"

Woodman was already on his way towards the door. "Forget it," he said curtly. "I just had a hunch about an entirely different case."

In Doctor Feltz's office, Enid Marley sat behind the desk and watched the small Viennese staring sightlessly out of the window.

"He's out there somewhere," she said, fingering her pearls and smiling. "Unless, of course, he's already inside the building. Poor Mangoyian! How he must hate you! He's been after you for . . . how many years? Fourteen?"

"Vivdeen," murmured Doctor Feltz.

"Tell me, when did he change his name?"

"Ach, a dozen dimes! When I med him in Durkey, it was Glive Axelrod."

She said relentlessly, "He intends to kill you. He knows that he can only hang once. What are you going to do?"

Doctor Feltz looked her over his shoulder. For an instant, he regarded her as a patient. In the old days, he would have enjoyed analyzing her. Beneath that bland, three-cornered smile, that almost tangible air of decorum, what a poisonous goulash there must lie! He said hopelessly, "I doand know."

She studied her nails. "As a loyal citizen, you should appeal for police protection."

He met her eyes across his desk. They were on the same level as his own although she sat and he stood. He knew – and he knew that she also knew – that were he to summon the police, he would have to tell them the whole dreadful story . . .

He saw again the huge, grand room just off the Ringstrasse; himself, bearded, precociously famous, sitting behind an austere desk which had once belonged to Metternich. He saw Mangoyian's flaming hair against the couch with the black leather buttons. He heard again the man's soft voice, speaking French with a heavy Armenian accent. *Doktor, Doktor, you must help me! My mother is mad. She refuses to believe me though I tell her every day, every day, every day that my father is mad . . .* And he? He had refused the case, sailed for America to comfort a film producer who was afraid of his wife.

He turned back to the window and laid his forehead against the cool glass. "Why do you dormend me?" he asked without interest. "You know well it is imbossible."

"I suppose so." She joined the tips of her fingers and added, "Perhaps *I* should appeal to them on your behalf."

He was not surprised. He had expected it. He was already resigned to the fact that until Kayes was caught and hanged, Enid Marley would not be satisfied with her usual expensive monthly present.

He said dully "Yar. Will you dake a jegg?"

"*Terrible, 'orrible, 'omicidal killer right 'ere, right now!*" bawled the news vendor on the corner. "*Read all about your deadly peril!*"

Mr. Jackson hurried through the crowd and glared at him. "What do you mean killer?" he demanded. "I gave you ten bob to say it was Both."

"That wasn't your caper, guv," said the news vendor. "Was the other, this Kayes cove. I'm bashin' 'em sort of alternate, see?"

Mr. Jackson said angrily, "Well, don't! Shout 'Baffling Enigma Case!' "

"I'd feel silly."

"Then shout, '*You* mystery baffles Yard!' "

"*You Mystery baffles Yard!*"

Mr. Jackson began to struggle towards the archway. He caught a glimpse of the Hungarian photographer, who was signing autograph albums, and O'Leary, who was eating plums off a barrow and looking thoughtful. One of the *Echo* team was leaning against an enormous camera by the railings. He winked at Mr. Jackson.

"How's it coming you-wise?" he asked.

"Terrible. I have to tell Kidder." Mr. Jackson eyed the camera. "That the one for smashing?"

"Yep. Kick it right *here* and you'll be okay. No point in wrecking your shoes."

"No."

"Will you tell Kidder I have a date at six?"

Mr. Jackson edged his way through the staring group outside the archway. The janitor stood in a pioneer attitude at the foot of the lift shaft, posing for a youth with a box camera. There were two policemen at the bottom of the stairs. They stood aside to allow Mr. Jackson to pass.

One said, "No offense, old man, but are you honestly a general?"

"No. Are you really a policeman?"

"Good Lord, no! Will you remind Kidder that my train leaves at 7:04?"

"Your helmet doesn't look right."

"Not to worry."

On the second floor, Mr. Jackson met Carstairs, the private detective. The man was holding his left elbow in his right hand, straining over his shoulder to reach some point between his neck and the small of his back. He achieved it, scratched, and mumbled, "Hear your blushing bride took a powder. Want a divorce?"

"Not now. I have to see Kidder."

"Okay," said Carstairs, rubbing his back against the wall. "Your funeral."

Kidder sat in the lift between the third and fourth floors. He had a typewriter between his feet and he was tapping out copy at machine-gun speed. He looked up, saw Mr. Jackson and said, "Tell."

Mr. Jackson told. "It's this blasted brother chap," he finished. "I knew we'd had it as soon as he started about the sandwiches. Now they're all a hundred percent for *You* and Misadventure, and four hundred percent against the *Echo* and Murder."

"Well, aren't you the original bright boy?" Kidder asked bitterly. "I promise the Old Man a riot, so you souse my honest rebels with brotherly love! Frankly, general, you make me puke."

Mr. Jackson scowled. "How about you?" he demanded hotly. "You promise him three days of exclusive murder spreads and you can't even rustle up a corpse."

"I can't understand it," Kidder said, outraged. "People get knocked off every day. Why not yesterday? Or the day before? Or even today? What's the *matter* with me? Am I slipping?" His eyes narrowed suddenly. He lit a cigar and looked at Mr. Jackson sideways. "Hey, you don't think your wife would . . ."

"Browneyes?"

"Yeah, her. You don't think she'd . . ."

"No."

"Sure?"

"Quite."

"Be a nice tie-up there," said Kidder, making no attempt to conceal the wistful note in his voice. "Banner, Puzzle Case Claims Second Victim!"

"She'll turn up."

"Might be worth checking. You can't prove it."

"Yes, I can." Mr. Jackson produced Browneyes's farewell note and offered it through the bars of the lift gate. "She's atoning. It's not the first time."

Kidder took the sheet of paper. " 'Dear *You*,' " he read aloud. " 'The present situation, obviously, is intolerable. I can no longer bear so heavy a burden. I have, quite calmly, given the matter . . .' "

"Turn over," said Mr. Jackson. "Other side."

Kidder turned the letter over. He frowned at Browneyes's tear-blotched scrawl. " 'I know I only married you yesterday,' " he read. " 'But I have already repented of this . . .' " He crushed the paper into a ball and tossed it over his shoulder. "Ah, to hell with it! Okay, she walked out, she's atoning, she'll be back alive and kicking. Pity!"

For the second time, Mr. Jackson found himself disliking Kidder. He would have liked to challenge the man to a not-too-enervating fight, but he could not get at him. He said curtly, "I'll get back to the Walvis Hall. I'm going to take a poke at that brotherly swine."

Kidder was already deep in another train of thought. He said absently, "Attaboy! Do that thing."

Mr. Jackson started down the stairs. He was on the ground floor when he heard the journalist shouting down the lift shaft.

"*Hey, General! Jackson! General Jackson!*"

"*What is it?*"

"Shoutin's not allowed," said the janitor. "It's in the lease."

"*You notice a tall, red-haired bird out there who looks Armenian?*"

"*No. Why?*"

"*As you were! Forget it!*"

". . . six foot five, scar left cheek, heavy blond brows, probably wearing a khaki trenchcoat?"

Inspector Woodman had asked the same question at two public houses in the immediate neighborhood, three cafés, a post office, an espresso bar, and every front door in Bilton Street. Nobody had seen Kayes, but he was in no way discouraged. He waited for the proprietor of the Indian restaurant to answer him with precisely the same eagerness yet lack of hope as he had waited for the first publican half an hour before.

The Indian clapped him on the back. "You johnnies surely are familiar with your onions!" he said warmly.

"Did you see him?"

"Yes indeed, man! Oh, a naughty fellow! He was in my cookhouse two minutes hence, demanding sandwiches. While my *khansama's* back was in reverse, he vamoosed with one pound ham, five *chapatis*, one banana. My *khansama* – very funny joker, drives me up the wall! – he cries after him, 'Come back now! You got no mustard!' "

"Which way did he go?"

"Into yard, on to henhouse, over wall, into limbo."

"Show me! Hurry!"

The Indian's eyes glittered. "Further drama, eh?" he asked eagerly.

"Show me!"

The back yard was littered with empty crates, boxes, cartons, tins, and bottles. A fat old woman in a grimy sari sat crosslegged among the rubble, shelling peas into a bucket.

She looked up indifferently as Woodman dragged off his coat, spat on his hands and charged at the henhouse. She watched impassively as he jumped, caught at the edge of the roof with one hand, and swung there apparently trying to kick down the wall. She lost interest as he got a grip with his other hand and, grunting, began to drag himself upwards. As he got one foot over the coping and hung for a moment trying to regain his breath, she remarked to the proprietor of the restaurant in Hindi, "The second in as many minutes! Your friends are trash, son."

With an immense effort, Woodman heaved himself on to the roof. He lay there panting while the landscape reeled. Then he embarked on a scrabbling, crablike crawl towards the apex. This achieved, he swung a leg over it, banged his left elbow, swore, and cautiously stood up.

He looked down into the yard. His head was less than twenty-five feet from the ground, yet his stomach curdled. He knew an instant of panic. And in that instant, he knew also that he had solved the Marley Case. Nobody who feared heights – as the idiotic woman had admitted in a signed statement – would have ventured on to a window sill eighty feet up in the air in order to save a wounded bird, or a pot of gold, or anything or anybody else. There would have to be some motive as compulsive as life itself, for instance, death. Enid Marley had attempted to commit suicide.

He could not, of course, prove it, nor did he particularly want to. But he could and would force her, and Egon, and Kidder, to accept a Misadventure verdict, which meant that he could drop the case, have nothing more to do with it, by quite simply inviting her to repeat the experiment . . .

By edging a few feet, he gained a hold on a blessedly solid wall. He clutched it with both hands and looked over it.

On the far side was the narrow lane which, twenty yards away, sloped underground to the packaging department of the *You* and *Me* building. At the top of the ramp lay a half-eaten banana.

Woodman grinned. He hauled himself on to the wall, sprawled for an ungainly, painful moment on his stomach, then lowered himself towards the lane to the full extent of his arms. He hung there, smiling. He knew that the drop would hurt his feet terribly, perhaps sprain one or both ankles, but he looked forward to it with relish.

For Kayes had passed this way! Kayes with his mad, secret smile and his broken tooth! Kayes of the shifting, khaki-colored eyes and the vast red hands! Kayes who once, years before, had made a fool of him in public, in the presence of six distinguished barristers, in Court! Kayes who, a day ago, had boasted in jail that he was willing, even eager, to be hanged, but not until he had liquidated his one last sovereign enemy!

And that enemy, as Woodman's hunch had told him, was obviously somewhere inside the huge *You* and *Me* building! For otherwise Kayes, who was as foxy as they came, would never have headed for the metropolitan area. He would never, unless he were within striking distance of his quarry, have been rash enough to steal food, to show his distinctive face.

And, above all, he would never, never, never – unless he were desperate, closing in for the kill in one of his wild moods of manic elation – have thrown away a half-eaten banana, his favorite fruit.

"Is it *my* fault?" Kidder roared into his transmitter set. "Who ordered that brotherly swine? Who ordered charabancs that were all tied up with the Gas Workers' Union? Now listen to me, you chairborn bum! I want action, and *fast*, or this thing's going to blow right up in our faces. Kayes is dodging around out there. Find him, follow him, hang on until he bumps somebody, then grab him, hole up somewhere, and get an exclusive. Get it? Over. How do *I* know where? Get him into the Walvis Hall! Get him in among the Gas Workers! Get him into Enid Marley's office! But get cracking! Give me something, anything, and I'll tie it up! Signing off!"

He sat back on his heels breathing heavily and fumbled for a cigar. He pulled his typewriter towards him and began to work. He had tapped, *While scores of Special Branch C.I.D. men combed the dark alleys behind London's present center of doubt and intrigue*, before a sudden thought struck him. He turned slowly, as if he were afraid of what he would see, and looked over his shoulder.

For a second, he thought that the letter had somehow disappeared. Then he saw it half hidden under a mound of rugs and cushions. He listened carefully to make certain that he was not going to be interrupted. He heard Carstairs, the private detective, making the most of a coughing bout on the second floor, but nobody nearer. He reached for the crumpled ball of paper which had been Browneyes Jackson's farewell note to her husband, and smoothed it out.

He turned it over with mixed feelings. He noted the stylized green lettering in one corner, the telegraphic address – US WE, LONDON – the green-typed date, the purple stamp of Enid Marley's ill-tempered signature.

. . . situation, obviously, is intolerable, he read. *I can no longer bear so heavy a burden . . . only solution lies in a swift, final exit.*

Well, well, well!

His immediate thought was, as usual, in the form of a headline. TRAPPED REPORTER SOLVES *YOU* RIDDLE! Then he drew deeply on his unlit cigar and thought again.

Either the letter was a forgery, or it was not. If so, it proved that one of the seven suspects had not only murdered Old Sister Toothache, but had also planned the crime with some care. If not, it proved that Enid Marley had, in a premeditated manner, intended to bite the dust.

Kidder's hands sprang automatically into position over his typewriter, flexed, dived to the attack. *Meanwhile*, he hammered out, *the police had not been idle. In the experienced hands of the laboratory experts at the Yard, this amazing document soon yielded its gruesome secret . . .* He realized what he was doing, and stopped, eyeing the letter sideways. It was probably absolutely lousy with fingerprints. Either Enid Marley's were present, for suicides did not wear gloves to write their final notes, or they were not. If Woodman did in fact get his hands on it, and passed it on to the Lab birds, then it would point the way beyond doubt to a verdict of either Homicide or Suicide.

But . . . and how was this *Echo*-wise? . . . it killed Misadventure stone dead. It was good-bye, Both! Both, which should have been good for at least another three editions!

As always when presented with an indisputable fact, Kidder's agile mind shied, dodged, took cover, at once split into several warring sections.

Take it easy, Boss! warned the cautious one without hope, and retired from the discussion, never to be heard again.

Boy! What a break! cheered the one Kidder knew as Eager Beaver. *Plug it! Sock it for six! Give it the works!*

The realist growled, *Relax! You know the Old Man won't touch Sui-*

cide. Look what happened to Bill when he scooped that starlet prang, he still owes you ten quid. Be reasonable, this has to be Homicide, or else!

The practiced crook whispered beguilingly, *Lookit, suckers! If we ventilate this document, we may get stuck with Suicide! which is strictly page 4. Why not let's stick to Both? Ever heard of destroying evidence? Velly! velly wicked, no?*

The realist said abruptly, *Hold it, hopheads! Let's try this for size. Suppose Egon confronts the Marley with this lot? She's got to come clean, hasn't she, yes or no? No, she denies writing it, okay, we've got Murder. Yes, she admits it, okay, we've got her cold. She's committed a felony and she'll be right in the right mood to write us an exclusive little Misadventure piece. How's that? Am I clever?*

You'll do, baby! admired the crook. *You'll get by!*

Okay, boys! shouted Eager Beaver. *Action stations! On the left, there! And the right! Let's go!*

Kidder stood up, loosened his tie, and drew a deep breath.

"HEY!" he blared up the lift shaft. "*You! You* up there! Come right down here, and make it snappy! Hey, *You! YOU!*"

"*A, Angel Three,*" droned the dashboard radio. "*A, Angel Three. Blue Morris LPZ 2001 obstructing traffic Lesley Terrace. Proceed. M, Mary One, M, Mary One. Boy trapped in barrel 14, Nagpur Street. Proceed . . .*"

Inspector Willis sat in the back of the police car and ate sausage rolls from a grease-spotted bag. He was thinking of Woodman, trying to understand and forgive his old friend's extraordinary loss of temper at the bus stop that morning. The poor fellow was, of course, peeved that he had not been assigned to the Kayes case, but . . . well, he had had his chance once before and he had muffed it. But surely he knew that he, Willis, would also have preferred to be working on an entirely different case? He must know that Willis would have abandoned Kayes with pleasure to catch and arrest the four young delinquents who nightly knocked off vegetables from his allotment just outside . . .

"*T, Thomas Four, T, Thomas One, H, Harry Three, G, Gertie Five, are you receiving me? Are you receiving me?*"

The detective-sergeant in the front seat flipped the switch and said, "H, Harry Three, H, Harry Three. Receiving you. Over."

"*Guy Kayes, Guy Kayes, last seen Indian restaurant, 22, Croissant Street, 22, Croissant Street. Proceed fastest, stand by for further instructions . . .*"

To his driver, Willis said, "Okay, step on it!"

The sergeant remarked, "Tough break for Inspector Woodman, sir. He'd give his left ear to be in on this."

Willis lost his temper. As usual, he gave no sign of this. His face remained expressionless, but he dropped the remaining half of the sausage roll into his briefcase and kicked himself hard and painfully on the ankle. He told himself silently, *And I would give my right ear to give Woodman's left ear a thick ear. How dare he tell my mother to go to hell? He's got a ruddy nerve! What about* his *damnfool mother? To hell with her too!*

Rex laid aside a letter from a disgruntled woman whose husband, after fifty-two years of marriage, had suddenly started to take fencing lessons for no apparent reason. He leaned across his desk and tapped Doon on the shoulder with a pair of scissors.

"Angel," he said anxiously, "just suppose this *was* Misadventure, and it had been you who tried to save Madam, you would *declare*, wouldn't you, anyway to me?"

Doon finished her pear and threw the core out of the window. "If I had," she asked, "would you hold it against me?"

"Of course not."

"Honestly?"

Rex hesitated. "Well," he admitted reluctantly, "I might look at you sort of askance just for a second."

"You mean, seeing as how it was Madam, you could sympathize with Murder, but Misadventure's rather . . . rather . . ."

"Well, it *is*, angel. I mean, isn't it?"

"It is rather."

"She was so absolutely *vile*."

"You mean *is*."

"So I do."

Ellie hurried into the room, pulled up a chair, and eased off her right shoe. "I bring news," she said. "Misadventure's no longer fashionable. Look what Kidder's just pressed into my hot little hand."

Rex took the offered letter. Doon put on her spectacles and peered over his shoulder. He read aloud, " 'I know I only married you yesterday, but I have already repented of . . .' "

Ellie eased off her left shoe and said, "Other side, dear."

Rex turned the letter over. " 'The present situation, obviously, is intolerable,' " he read. " 'I can no longer bear so heavy a . . .' "

Behind him, Doon drew a sharp breath. "Oh, *corks!*" she whispered.

"*Well!*" said Rex, and added weakly, "Whatever next?"

"The end of the trail, dears," said Ellie. "Kidder's praying it's a forgery, but we all know very well indeed that it isn't."

Rex rallied. He said, "No, we don't! *How* do we?"

"Make with the little gray cells, love," said Ellie impatiently. "It's signed with seal, no? Madam kept that seal on her key ring, yes. And she kept her key ring in her handbag. And she was wearing her handbag when she did her honorary bird act."

"How do you know?" Rex asked suspiciously.

"If you're going to start being shrewd, dear," Ellie said, "mum will go elsewhere."

Doon took off her spectacles, polished them on one of the *Knit a Square!* competition entries, replaced them, and said, "Did you tell Kidder?"

"No."

"Why not?"

Ellie gazed out of the window. *Why not?* she silently asked the cloudless sky. *Because Sammy did so want Both, bless him, just like a little boy with two splendid new toys! I might have taken one away from him, for his own good, or the other likewise, but not both. No, not Both!* Aloud, she said, "Kidder told me that I looked like a reasonable woman. It was the "woman" that made me so hopping angry . . ."

As Mr. Jackson hurried into the assembly room of the Walvis Hall, the swing door jerked back and struck him hard on the elbow. He compressed his lips, closed his eyes, and thought a string of foul oaths. Then he opened his eyes and looked around him. For an instant, he thought that – except for the two dogs, who now stood immobile, their fangs sunk into each other's throats – the room was deserted. Then he saw the old-young man who claimed to be everybody's brother sitting behind an upright piano and staring moodily at the keyboard. He strode across the splintered wooden floor, his footsteps echoing, and demanded fiercely, "Where are they?"

The old-young man looked up and said passionately, "Oh, go *away*, will you?" He rested his forearms on the keyboard, striking an unholy chord, and sank his forehead on to his clenched fists.

Mr. Jackson resisted the impulse to snatch the chair from under him. He asked in a controlled voice, "Where are they?"

The old-young man said dully, "Call me Brother."

"All right. Where are they, Brother?"

"They've gone."

"Obviously. Where to?"

"The *Echo*."

"What for?"

"I can't *understand* it," said Brother, raising his head and gazing at the ceiling. "I *had* them. I felt it. You always know." He played middle C with his left thumb. "I'd *got* them, I tell you. I'd talked them right out of the mood for trouble. Their hearts were full of love and kindliness. I'd talked them right out of hating *You*. They're all going to write letters of apology and renew their subscriptions. They meant it, I swear they did." He played C sharp with his right thumb and asked, "Why, why, *why*?"

"Why what?"

Brother looked over his shoulder and said sharply, "Caesar! Janus!"

Following the direction of the other's eyes, Mr. Jackson realized that he was speaking to the two dogs on the far side of the hall. They immediately released each other and turned to look at him.

"Biscuits!" said Brother.

The dogs shook themselves. The Airedale yawned hugely. Then both trotted over to the piano. The Alsatian, tongue lolling, placed his chin on Brother's lap. The Airedale sat down, wagging his tail.

"Good dogs! Good dogs!" said Brother, giving each of them a small yellow biscuit. "You did your stuff, didn't you? It wasn't your fault, was it? It was Dad. Dad went wrong somewhere, didn't he?"

Mr. Jackson said, "They're *both* yours?"

Brother brushed a lock of hair off his forehead. "If you want to spread the gospel of peace," he said morosely, "you've got to have your violence first, then build into the contrast. I trained them myself. It's not cruel. They don't hurt each other."

"There's a boy!" said Mr. Jackson, not touching the Alsatian.

"He's got a touch of mange, poor old man, haven't you?" said Brother, stroking the Airedale, who was a messy eater. "It's the same old story every summer."

Mr. Jackson drew a shallow breath. "Brother," he said, tapping the other gently on the shoulder. "Shall we talk about my Complainers?"

"I can't *understand* it," said Brother. "I united them all right. They were clapping and stamping. They sang *For He's a Jolly Good Fellow*, then they gave three cheers for *You*. Then I asked, very quietly – always more effective, you know, after a demonstration – 'Friends, are we going to treat this troublemaker, this scurrilous organ, this *Echo*, with the contempt that it so richly deserves?' And they yelled '*Yes!*' fit to raise the roof. Some damn fool started singing *Knees Up, Mother Brown!* then they all started shaking hands, then . . ." Brother took a half-eaten sandwich from the top of the piano, looked at it, then dropped it on to the floor. "Eloquence is a dangerous thing," he said, grinding the sandwich into the floorboards with his heel. "It runs away with you. Somewhere, somehow,

I must have overdone it. Because they all quite suddenly . . .”

"Yes?"

"*Sit*, Janus!"

"They all *what*?"

"Ironic, isn't it? My greatest triumph and my greatest failure . . .”

"Look, Brother, do I have to bash you about? They all *what*?"

Brother bit his lip and slumped back over the piano. He said in a low, defeated voice, "Before I could get a word in edgewise, they'd all stormed off to take the *Echo* to pieces!"

"You're too *keen*, Woody," grumbled Carstairs outside his office. He peeled a bar of chocolate with thick, lazy fingers. "Relax, that's my motto. Remember that Kayes boob? If you hadn't gone off half-cocked . . .”

Inspector Woodman was in an ugly mood. In dropping from the wall behind the Indian restaurant, he had torn his jacket and twisted his left ankle. He barked, "You listen to me, you flatfooted flop! Kayes is in this building right now. He intends to kill somebody." His voice rose. He began to speak slowly and clearly as if Carstairs were deaf, mad, and illiterate. "All previous victims foreigners, right? Not unreasonable to suppose next victim also foreign? So you tell names of all foreigners in this place, eh?"

Carstairs shrugged, slapped a large piece of chocolate into his mouth, and masticated noisily. "Well now, let's see," he said at last. His tiny eyes ranged around the landing in silence. "Good stuff, this," he remarked. "Nuts and such. Have some?"

"No."

"Well, there's . . . Quite sure? Got bags of it."

"Quite."

"Nuts get in the old molars, of course, but you can't have everything, I always say."

"Look," said Woodman. "These foreigners?"

"Well," said Carstairs in a leisurely manner. "There's my Hungarian photographer, three or four ooglies with the Escort people, nifty little Russian bint with the Dancing School, couple of funny furriers on the Third, and . . . I'd say your best bet was the smarmy swamis on the Fourth. Whole tribe of 'em, speak no known lingo, give you the creeps, name of da Gongas. Then there's that . . ." Carstairs tore his eyes from the slab of chocolate he intended to eat as soon as his mouth was half empty, and saw that Woodman had left. He heard him running upstairs.

For an instant, he wondered whether to call after him. Then he realized that in the first place he could not be bothered, that in the second, he could not remember the name of the old joker on the Fifth. Heinz, or Wein-

burger, or Belts, or something. Trick cyclist or some such, ate spiders . . .
Oh, well! *Who cared?*

"Sa . . . I mean, Mr. Egon, dear," said Ellie, hastening into Egon's
office. "This is going to hurt you far more than it hurts *You*." She offered
the double-sided letter with an apologetic flourish.

Egon, his hair on end, his eyes glittering, was making a heroic effort not
to lose his temper with Paul. "I tell you we've got to introduce a who-
dunnit element," he was saying with dangerous calm. "Okay, you won't
bump off Hannibal. All right, I respect that. So we find this elephant dead
in curious circumstances . . ."

"No," said Paul. "No, we don't."

Ellie put the letter into Egon's hand.

He glanced at it and gave it back. "So she's atoning," he said impatiently. "What do I care? Paul!" he pleaded. "Don't you *see* it, kid? This
bloody great elephant dead in the driving snow! Marvelous elephant, a
real trouper. Pathos, drama, frostbite! You turn black. Don't you see the
illustration?"

"No," said Paul.

Ellie turned over the letter and handed it back to Egon. "Read, dear,"
she said. "And *you*'ll turn black."

Egon read the letter, closed his eyes for a moment, then handed it to
Paul with a brilliant, haggard smile. "You win," he said pleasantly. "Nothing happens to the elephant."

Paul read the letter. "Suicide," he said. "Well, well!"

"Ruin," said Egon. "Ruin, that's all."

Ellie said, "With love from Kidder."

Egon slopped gin into a teacup and drank it thirstily. He said in a small,
quiet voice, "I may kill Kidder."

Paul put the letter on to the desk and held it down as if it might escape.
"Where did he get it?"

"Mr. Jackson," said Ellie. "Who got it from Browneyes, who got it
from Madam. Sylvia obviously posted it in one of her girlish moods of
dementia tremens." She noted that Egon was very slowly turning an odd
shade of mauve. She said quickly, "All is not lost, dear. We'll have to ditch
Both and Murder, but we aren't necessarily stuck with Suicide. You see,
Kidder's got a rather bright idea . . ."

"Very, very *big* man," Inspector Woodman told the da Gongas tribe on
the fourth floor. "Huge, like tree. Savvy?"

"*Nok*," said the oldest da Gongas. "*Innimik?*"

"Red hair," said Woodman. "Red, get it?"

"*Sharlintikilyga*," said the wall-eyed da Gongas. "*Hoaka?*"

The others laughed.

"Mangoyian," said Woodman. "Gyko Khosrove Melik Mangoyian. You know?"

"*Hurrumpitiga*," said the woman. "Gyko?"

"Yes," said Woodman eagerly. "You know?"

"*Nok*," she said, blowing her nose. "*Innimik.*"

". . . *T, Thomas Four*," droned the dashboard radio. "*H, Harry Three, G, Gertie Two. Seal Croissant Street north and south, Bilton Street east. Guy Kayes, Guy Kayes, believed to be in* You *and* Me *building. Proceed on foot. Premises being surrounded.*"

Inspector Willis brushed the sausage roll crumbs from his knees and heaved himself from the car. He told the sergeant in the front seat, "You come with me, Benson," and said to the driver, "You stick around and surround yourself." Then he turned and began to plod through the crowd towards the archway.

A woman carrying a cat in a basket said, "They'll be reporters, see. You can always tell by their feet."

Willis asked one of the false policemen at the foot of the stairs, "Any sign of him?"

"Who?" asked the one whose helmet looked wrong. "And who are *you* for a start?"

The other one said, "And don't try to swing the rozzer act, either! We've been on to that lark for hours."

Mr. Jackson was forced to stop running by the queue outside the Indian restaurant. He was excusing his way through it when he met Colonel Quincey. He asked bitterly, "Why aren't you smashing up the *Echo*?"

The Colonel blew up his white mustache. "Mutiny," he said vaguely. "Definitely dicey." He jerked a thumb in the direction of the restaurant. "Sound advice, don't eat there. Ever. Muck. Misadventure *Birhane*, Murder *Vindaloo*! Tourist muck." He began to move away.

"Where are you going?"

"Home," said the Colonel simply. He waved his umbrella at a taxi driver, who ignored him. "Old days, transport reliable. Foot, horse, odd camel. Remember young Ferguson, '19, tight as tick, jumped nullah, thrown, lost nag, up Khyber in rickshaw. Shot, of course. No loss."

Mr. Jackson looked at him with hatred and turned away. The crowd on the pavement obliged him to walk in the gutter. The news vendor on the corner saw him and roared, "BOTH! *Read all about 'em! 'Ow am I doin', guv?*"

"Mind the car, sir," said a policeman on a horse.

Mr. Jackson jumped aside as a police car bore slowly but purposefully down on him. There was a plain clothes man sitting beside the driver, speaking into a microphone. Twin loud speakers on the roof boomed, "Clear the road, please! Clear the road! Please leave Croissant Street in an orderly manner to the north or south. There is no cause for panic. You are in no danger, yet. Now move, please, move along! Please pass through the police cordons at either end of the street in single file, in single file. Come along now! Come along, please!"

The crowd parted stagnantly before the car. A few people began to turn obediently towards the main road. Mr. Jackson grabbed the news vendor's arm. "Stop them!" he hissed. "Kidder needs them! Shout something!"

"*Something!*" bellowed the news vendor, confused.

"Shout 'Dramatic Developments Expected Hourly in Croissant Street!', you fool!"

The news vendor shook himself free. "'Ave a 'eart, guv? I'd get nicked. An' I got a wife an' nine cats."

"Shout 'Stay and See the Riots!' "

"Now pack it in, sir," said the policeman on the horse. "You wouldn't want to cause a breach of the peace, now, would you?"

Mr. Jackson swallowed, cleared his throat, said, "Nice horse you've got there," and walked rapidly towards the archway.

The crowd was already thinning, moving reluctantly north and south in grumbling groups. Mr. Jackson looked over his shoulder and saw that the police horse was still watching him. A girl in a blouse which failed to conceal five pairs of shoulder straps nudged him and murmured confidentially, "It's this escaped convict they're on about, see. Was engaged to one of these deaf mutes – sad, isn't it? – and before they hang him, he wants to thank this blind one that stopped the murderer cutting her up and lacerating her. You lonely?"

"No," said Mr. Jackson, pushing past her.

"Positive?" she asked, clashing a ring of keys as if they had been castanets. "I got a nice little . . ."

Mr. Jackson plunged through the archway. At the foot of the stairs, the false policeman with the odd helmet hailed, "Watcher, General! I've just made the biggest clanger of all time!"

The other one said, "Fellow said he was Detective-Inspector Willis. Floyd here tried to arrest him. He *was* Detective-Inspector Willis, and he jolly nearly arrested Floyd."

"Where is he?"

"Mumbled something about sealing off the fire escape, poor chap. I hear it's madly dangerous. That's why the joint's condemned."

Mr. Jackson ran up to the fourth floor. Kidder was prowling around in the lift, scowling and smoking a cigar. "What's all that deathly hush out there?" he snapped the moment he saw Mr. Jackson. "What's going on?"

"Police cars," said Mr. Jackson. "They're clearing the street."

"Oh, hell!" said Kidder explosively. "Hell, hell, *hell*! Where's O'Leary?"

"In jail. He slugged a constable. Some chap said he'd get about ten days."

"Where's Fred Turner?"

"Feeding Tinker."

"Where are Cream and Jepson?"

"With the Complainers, taking the *Echo* apart."

Kidder reached through the bars and seized Mr. Jackson roughly by the lapel. "Say that again," he ordered.

Mr. Jackson said it again, adding two epithets.

Kidder let him go. "Oh, God," he said. "Isn't Life a great big bowl of bad tomatoes!" He walked to the back of the lift, and banged his head lightly against the rosewood panels. "Am I in trouble or am I in trouble?"

"Both," said Mr. Jackson.

Kidder began to curse. He cursed, thoroughly and with attention to detail, Misadventure, Murder, Both, the police, *You*, Egon, Mr. Jackson, O'Leary, the Complainers, Enid Marley, Tinker, everyone he knew, had known, would know, ever, anywhere, alive or dead. He had started to tell Mr. Jackson why all journalists had to have whatever a really classy saint had, only in triplicate, when he interrupted himself abruptly, fell on his knees, and grabbed his transmitter set.

"Kidder calling, Kidder calling! Stan? Listen, there's been a slight technical hitch . . ."

"Please," said a thick, low voice behind Mr. Jackson. "You help me, please?"

Mr. Jackson turned, startled, and looked up at a huge red-haired man with a scar on his left cheek and small hazel eyes. "Where did you appear from?" he asked sharply. "What do you want?"

"I appear from paggaging department," said Gyko Khosrove Melik Mangoyian. "I must see the Doktor."

". . . may manage to dream up something," Kidder was telling his transmitter set. "Have these fool Complainers hit the *Echo*? Over. No? Well, do you hear a dull, sullen roar?"

"Which doctor?" asked Mr. Jackson.

"The name will be different," said Mangoyian. "A small man, head like *ein Kürbis* . . ."

"*Ein* what?"

". . . can't explain now," Kidder was saying. "Yeah, they're mine, but they got diverted. No dice on this front, but be prepared to defend your sector . . ."

"Small," said Mangoyian. "Very small, many hairs on head like . . . you call pumpkin?"

"What do you call?"

"*Kürbis.*"

"A stiff could still swing it," said Kidder. "For the last time, do you have any in stock? Over."

"Is matter of life and death," said Mangoyian.

"I wouldn't know," said Mr. Jackson, disliking the slight tic in the corner of the man's mouth. "I live in Seaford."

". . . the usual precautions," said Kidder. "First call the riot squad, then tell the Old Man I can explain everything. Just keep that mob out of the *Echo* with minimum song and dance . . ."

"Please," said Mangoyian, taking his vast red hands from his pockets. "Every second counts."

"Oh, damn you to hell, man!" shouted Kidder into his transmitter set. "I *know* that last year's *Echos* if placed end to end would girdle the universe. I *know* they're holding the front page. I *know* they're having heart attacks left and right. I know they've got the Kayes stuff all teed up."

"Is from Wien," insisted Mangoyian. "Vienna, brain man, very small."

"Feltz, Feltz, Feltz, for God's sake!" said Kidder without looking up. "Fifth floor, fourth door on the left. Now, look, Stan, give me ten seconds alone with my mind. Haven't I dredged us out of tougher spots than this before? Hasn't something always broken? Ask the Old Man have I ever let him down yet?"

"Feltz?" Mangoyian smiled, disclosing chipped, discolored teeth. "Ah! Thanks, thanks much. I promise you something will break. You will obtain your *Überschrift*. Tell your friend to halt the front page. Good-bye, mister."

"Scram, will you?" said Kidder. "I'm thinking." He glanced up frowning, but Mangoyian had gone. He remarked to Mr. Jackson, "These birds get in my hair. Who was he?"

Mr. Jackson shrugged. "I don't know. Some nut."

Kidder squinted at the end of his cigar. "General," he said. "I begin to see the light. Get hold of a megaphone, get up on the roof! Then . . ."

"No."

"Yes. A personal appeal to killer Kayes! The *Echo* will not only outbid all other publications for his exclusive life story, but . . ."

"No."

"Yes."

"No."

"No?"

"No."

"Why?"

"I've had enough," said Mr. Jackson. "I resign. Good luck, Colonel. You'll need it."

"Where are you going?"

"Seaford."

"What for?"

"I need a shave."

"What about Enid Marley?"

"To hell with her!"

"What about Browneyes?"

"To hell with her too!"

"What about me?"

"Do you want me to tell you?"

"Oh, you low, lousy rotten rat!"

"Quite frankly, I lost interest in this campaign when you had General O'Leary pinched."

"Oh, you fifth columnist!"

"I don't like you either. Admit that you couldn't wait for my wife to commit suicide! Admit that you couldn't care less that my best friend's in jug for ten days! Admit that you've had me playing baby-sitter to all your lost causes with the worst hangover I've ever had in my life! Admit that you're a bungler! Admit that you're callous and pigheaded and just awful!"

"Deserter!"

"Swine!"

"Spy!"

"Poop!"

"Saboteur!"

"Oh, shut up!" shouted Mr. Jackson. He badly wanted to hit Kidder, but he could not get into the lift. He hunched away and started down the stairs. He had reached the first floor before he hesitated, chewing his lip. He stood for a moment listening to the accusing silence from above. Unwillingly, he admitted to himself that he felt slightly guilty. He wondered what Enid Marley would have done in his position, and immediately knew the answer. Had he – as that persuasive Brother so-and-so had tried to convince him – underestimated her? Had she, in the long run, done him a sterling service by removing Browneyes, who was a thief, from his life? Perhaps, as Brother had said at length, she was a crazy old hag, but dedicated, and meant well. It was not enough, of course, but it was a start. Had he, in his cups, misjudged her? Was Brother right? *Was* violence wasteful, sordid, and middle class?

Pleasantly conscious of a glow of righteousness – *Never part from friend or foe in anger*, Enid Marley would have advised – he took a step sideways and shouted up the lift shaft, "Colonel! Colonel Kidder!"

"*Scum!*" bawled Kidder.

"Maybe," said Mr. Jackson reasonably, from the heart of his strange new mood. "Maybe, maybe. But try to see this thing from the other chap's point of view, Colonel! Try not to forget the human element!" He realized that he was quoting Brother and wondered for a wild moment whether the man had in some way hypnotized him. "Remember that nobody is infallible!" He felt his hands begin to shake, his collar to grow uncomfortably tight. He wanted only to get on to the first train for Seaford, to write to Enid Marley asking her how soon he could divorce Browneyes for desertion, to avoid all further trouble. But he found himself kicking first the wall, then a bucketful of sand, then the gates of the lift. He heard himself saying upwards in an almost incoherent roar, "*And don't call me scum either, you silly sod!*"

"All right, all right! Quiet, *please*!" said Woodman for the third time. He took off his trenchcoat and threw it over a chair, indicating that he intended to remain until he received a straight answer from one of the da Gongas tribe. "So you don't know any Mangoyians. All right. You savvy any Kayes? Guy Kayes?"

"*Misme dasotahong*," said the old man. "*Hif?*"

"*Harrossamosa twigpin?*" said the woman.

"*Duello simhif?*" asked the one who was eating yoghurt.

Woodman swallowed. He said with a patient, reassuring smile, "Okay, as you were! No Mangoyian. No Kayes. How about Axelrod? Clive Axelrod?"

The walleyed one looked up from a small red phrase book and inquired laboriously, "You . . . wish . . . tea . . . coffee . . . arak?"

The glass door marked *Inquiries* opened and Inspector Willis walked into the room looking heavy and official. He saw Woodman and his expression changed.

"Oh," he said curtly. "You're here, are you? Great minds, eh? Have they seen him? Do they know anything?"

"*Nok*," said Woodman. "*Innimik*. Tea, coffee, or arak?"

Jimmie put the two-sided letter back on to Egon's desk. "Well," he said regretfully, "I suppose that means good afternoon to Murder. Pity!"

"Let's eat it," suggested Rex brightly. "Like secret agents do."

Egon turned from the window, from a long, moody contemplation of the now deserted street below. "I may begin to hate you, Rod," he stated flatly. "Quite soon."

"Let's face it, Sam," said Mrs. Ryder gruffly. "It's Suicide."

"*No!*" said Egon, shooting his cuffs. "No, it's not! Not if I can help it!"

"You *wanted* Suicide once," Paul reminded him.

"Never!"

"You did. I remember it distinctly."

"It was only for a moment," said Ellie, springing to Egon's defense. "And he wasn't thinking at the time."

"It was just after you scrapped Murder," persisted Paul, "and began to take a shine to Misadventure. Or was it the other way round? Or can't *you* remember either?"

Egon looked at him. He noted the angle of Paul's hat, the set of his jaw, the gleam of rebellion in his eyes. He glanced quickly around at the others. Mrs. Ryder sat squarely, biting her upper lip and staring at her brogues. Ellie was examining her reflection sternly in the mirror of her compact. Jimmie sat on the floor absently pulling threads out of the coconut matting and measuring them against each other. Doon yawned openly, touched Rex with her toe, and murmured, "Darling, did you remember the bread?"

Egon laid hold of the lobe of his left ear and shook it. He knew that he had to do something, to make another of these terrible, debilitating decisions. The fact that this one had already been made for him, that he had no choice, in no way comforted him. He knew that Kidder's was the only solution, that Enid Marley must be threatened with the farewell note, blackmailed into writing a decisive Misadventure confession for both the *Echo* and *You*. For Suicide would spell loss of circulation for both publications, and a lot of awkward questions from both Boards. Had he ever, even for a second, really considered it seriously? Of course not! It had been rather like seeing a pretty girl hurrying in the opposite direction during the rush hour. *Good for a cover picture? No, too many teeth.* Out, forgotten, *finito*! Whereas Misadventure had been like a friendly woman with whom one could spend many dull, pleasant evenings until one met an altogether more exciting creature . . . a creature who admitted frankly that she was Murder. He had become infatuated with her, chased her relentlessly, only to go smartly into reverse when he spotted Both. With Both, it had been love at first sight. So he had, so to speak, called Murder a taxi, ditched her, and run back hotfoot to propose to Both. Who had welcomed him with open arms, led him up the garden path . . . and, now, had jilted him!

How could he explain all this to his staff? How could he persuade them that he was not mad, weak, and fickle, but merely human? How could he even persuade himself? He knew that he had to start talking before he began to think how human he was, and how misunderstood . . .

"Kids," he said warmly. "Am I a nice man? A clever man? Would I lie to you? Will you believe me when I tell you that I love you, I love you one and all? We've come a long, long way together in the past few days . . ."

Paul moved restively. He said in the manner of Stephen Ambler, "And when you think of our unswerving loyalty, our blind devotion to not only you, but *You*, you feel a warm glow just above your indigestion." He laughed, and added, as Spike Raven might have done, "Spill! What gives?"

Egon walked across the room and stood looking down at him. "Kid," he said softly, bending forward, hands spread as if he were judging the weight of a huge baby. "Didn't I give way about your elephant, a major policy decision? Didn't I?"

"Let's have it," said Paul coldly. "What is it this time? Arson?"

"Not to nag, dear," advised Ellie. And, not looking at Egon, added non-committally, "Kidder says that the Beefers are absolutely dying for Mis-adventure."

Egon shot her a look of dumb gratitude. "Our public," he cried, slapping his desk. "Our great big-hearted public, who can make or break us . . ." He faltered, thinking of his public, of the two main groups into which it fell, both equally nauseating . . . the cretins who had become addicts, and the addicts who had become cretins. He asked abruptly, "Where's Enid?"

"In her office," Rex volunteered. "She's helping Doctor Feltz to make a will, bogey, bogey."

"Mmm," said Egon. "Mmm-hmm!" He knew that he must go, at once, before he threw something at Paul. He picked up his bottle of gin, a tea-cup, the two-sided letter, drew a deep breath through his nose, and left the room.

Paul shook his head, sighed loudly, and followed him. Mrs. Ryder jerked at her corset, passed a hand over her hair, and followed Paul.

Jimmie raised an eyebrow at Ellie. "How now? Misadventure I pre-sume?"

"Herself."

"In fact, we're right back where we came in?"

"Correct."

"Where are you going?"

"I'm a decent, normal, healthy girl," said Ellie. "Therefore I can't wait to see Madam taken down a peg or two or even three." She turned right into the corridor and disappeared.

Doon put on her spectacles and frowned at Jimmie. "Ducky," she said. "Has it occurred to you that even if it *was* Suicide, somebody either pushed or pulled Madam? Now if that somebody had *pushed*, Madam would have dined out on it for twenty or thirty years. True or false?"

"True."

"Exactly. So that somebody almost certainly *pulled*. So, in a *way*, although we know it was Suicide, it's still Misadventure."

Rex offered helpfully, "And if it was Misadventure, then whoever didn't do it kept it under his bonnet because he wanted Murder."

Jimmie scratched his crew cut. "You mean that somebody knew it was Suicide, wanted Murder, and got weaving on Misadventure? *Why?* He could have had Murder without lifting a finger. He only had to hang around and let it be Suicide."

"You're not *trying*, ducky," said Doon. "Don't you see that somebody knew that Suicide would indirectly have been Murder, and anyway, fundamentally, he wanted Misadventure all the time?"

"But you mean he's been stymied? Because as soon as Kidder got busy, first it was Both, and now it's all three?"

"Exactly."

"You know what I deduce?" asked Rex after a long pause. "Having sifted all the evidence and questioned all the suspects, I deduce that the whole thing's distinctly spooky."

Doon said philosophically, "Well, I suppose Suicide's a bit better than Both. Except, of course, it *is* Both because it's all three. Shall we go and watch?" In the corridor she took off her spectacles and peered at Jimmie. "In the light of everything," she said, "do you still fancy me?"

Jimmie laid an arm around her shoulders. "Of course," he said gallantly. "In my carefully considered opinion, you're an absolute poppet."

In Enid Marley's office, Egon, pale with some strong emotion, was holding a dramatic big game hunter's pose, standing with one foot on a chair as if he had just shot it. Doctor Feltz sat behind the desk with his head in his hands, whispering to himself. Mrs. Ryder was trying to persuade him to eat two aspirins, Paul and Ellie were witnessing his will. Enid Marley, her head proudly back, stood confronting Egon with an expression of sorrowful contempt.

"Samuel Egon," she said. "I must accuse you of deliberately and maliciously manufacturing spurious clues."

"No, you mustn't, dearie!" barked Egon, waving the two-sided letter. "If you'd signed it yourself, it might have been a forgery. But you didn't. You used your own personal little stamp which never left your own personal little key ring. So it's genuine. Ironic, isn't it?"

"It's absurd," she said, knowing that she had to keep icily calm. *How could she have forgotten about that damned stamp?* 5LP + DMy3, she thought, brushing aside the first niggle of panic. "It's ridiculous!"

"Isn't it just?" Egon agreed, nodding, beaming at her in a genial manner. "Poor old Woodman'll laugh no end. He fancied Suicide all along."

Doctor Feltz raised his head. "Zuizide is very bad," he said with emphasis. "In this gountry, id is a *grime.*"

"Unless, of course," said Egon, closing one eye, "you and I and Kidder can persuade our public that it's Misadventure."

"Kidder?" Enid Marley stiffened.

"Him. In fact, you and *You*, and the *Echo.*"

"No!"

"Yes. *Or else!*"

"Are you attempting to threaten me, Egon?"

"Yes, dear," said Egon, pinching her cheek. "Aren't I awful? You come back to work Monday with the first installment of a meaty great four-part serial entitled *The TRUTH About My Amazing 'Death'!*"

She hesitated. She too wanted Misadventure, but by publicizing it and thus closing the case, which was desirable, she admitted Suicide to Kidder and the staff of *You*, which was most emphatically not. They would forever have a hold on her, have her exactly where they wanted her. She would not even be able to . . .

She glanced quickly at Doctor Feltz and saw with a spurt of anger that he had already assessed the implications of the situation. He was, without any pretense of stealth, indeed with a triumphant little flourish, removing his check from her handbag and applying a match to it. If he, the worm, had turned, what about Kidder, the cobra? What would *he* want? An article of three thousand words headed *I Flew Through YOUr Window!* and signed *Enid Birdwoman Marley*? A picture of her lying naked on a cushion at the age of six months? A picture of her lying dressed on the pavement outside the Indian restaurant at the age of fifty-eight? *Oh, horrible*, HORRIBLE! Yet what choice had she?

She asked sarcastically, "And who, may I ask, attempted without success to save my life?"

There was a short silence. The staff looked at Egon. Egon stubbed out his cigarette on the cap of a bottle of ink, passed a hand across his eyes, and said with sudden tremendous assurance, "A fair question!"

"A fair question!"

There was a loud, impatient knock on the door. Rex, who was nearest, unlocked it, put his head into the corridor, and said, "Go away! You can't come in!" He then staggered back and sat down hard on the floor.

The door swung inwards and crashed against the wall.

"I am come for Doctor Feltz," boomed Killer Kayes. "My name is Clive Axelrod."

Chapter 15

DOCTOR FELTZ stumbled to his feet. His chair fell over behind him. "Blease!" he said urgently. "Now listen, blease! I shall eggsblain everything . . ."

"How *dare* you push me around, you rude beast!" said Rex angrily from the floor. "Assault, that was! I could *sue* you!"

Egon, his head lowered, marched forward ten paces and scowled at the red-haired giant in the doorway. "Beat it!" he barked. "This is a private, personal staff conference. *Scram!*"

His confidence evaporated as he realized that he was looking up the other's nose. "What do you want?" he asked, retreating a step.

Doctor Feltz spread his hands. He said in an oddly documentary manner, "He wands to mörder me."

"Murder?"

"Yar."

"You? Why?"

"He does not like me."

"Who is he?"

"Clive Axelrod," said Enid Marley. "Gyko Khosrove Melik Mangoyian, and . . ."

"Mangoyian?" asked Doon. "Charlie's chum?"

"They've met, in an official capacity. As I was about to say, this . . . gentleman . . . is also Guy Kayes."

"*Kayes!*"

"No," said Egon. "No, he's not! I won't *have* it!"

"Is drue," said Doctor Feltz. "He is the Bush Killer vrom the babers."

"Oh, God!" said Ellie. She sat down abruptly on the window ledge.

Jimmie said, "Crikey! I never met a . . . well, *crikey!*"

Doon put on her spectacles, then took them off again.

"Don't just stand there, man!" Mrs. Ryder ordered Egon. "*Do* something!"

Kayes sloped into the room and kicked the door shut behind him. He said heavily, "How you do? Good evening."

Egon retired behind the desk. He cleared his throat unsuccessfully. "Sit down, old man," he said huskily. "Make yourself at home. Tell us why you want to kill Doc. Have a cigarette. Have a gin." *Here, at last*, he reflected wildly, *was old Mother Murder!* Murder, which he had once yearned for, prized so highly! *Why?* He must have had good reasons at the time; could he no longer remember even one of them?

He knew only that, now, he wanted no part of it. Perhaps a complete stranger, a *fait accompli*, somewhere else in the building, maybe on the fourth floor, just to please Kidder . . . but not this! Not here, or now, or Doc either! Particularly not Doc, who was also – irreplaceably – *A. Friend, Viennese Psychiatrist, G.P.*, and *Romany Nemo*!

He reached for his gin, saw that there were only two cupfuls left, both of which he would need himself, and amended, "Have some champagne."

Rex laughed nervously. "That man *said* to give it to the murderer," he chattered. "He *would* be pleased!"

Paul moved suddenly. He pushed past Jimmie, leaned across the desk, and snatched up the telephone receiver. He heard the girl at the switchboard say, " '*Why?*' I said, raising my eyebrows like this. 'Well, you may well ask!' Then *he* said . . ." Then a huge hand clamped around his wrist, and twisted viciously. He looked down and saw the tufts of fierce ginger hair on the backs of the knuckles. He looked up and saw Kayes looking down at him with an expression of mild concern. He dropped the receiver and heard it clatter on to the desk.

"You want trouble?" asked Kayes.

Paul massaged his wrist. "No."

"If you want, you say now."

"No. No trouble."

Kayes pulled a button off his jacket, frowned at it, and dropped it on to the floor. "I have trouble," he remarked. "Isn't it?"

"Yes."

"Yiss. Much, very much." Kayes eyed Doctor Feltz and added in the same tone, "Now I kill him."

"Gyko," whispered Doctor Feltz. "I was wronk. I beg your pardon."

"You can't bump off people just like that," Doon protested, putting on her spectacles. "They'll hang you."

Kayes nodded. "Yiss," he agreed. "Is right, proper. I kill him, then I go hang. Good." He reached forward, took Doctor Feltz by the shoulder and lifted him across the desk. "So small," he marveled. "The last one – you know, Sven K. Paullsson Esquire – very tall, very thick, and strong." He shrugged. "But easy, when you know."

"Sam Egon!" snapped Mrs. Ryder. "*Do* something!"

"Sammy!" cried Ellie simultaneously. "For God's sake don't do anything rash!"

Egon poured himself a gin and drank it greedily.

Rex picked himself up from the floor. "Why don't you all rush at him?" he suggested faintly, edging towards the door. "Then you could tie him up while I go and find Charlie."

"No," said Kayes. "You stay. Yiss."

"Yiss," said Rex. "Just a joke."

"You say thank."

"Thank."

"Joke?"

"Yiss. Funny. You know, comical."

Egon darted a glance at Kayes and saw that the man had been temporarily distracted by Rex. He bent quickly over the fallen telephone receiver. He heard the tiny, tinny infuriating voice from the switchboard saying, " 'And since *when*,' I said sort of sarcastically, 'do I live in Marble Arch?' "

He said, quiet but dynamic, "The police! Marley office, *You*! Get the police. *Police!*"

"What?" said the girl at the switchboard. "Did you want the building?"

"I don't understand," Kayes told Rex. With his free hand, without looking, with practiced efficiency, he began to pull off Doctor Feltz's tie.

"Funny," said Rex. "You know, har har." He tried to laugh, stopped, turned pale, and explained earnestly, "That sort of thing, you understand, only about an octave lower . . ."

Kayes lost interest and turned back to Doctor Feltz. Egon straightened up hastily. He heard the girl at the switchboard say, "*You* again; they've been absolutely soppy ever since this whatever-it-is. Daft, I call it, not as if anyone's dead . . ."

Kayes removed Doctor Feltz's collar and handed it to Jimmie. "You wish to say a thing for your mother?" he inquired.

"Gyko," said Doctor Feltz. "Nod here. In the gorridor."

"Good." Kayes clicked his tufted fingers. "We go now." He opened the door, looked out into the passage and added encouragingly, "Is nobody."

"Blease," began Doctor Feltz. "Gyko, I musd eggsblain."

"No," said Kayes. "No time now. There is hurry. Inspector Willis will be worried, running, running, searching." He steered Doctor Feltz towards the door.

Egon started forward, his hands raised into fists, then hesitated. He knew that he ought to hit Kayes, to deliver some spectacular uppercut to the chin, but he doubted if he could reach that far. And even if he could and did, he would probably break his hand in a lost cause for Kayes would not feel the blow.

"Now look here, old cock," he said without hope. "I swear you're making a big mistake . . ."

"Mr. Mangoyian," said Enid Marley clearly, formally, from the far side of the room. *"You will never hang!"*

Still gripping Doctor Feltz, Kayes turned in the doorway. His fiery, wiry hair brushed the lintel. He examined Enid Marley carefully as if she had been some piece of intricate machinery which he did not fully understand. Then he said, "You shut up!"

Enid Marley raised one eyebrow, laced her fingers together, studied them with a slight, superior smile, and, maddeningly, said nothing.

"I hang," said Kayes. "Yiss."

She shook her head. "No."

"Yiss."

"No."

Kayes kicked the wall. A piece of plaster roughly seven inches square and three inches deep fell on to the coconut matting. *"Yiss,"* he insisted, arching his neck. He shook Doctor Feltz. "Ask *him*! He will say."

"Mr. Axelrod," said Enid Marley as if she were addressing a fractious child. "Have you never heard of the McNaughten Rules?"

Kayes stood bull-like, his head at an unlikely angle. He watched her suspiciously, his small eyes bright with cunning. "Which is this mister? You bring him in this room."

Enid Marley asked in a conversational tone, "How many people have you killed, Mr. Kayes?"

Kayes raised rocklike shoulders. "Ten, eleven, maybe twenty, I don't know. What difference? I hang the once only."

"No, you don't," she said. She crossed to the smallest of the charts on the walls, the one headed, *Death, Unnatural*. "I shall prove it to you." She took the dangling strings and placed one end of the first on *Homicide, Ipso Facto, Mea Culpa*. She looked over her shoulder and saw that Kayes had not moved. She asked sternly, "Can you read?"

He stood for a moment, his lower lip slack, then he said, sullenly, "You are silly bitch."

"Come here!"

"No."

"Yes."

"I don't."

"You do."

She laid the far end of the first string on *Male, Foreign*, took the second and stretched it between *Previous Record* and *Amnesia, Partial*. Her nostrils flared as she caught a strong whiff of garlic and banana. She turned and found Kayes towering over her. Beside him, Doctor Feltz gave her a stricken look.

"Is about me?" Kayes asked.

"Yes." Enid Marley indicated the point where the two strings crossed. "Read it."

"No," he said, moving closer. "You."

She struggled against an almost overwhelming impulse to dodge past him, run out of the room, lock the door, and let him kill them all. Then she thought how the story would read in the newspapers, and bit her lip. Behind him, she saw Egon nudge Paul, whisper something. Paul nodded and glanced at Jimmie. Egon moved stealthily around the desk, picked up the bottle of champagne, and weighed it in his hand. Ellie stood up, caught at his arm with both hands, and held on. He glared at her, trying to prise her fingers loose.

Enid Marley turned back to the chart. " 'My dear,' " she read. " 'This is a very serious matter, as you yourself must realize or you would not have written to me. I know that it can be unsettling, even at times irritating, to find yourself in a country whose people, customs, and language you understand only imperfectly. But, you know, for your own sake and that of others, you really must learn to control your temper.' "

"Why?" said Kayes.

She realized that his interest was waning. Behind him, she saw Jimmie take off Doon's spectacles, put them into her pocket, and move quietly to Paul's side. Ellie let go of Egon and closed her eyes. Egon hid the bottle of champagne behind his back and took a cautious step towards Kayes.

"Here," said Enid Marley, tapping the chart with a plump, pink finger, "is the formula. $6L + 3Bw$. Now follow me, please."

She moved on to a filing cabinet, not daring to look back. Would Kayes follow her? *Would he?* Or would he for no reason fell her with one slap of a hand that must weigh as much as a normal arm? Was she out of her mind to risk her life in order to prolong Doctor Feltz's No, of course, she wasn't! She was not trying to save his skin – he had that curious aura of expendability of so many displaced persons – but her own. For if Kayes murdered him now, in her presence, the case, the *whole* case, *the-truth-and-nothing-but-the-truth-so-help-me-God*, would be probed, prodded, ventilated in a Court of Law . . . and she would almost certainly get stuck with Suicide.

She pulled open a drawer and selected a file. She forced herself to turn the pages without haste. She wanted savagely to know what Egon was doing, but she knew that she must not look. Was he about to make yet another of his complicated bloomers? Could even he, Paul, and Jimmie deal with Kayes? Or would they merely madden him, drive him to some hideous atrocity? Could she hold his interest while they at least tried?

She had found the appropriate entry before she heard Doctor Feltz's shallow, terrified breathing, smelt garlic-banana, and knew that Kayes was again at her shoulder.

She saw that the page was headed, in red, *Paranoiac, With/Without Hallucinations. CAUTION.* " 'First, my dear,' " she read calmly, " 'believe me when I assure you that you have my deepest sympathy.' "

"I don't want," said Kayes.

There was an asterisk. Her eye flew to the bottom of the page where a note, also typed in red, informed her *Psychoses. Possible Brain Lesions with Virulent Toxins: Systematized, Delusional Insanity: Habitually Homicidal: N.B.: V. Dangerous.* She placed her hand over it in an absentminded manner, wondering whether Kayes could read English.

" 'Your problem,' " she read, " 'as I am convinced you know in your heart, is easily solved! There is one – and *only* one! – course of action which will secure your future peace of mind. You must immediately contact a solicitor. Tell him frankly all you remember of the manner in which you killed the people you mention. Suggest that he then accompanies you to the nearest police station. On no account must you lose your temper. Remember that these men are your friends. Between them, they will settle all your problems for you.' "

"Yiss." Kayes inclined his head approvingly. "They take me for hang."

Enid Marley read on. " 'Should there be any doubt in your mind about capital retribution, dismiss it. Trust me when I promise you that you will never hang.' "

Kayes stamped one huge foot, then the other. The room shook. A pencil, two letters, and a packet of paper clips fell off the desk. "Why *not?*" he shouted.

Behind him, Paul glanced at Egon. Egon looked at Jimmie. Paul mouthed, "*Now?*" Jimmie swallowed and moved about an inch and a half forwards. Egon, clearly intending to whisper, said loudly, "*Zero one!*"

Enid Marley turned her back, wondering whether she could trust her voice. " 'Because, my dear,' " she read, " 'legally, you cannot be punished for an action or actions for which morally and psychologically you are not entirely responsible. Let me explain. Imagine for a moment that you are two quite different people . . .' "

Kayes snaked out a hand, seized her by the collar of her blouse, and dragged her towards him with a twisting movement which threw her off balance.

She felt her pearls break, heard them pattering on to her feet, his feet, the coconut matting. His red face was less than a foot from her own. He gave her the intense, flat stare of an infant prodigy. He let go of Doctor Feltz, applied the heel of his other hand to the point of her chin and began slowly, tenderly, to force her head back.

She felt her hat slide off, heard Doctor Feltz collapse onto the floor. She trod on her own foot and knew that in one more second Kayes would break her neck.

"*Zero!*" bellowed Egon.

"*Let him have it!*" shouted Paul.

"*Banzai!*" yelled Jimmie.

Beneath Kayes's arm, Enid Marley caught a brief, slewing view of Egon plunging forward, raising the bottle of champagne above his head, bringing it down with all his weight behind it. As she had known with awful certainty, it missed.

It caught Kayes a glancing blow on the elbow, bounced off him, struck her a paralysing blow on the shoulder, hit Doctor Feltz on the left temple, rolled harmlessly away into a corner.

Kayes looked puzzled. He stirred Doctor Feltz's small unconscious body with one foot. He was turning, his mouth loosely open, when Paul and Jimmie hurled themselves at him.

Paul reached him first, mistimed a left hook to the diaphragm and hit him on the right hip. Jimmie, a fraction of a second behind, collided with Paul, struck Kayes in the small of the back, stumbled, and, falling, grabbed him around the knees.

Enid Marley clawed at Kayes's hands which now, casually, almost affectionately, had fastened themselves around her neck. She felt his hot breath on her face. Her feet swung clear of the floor as he lifted her off the ground and shook her as if she had been a length of dusty material.

Her left shoe fell off. The room began to darken around the edges, to slide softly out of focus. It turned red, a nice bright red lit by tiny stabs of green lightning . . .

For the second time that week, she knew that she was about to die.

From a long way away, she heard a crash, a scream, a grunt, another crash, voices shouting, getting further and further away.

"Charlie! Where are you, Charlie? *Charlie!*"

"*His foot, you fool! Hold on!*"

"Duck, ducky! *Duck!*"

"Get him! Now! Now, now, NOW!"

Then her mind began to revolve in smooth, red-hot circles, and each time it passed North, she thought, *How foolish they are! Ignorant creatures!* For her husband's name was not Charlie, but Harold, or Wentworth for short. And his hairy consort was called Miss Adventure . . . Ah, how delighted they would be when they heard that she was dead! A discreet celebration, a furtive bottle of champagne! He would hit her on the head with it, but miss, and honk his silly laugh, and say in his idiotic City manner, "My dear, I hereby christen you Mrs. Harold Wentworth Marley! What about it, eh?"

Miles away to her right, she heard a telephone begin to ring, then another. She felt herself capsizing gratefully into soft, warm, spinning nothing. She was no longer afraid, because it had all happened before. *It is only the Unknown which is alarming, you know, my dear!* B3f + K. So right, so true! She was not alarmed because she knew exactly what to expect. She would not die just yet because she would at any moment now bounce on the awning of the Indian restaurant. As if she were drowning, her mind was swirling backwards through the great, dark, booming tunnel of her life . . .

It was all just the same!

There again were the voices of the crowd below her office window! One, above the general hubbub, was saying, over and over again, "No! Oh no, Sammy! *No!* Honestly, he'll *kill* you, Mr. Egon, dear!" Another bawled, "Go on, you ape! Go *on*! Have a bash!" Some large object fell over with a shuddering crash, then there was a momentary silence.

Somebody said wildly, "Jimmie! Jimmie, *say* something, ducky! Are you dead? Now make an effort, love! You aren't dead at all! I mean, *are* you?"

Jimmie? That was strange, wasn't it? Perhaps not. How was she to know? She had never been drowned before, had she? But where were those hands which had snatched at her skirt, her legs, dragging, tearing? And the voice, that breathless, desperate, anonymous voice? It should, just about now, be panting "It's all right! I've . . ."

But it did not. Nor, when it came, was it breathless. It was assured, curt, authoritative. And it said, "Evening, all. Well well, what a mess!"

She lay still, groggy, confused. The voice had sounded like Inspector Woodman's. Surely it could not possibly be so? Could it? She opened one eye an eighth of an inch and registered dimly, without understanding, that she was not lying on the pavement outside the Indian restaurant and Mrs. Frederick Turner, but on coconut matting in her own office and Doctor Feltz. Something was very wrong. She closed her eye quickly and tried to concentrate upon listening . . .

A guttural voice she had heard before, quite recently, not long before she was drowned, cried enthusiastically, "Woody! Is Woody! My funny old friend from many years! You were waiting?"

Woodman said, "Yes. Yes, I was waiting all right."

"Little old Woody!"

"And little old Kayes!"

"The other time, I am still young," said Kayes. "I am not *ready*, there is still the Doktor . . ."

Woodman cleared his throat. "Shall we check that?" he asked. "*Is* there still the Doctor?"

Kayes began, "Is dead, finish, all gone. This mister, he takes bottle and *zonk*! The Doktor, he don't complain, he just . . ."

Enid Marley heard footsteps padding towards her over the matting. She sensed that somebody was above her, heard a soft movement of clothes as whoever it was bent over Doctor Feltz. Who was it? Kayes? Woodman? Egon?

Without warning, a thumb descended on her right eyelid and pulled it back. She found herself staring at Paul East. There was a livid bruise on his jaw and he had lost his tie. He was squatting on his heels and with his other hand feeling Doctor Feltz's pulse. He looked at her for an expressionless moment, removed his thumb, stood up, and said quietly, "All present and correct."

"Me, I did never use a bottle, not full," Kayes was saying. "Once, in Smyrna, just a boy, I did take a bottle, but was empty also broken . . ."

Enid Marley closed her eyes. So she was alive all over again, was she? Or was she? Was she, for the third time within a week, sprawling on the ground, absurdly alive when she should have been shockingly dead? Kayes was boasting about two brothers whom he had killed and partially filleted with a large sliver of glass. Was she his first failure?

"Let's go, Kayes," said Woodman. He sounded young and happy. "Be seeing you, Egon. Kidder tells me that we've finally got ourselves a cast-iron Misadventure. Fact?" He laughed jauntily. "Oh, well, who cares? I'd have settled for Loitering With Intent, just as long as I can close the case, if you can call it that, which I don't and never did. Too bad about your Both stuff!"

"Clear out, will you?" Egon asked aggressively. "Take your dinky little chum and disappear! You're trespassing."

Woodman said, "Tell Mrs. M. I'll take her statement tomorrow. Tell her I'm gratified that she's still in one piece. Been ironic, in a way, under the circumstances, if she'd finally bought it, wouldn't it?"

Enid Marley shook her head, trying to clear it. She knew only, compellingly, that she must get on to her feet, do something about the detective's blatant impertinence. But what? Demand an apology? Take his number, report him to the Commissioner? Or deal him, as she longed to do, a telling blow with her handbag?

She pushed ineffectually at the matting, forced herself to struggle on to one knee. The effort left her breathless. The room swam towards her fuzzily. She caught hold of the window ledge and dragged herself to her feet. She felt weak, light-headed, as if she had been dangerously ill for a long time.

Nobody was paying the slightest attention to her. Kayes towered over Woodman in the doorway. He was wearing handcuffs, smiling down at them, inviting Woodman to admire them. A few feet away, Jimmie sat on the floor, leaning against the overturned desk, holding a bloody piece of blotting paper to his cheek. Beside him, Doon was crouched over the fallen telephone. Her hair hung over her eyes and she was whispering into the receiver, "Give me 999, you donkey! Give me 999 absolutely immediately!" Paul and Mrs. Ryder were occupied with Doctor Feltz. Paul was loosening his collar, Mrs. Ryder was slapping his hands. Rex was sitting on a pile of spilt mail and a large parcel which had exploded to reveal a salmon pink cardigan, and combing his hair. Egon, one sleeve partially ripped out of his jacket, was being supported by Ellie while he stood on one foot, tied up a shoelace, and glowered at Woodman.

"Good-bye," said Kayes, displaying his discolored teeth. "Isn't it?"

"Yes," said Egon roughly. "It is. Absolutely."

Woodman piloted Kayes into the corridor, looked back over his shoulder and said mildly, "Next time you ladies and gents decide to have yourselves a Murder, or a Suicide, or a Misadventure, or a what-have-you, will you do me a favor? Will you ring the Yard and ask explicitly for Inspector Willis?" He took Kayes by the elbow, nodded, turned left, and was gone.

Enid Marley staggered two steps backwards. There was something strangely wrong with her ankles. She groped for the window sill, and could not find it. She thought stupidly, *Must stop falling around like this! What would Browneyes think? Or Mags, Cornwall?*

As her knees buckled, the sill caught her painfully across the hips, jerking her forward. She heard glass shatter and knew that it had all begun again. Only this time it was no dream, no illusion. She saw a green car five floors below parked against the curb. The new awning over the Indian restaurant was neatly furled. There was nothing between her and that faraway pavement . . .

Behind her, somebody screamed.

She heard herself say thickly, "Help me! *Help!*"

Then a hand seized her by the left shoulder, another grabbed at her right calf. Somebody lunged heavily against her, fumbled, made a futile snatch at her arms as she slid downwards . . .

And the voice she had been waiting for but no longer expected to hear, said, not breathlessly but almost casually, "Relax! It's all right! I've got you!"

She recognized it immediately. She sat down hard on the floor and looked up. "You!" she said accusingly. "I knew it! It was *you!*"

Egon stared back at her. A slow, guilty flush crept up his neck. He let her go, turned away, and kicked at a filing cabinet. "Getting monotonous, isn't it?" he mumbled. "Mmm?"

Chapter 16

EIGHT minutes later, two of the telephones were both silent for five seconds at the same time. Egon replaced the receiver of the third and said to nobody in particular, "Some old goat called Holmes. Wanted to apologize for her unreasonable attitude about juvenile delinquents, so do ninety-one other Old Beefers. They all want to renew their subscriptions and they're in the Strand canvassing new readers. Somebody's brother's been at them, and now, God help them, they love everybody, but juvenile delinquents and us best of all." He sprawled across the desk, pulled at his lower lip and added, "Well, I don't know. How mad can you get?"

Doon, wearing her spectacles and hanging out of the window, said, "Honestly, I never *saw* so many rozzers. One of the horses is creating! There go Kayes and Charlie! They do look *happy!* Can you *arrest* horses?"

Beside her, Rex produced a handkerchief and waved it vigorously. "'Bye-bye, Charlie!" he shouted. "See you in the papers! Give my love to your aunt!"

Doctor Feltz levered himself on to one elbow, then sat up on the floor and pushed away the cup of scalding tea which Mrs. Ryder was trying to persuade him to drink. He looked across at Enid Marley, who sat rigidly in a chair staring at Egon. He asked stupidly, "Alive again? So soon?" He flushed at his lack of tact and said earnestly, "Gongradulations!"

"There goes that odd burglar I saw on the fire escape," remarked Doon. "He said his name was Willis. He's going off in a police car. I suppose he's under arrest."

"Egon," said Paul for the fourth time. "Don't you think you owe us an explanation."

"What's that, old man?" asked Egon, in order to gain time.

Paul said with elaborate patience, "If you knew the whole time that it was Suicide, we'd like to know why the hell you didn't say so."

"You would?"

"Yes."

"A fair question!" said Egon without enthusiasm. He walked rapidly around the desk, over to the door, and back again. He turned slowly, managing to give the impression that he was speaking from a rostrum, that he was subduing a vast audience of hecklers. "Perfectly fair!" He paused, raked a hand through his already dishevelled hair and asked with burning sincerity, "Mmm?"

"Mmm," said Paul.

"Start from the beginning, dear," Ellie suggested tactfully. "There was Madam staggering around on the window sill . . ."

"I was not staggering," said Enid Marley clearly. "I have never yet staggered, and I never shall." Nobody even turned in her direction. Obviously, by some unspoken agreement, the staff of *You* had decided to put her in Coventry. *Why?* Just because at one time she had happened to accuse an unspecified one of them of Murder? It was not fair. What about Egon? He had accused all of them of Suicide, Misadventure, Murder, and Both while being fully aware that it had been none of these and that anyway he had done it himself!

"Let's look at it this way," said Egon, wondering what he was going to say. He picked up his empty gin bottle, looked at it, then threw it into the wastepaper basket, which fell over. "Now in a situation which demands immediate action, you'll agree that some characters react fast, some slowly. Some automatically take action, some automatically don't. Right?"

"Right," said Paul.

"Right," said Egon, scratching his ankle, wondering for a split second why his kind, helpful aunt had not sent him a birthday card. "Now papa's in the automatic *Do* class, so let's break that down for a start. Okay? Okay, some of us automatically do too much, some do too little. Some of us know exactly what we're up to, some don't. Some of us do the right thing, some know they're going to pull a dirty great boner . . . and go right ahead and pull it. Some of us fundamentally know ourselves inside out, some of us fundamentally think we're some other chap. Okay?"

"Go on," said Paul.

Egon aimed a halfhearted kick at the wastepaper basket. "Now take me. I've known myself for a long, long time, under all sorts of circumstances, in all sorts of climates," he said slowly. "And . . . mind you, I'm not arguing, I'm *telling* you . . . that I fundamentally understand myself inside out. When I get in a situation which demands immediate action, I react just like *that*!" He snapped his fingers. "I switch on automatic *Do*. Automatically, I do too much. And all the time I know that, temporarily, I'm some other chap and that he's fundamentally dead wrong. Any questions?"

He scowled around the room, waiting for somebody to question him so that he could substantiate his case by listing twenty or thirty of his classic blunders. But nobody spoke. He raised his shoulders, let them fall. "So, naturally," he said, depressed, "I've learned to distrust my immediate, automatic, fundamental reactions."

Paul said, "So your I.A.F.R. having been to save her life, you at once assumed that this must be basically wrong? Right?"

"Absolutely."

"Which let out Misadventure?"

"Obviously."

"So you and Murder slunk back to your office and decided to come to some sort of misunderstanding?"

"You have a mind like a man."

"Have you?"

Egon swallowed. He said in a controlled voice, "Look, kiddo, I was in a state of shock. Maybe I *was* a trifle nutty, but only because there just wasn't time to go mad really professionally. I had to think of *You*, didn't I? I knew the provinces wouldn't buy Suicide, Misadventure was suspect, so by an effortless process of elimination, I was stuck with Murder. Fair?"

"Fair," said Ellie loyally. "More or less."

"I love you," said Egon. He paused, pointed one finger at the ceiling and added impressively, "*But!*"

"But what?"

"But, dear, if it was Murder, then somebody must have dunnit. Question, who? One of *You*? Answer, well, yes and no. Not one of you, who I can't spare for a day, let alone a life sentence, but me! *Me*! And, hell, I'm the *editor*!"

There was a long pause.

Mrs. Ryder cleared her throat and asked gruffly, "Tea, anybody?"

Simultaneously, Paul said, "So you tossed Murder over your left shoulder and swung briskly back to Misadventure?"

Egon rested his elbows on the desk and laced his fingers together. He propped up his nose on his knuckles and said in the mild, over-courteous voice which meant that he was about to lose his temper, "Correct. Murder's backward little sister. Which, you understand, was also dicey. Because if it was Misadventure, then *nobody* dunnit. And whereas nobody in the mob down there could have seen my face, some worthy swine had certainly seen my maulers."

His eyelids drooped, then flicked up. He stared at Paul and asked in a snarling whisper, "Do you begin to get the sketch? I had a choice of three possible verdicts, all of them impossible. I had to make a snap decision. I have no faith whatever in my snap decisions. I know, basically and fundamentally, that they're radically, cosmically, invariably wrong. You'll perhaps admit that the whole business was distinctly dodgy?"

His staff looked at each other in silence. Ellie sighed.

Paul pushed his hat even further back on his head and asked a filing cabinet, "Now what kind of a confession is that?"

Egon slammed a hand on to the desk. "Confession?" he barked, outraged. "What do you mean *confession?* What kind of wild talk is this? I'm not *confessing!* Why should I? What for? What *to?* I tried to save her, and I didn't, and I changed my mind once or twice, all perfectly legal. I want you to take a good, long look at me. Know me again, mmm? I want no mistake about this, old son, old son! I'm the geyser who *didn't* do it. Nothing, absolutely, precisely nothing whatever, was what I did, and let's not forget it."

"You deliberately suppressed evidence."

"I did?"

"Repeatedly."

"Prove it."

"How can I?"

"You can't."

"Charlie'd clap you in jug if he knew."

"If, chum, is the operative word. *If.*"

"*Evidence,*" mused Ellie. "What a funny word! Whatever does it mean?" She produced her compact and frowned at her reflection in the mirror. "Of course, Charlie needn't even suspect who did all this nothing, provided that we all completely forget what we've been talking about for the past ten minutes."

Doon took off her spectacles, polished them on her sweater, and replaced them. She said thoughtfully, "Considering that we've, so to speak, rather *had* Suicide, Misadventure, Murder, Both and All, and that we've all committed some fancy Perjury, *I* think that a drop of Amnesia would make a very nice change." She smiled brightly at Mrs. Ryder, "Don't you?"

Mrs. Ryder thought for a moment, then nodded. "Very restful," she agreed. She dropped four lumps of sugar into her cup of tea, splashed the front of her overall, and added placidly, "Drat!"

"Me, I heard nothing," murmured Doctor Feltz. "How gould I? I was ungonscious."

"I wasn't listening," said Rex. He raised his eyebrows at Jimmie. "Were you?"

Jimmie hooked his thumbs into his trouser pockets and looked at Paul. "I really can't remember," he said. "Can you?"

"Yes," said Paul. He lit a cigarette, broke the match in half, and flicked the pieces out of the window. "But I'm prepared to forget all I remember provided that Hannibal gets not only to the top of the Alps, but down the other side." He glanced at Egon. "Well, does he?"

Egon's face darkened, marshaled its reserves for a steep descent into fury. He opened his mouth, prepared to let rip with a flood of abuse, then hesitated, and changed his mind.

"Naturally, my dear old cock," he said suavely. "Hell, it's only historical!"

He stood for a moment, pulled at the lobe of his left ear, then crossed the room in a pantherish manner, and stalked in a tight circle around Enid Marley's chair.

"Which leaves *you*, dear," he mused, not looking at her, drumming his fingers absently on her shoulders. "I mean, which leaves you distinctly outnumbered."

She stared at him, hating him as much as she had ever hated anybody in her life, excluding Harold. She knew, and she knew that he also knew, that he had her exactly where he wanted her.

He could prove with that damned farewell letter that she had tried to commit suicide, which was bad enough, but he could also tell Woodman that she had intended to do nothing of the sort, which was infinitely worse. Nor could she accuse him of blackmailing her without revealing her absurd secret, which was unthinkable. She had a sudden ghastly vision of Egon telling it to Kidder. Dangerous Kidder of the despicable *Echo*! Kidder who knew probably better than any man, woman, or child in Europe, Asia, or Africa how to present an appalling libel – *blackening the reputation of an individual by bringing her into hatred, ridicule, and contempt* – without actually printing anything actually actionable!

She dug her nails into her palms, raised her chin, and forced herself to speak. "As, on second thoughts, I intimated to both Inspector Woodman and Kidder," she said icily, "I attempted to save a bird. I failed. Somebody attempted to save me. He failed."

Egon frowned. "He?"

"Or she," she said with an effort.

"Nothing and Don't-Know, mmm?"

"Mmm," she said savagely, "Mmm, mmm, *mmm*!"

At the window, assessing the crowd below, Rex said, awed, "*Look* at them! Watch them *teem*! They're standing in the aisles!"

"And *listen* to them!" said Doon, craning. "They're roaring, 'Down with Killer Kayes! Up with *You*!' Coo, our circulation'll whizz up to outer space!"

"Poor, poor *Me*!" said Egon piously. He hugged himself and performed a few steps of his curious, shuffling dance. "I predict that pitiful publication's about to take a terrible beating. We've been allocated half their paper already, and we've only scratched the surface. Isn't it *sad*?"

He skipped across the room, picked up the bottle of champagne with which he had failed to stun Kayes, and brandished it above his head. "Kids," he hissed in a hoarse, dynamic whisper, knowing that, as always when he was very happy, he was being childish, and not caring. "I propose to propose that we each propose a toast!" He snapped his fingers and told Ellie, "Pass the gem-encrusted goblets, missy!"

Ellie passed Mrs. Ryder's tray of teacups.

Egon prised the cork from the bottle and stood beaming as the wine overflowed and foamed up his sleeve. "Rally, you killer catchers!" he ordered, filling the cups. "I give you Mr. brackets Dog brackets Larkin, editor of *Me*! Any takers? Is there a madman in the audience?"

His staff, with the exception of Enid Marley, raised their cups.

"Larkin!"

"To hell with him!"

"*Me*! Down with *Me*!"

"Larkin! May he never become reconciled to our rejected material!"

"You," said Ellie, picking a piece of lint from Egon's ruined jacket. And added hastily, "I mean, of course, *YOU*! In caps!"

"Hannibal!" said Paul. "*Olé!*"

"Amnesia!" said Doctor Feltz. He began to shake with silent laughter. His head ached intolerably where Egon had inadvertently struck him with the bottle of champagne, but he was conscious of an overwhelming sense of reprieve. His future was again almost entirely his own property. Except for Kurt, Liesel, and Ali – and who knew where they were, or why, or even *if*? – who was left to tell the dreadful tale of the days in Old Vienna? Gyko? No, his career of carnage had plunged him irretrievably into madness; nobody would ever again believe a word he said. Enid Marley? With the counter threat of her farewell note in Egon's safe? No! He need not even send her the two-pound pot of caviar which she was expecting on the last day of the month! His secret was safe, or at any rate safer than it had been for many years. And if *he* forgot it, if he forgot his own real name . . . He began to laugh aloud. "Me," he said. "I doast to gomblede, dodal amnesia!"

"Charlie!" said Rex. "Maybe he didn't actually *solve* this case, but . . ."

"*What* case?" Egon asked in a loud, hectoring manner.

"No case. No case whatever."

"Poor old Charlie!" said Doon. "With the lift out of order and everything! Shall we buy him some new boots and all sign them?"

"We know nothing about his feet," Rex objected.

"Nor we do," said Doon. "Well, perhaps a little gold truncheon to put on his watch chain." She went on without a pause, "I give us Mrs. Frederick Turner. If she hadn't been groveling around under that awning . . ."

Jimmie asked, "Did anyone ever find out about Tinker?"

"I know it lives in a tank."

"Okay, I drink to Tinker's tank!"

Mrs. Ryder absently stirred her cup of wine with a spoon. "I propose," she said gruffly, "that we forget about the whole kaboodle. Water under the bridge, least said, and so on."

"Hear, hear!"

"Water!"

"Bridges!"

"Kaboodles everywhere!"

"May Larkin fall out with B.F., J.L., C.G., A.B., and all his advertisers!"

"*You!*"

"Hannibal! Damn good egg, old Hannibal!"

"Amnesia! Gomblede amnesia!"

"Charlie!"

"Mrs. Frederick Turner!"

"Tinker's tank!"

"Tank!"

"Tinker!"

"*Tinker's tank!*"

"Hold it!" cried Egon, pounding on the desk for silence. "I'm a lucky, lucky man. You don't deserve it, but I'm damn well going to make a speech."

"*Boo!*" said Rex.

"I don't understand you."

"I meant *Hoo*ray! *Speech, speech!*"

"Well," said Egon. He strode purposefully over to a filing cabinet, opened a drawer, peered into it, then slammed it shut. "I love you, I love you all," he said, blowing his nose, deeply moved. "We're a marvelous, sterling team. We always have been, we always will be. And the last few days have proved conclusively, vividly, beyond a shadow of a doubt, that *noth-*

ing can lick a really warm, cast-iron spot of teamwork. By which, of course, I mean that nothing can lick absolutely *everything*. We've sweated through Suicide, Misadventure, Murder, Both and the Lot. And what do we wind up with at the end of the trail? The one, single, sole, solitary solution that papa overlooked. Will you stand, please?"

He climbed on to a chair and raised his cup triumphantly. "Kids, comrades, colleagues, friends, raise your goblets and let us drink a solemn toast! I give you, in all humility, with profound gratitude, absolutely . . . *Nothing*!"

Chapter 17

HALF an hour later, Enid Marley alone remained in her office. She sat at her desk staring sightlessly at the opposite wall and, quite unconscious of what she was doing, cutting an indiarubber into minute pieces with a pair of scissors.

She knew only that she wanted to go home. She wanted to catch Mrs. Pickett before she left, to give the old pirate a final ten shillings, to impress upon her that the events of the past few days had been Nothing, nothing at all, not even Misadventure. She wanted to flop into bed, to send for Doctor Palmerston, who would madden yet soothe her by telling her for perhaps the five hundredth time that she was a great woman, a unique and irreplaceable woman, that she owed it to the countless thousands who so utterly depended upon her advice to take a long, long holiday . . .

The telephone rang. Automatically, she reached for it.

"It's about Tinker's meat," said Mr. Frederick Turner without preamble at the far end of the line. "On the bird floor, it is. Talkin' to that Kidder, I was, see, an' I put it down on this fire extinguisher thing an' . . ."

Mad, she thought, gently replacing the receiver, continuing her reverie as if she had not been interrupted. A holiday? She hated holidays and invariably returned from them so exhausted, in so savage a mood, that it took her three months of hard work to rehabilitate herself.

No! No holiday. Definitely.

But could she possibly work, even only temporarily as Egon had suggested, with Doon's dreadful brother as her assistant? No. No, no, *no*!

Very well, a holiday.

But. But, but, but . . . oh, the flies, the people, the sun, the peeling foreheads, the foolish laughter, the ozone, and the yelling birds at dawn. Egon had ordered her to return to work on Monday, and she would have to do so, because he now had the whip hand. But he had not said *which*

Monday. Which was the lesser of the two evils? Rex? Or a holiday? *Which?*

The telephone rang again. She ignored it. Waiting for it to stop clamoring, biting her lip, she picked up a sheet of paper on which Rex had scrawled a series of haphazard notes.

Tell somebody Mags, Cornwall rang up, doesn't understand about Madam, she read. *Wants to know all about it. Said didn't know, was past caring. Mistake? Shouldn't think so because woman's quite obviously mad as a weevil.* Below this was a small drawing of a waistcoat with double scalloped revers, beside which was written *Bit camp? Ask Neil.* Then, sideways, in red chalk, *Ideas for sinister articles: 101 WAYS TO LOSE YOUR MAN! Or maybe, HOW TO LOOK REPULSIVE ON £1,000 A YEAR!* At the bottom of the page, in large letters and surrounded by a carefully drawn border of creeping clematis, was the word *BREAD.*

Enid Marley tossed it aside. Rex, she mused, was of course a little mad, but not entirely because he was so sane about Mags, Cornwall, who really was subnormal. Restlessly, she got up, walked across to the window, and gazed down at the crowd below. It now filled the street completely. In the middle of it, a newsreel van was marooned; two men stood on the roof smoking cigarettes and tinkering with a movie camera. In the car park, a large group, the proprietor of the Indian restaurant among it, had linked arms and was plunging about singing *Underneath the Spreading Chestnut Tree.* Two policemen stood outside the café looking uneasy, obviously waiting for reinforcements. The street band had returned, the same band that on . . . on the day of the Nothing, had been shuffling without hope in the gutter. Now, they played with verve, smiling, doing a brisk trade. The old monkey was dancing with dangerous abandon on the drum . . .

Mad? All of them?

Enid Marley dug her nails into the palms of her hands, stalked back to the desk and slumped into her chair. For a long moment she sat with her head propped in her hands, wondering whether she was the last sane person in London. Then, suddenly galvanized into action, she seized a double handful of mail from her IN tray. She was about to vent her feelings on it, to tear it across and across, to throw it into the air in a purely therapeutic manner, when she saw among it the hatefully familiar envelope. It was mauve, sealed with bright pink wax. She withdrew it from the pile, turned it over. And there, as she had known, was her own name written in the round copybook script of Browneyes Jackson.

She realized that her hands were shaking and clasped them together tightly for a moment, closing her eyes. Browneyes! Who had ruined everything! Without whom she would never have landed in this invidious position! Who had elected to leave the incriminating farewell letter as her own farewell to her meddling husband! Who had passed into circulation the only clue in an otherwise cast-iron case of sober and dignified Misadventure!

Ah yes! Dear, dear little Browneyes!

Who now, no doubt, wanted advice? *My dear, I sincerely believe that your terrible problem can only be solved by immediate emigration . . .*

Enid Marley ripped open the envelope, withdrew the letter. The address announced that Browneyes was in a large industrial town in the north of England. *Darling Enid*, she had written. *I bet you are surprised to see where I am! I took your advice about the swift final exit you said and I promise I will never go back to Mr. Jackson, but will divorce him for collusion. You know you said once did I know the Mayor? So when I got here I didn't but I went to see him and he says I need the protection of an older man. I laughed jokingly because he is only 57 and says he feels much younger. He's got this smashing house and the room I'll have . . .*

Mad, of course.

Enid Marley crumpled the letter into a ball and threw it on to the floor. For the first time, she wondered whether *any* of her fans were entirely sane. What about *Anxious Mother* who had never had a child but owned four cats which all slept in prams? What about *Commuter* who for no reason at all started to laugh uncontrollably each time he set foot on an escalator? What about *Old Fashioned Girl* who had done it yet once again and who would appear before the same magistrate on the following Tuesday? What about *Worried, Bucks*, and *Wendy II*, and *Ex-Yogi*, and the macabre *Miss L. Maldive?*

Frowning, Enid Marley stirred the heap of mail with a forefinger. Had she for all these long, dedicated years been playing high priestess to a multitude of lunatics? *No!* her mind shouted. Her fans were *not* on the whole mad, not all of them, and, of those who were, only a handful had been actually certified, at least as far as she knew.

Take nice little Laura Morehouse, for instance, who lived in the best part of Hampstead, who was an indefatigable knitter, whose quiet, pleasant husband was so successful in the City. Take dear old Mrs. Jepson, who lived just outside Maidstone, content with her bungalow, her farmer husband and her beloved son, Billy. Take, above all, Lady Graystoke . . .

Smiling, reassured, she picked up Lady Graystoke's slim, elegant envelope. She admired, as always the small medieval script, the tiny, almost apologetic, crest on the back. What was it this time? An invitation to address the local W.V.S.? To sell flags? To open a bazaar in the castle grounds? She slit the envelope, drew out the letter.

Dear Mrs. Marley, she read. *When, last week, I applied for your Jacobean embroidery transfer, I was considerably startled to receive a handbook elucidating matters with which, as a great-grandmother, I am already familiar, and which, as a widow, no longer concern me. This I returned, only to receive an apology, which mollified me, and a pamphlet informing me how to enlist in the Royal Air Force, which did not. If this is your idea of humor, Mrs. Marley, I can only assume that your recent and extraordinary fall has unbalanced you. Briefly – and I pen this in sympathy rather than anger – are you mad?*

Enid Marley dropped the letter on to the desk and sat staring at it as if it might explode at any moment. A sickening doubt began to simmer in her mind, a doubt so unnerving that she felt a light sweat break out on the palms of her hands.

Was Lady Graystoke mad?

Was she? No! Never! Ludicrous!

But she *must* be, because the alternative was equally absurd. If Lady Graystoke were sane, then . . . She was reluctant even to think the words. But she knew that she owed it to herself, and to Lady Graystoke, to settle the problem beyond argument.

She forced herself to move. It seemed to take her a long time to cross the room, to reach the appropriate chart. She reflected with a sense of outrage that she had never expected to approach it, or indeed any of the others, on her own behalf. What precisely was her query? How, had she been writing to herself, would she phrase it?

Simply. Clearly. Succinctly. And, unlike the majority of her fans, with no unnecessary detail, no beating around the bush. And would she, also unlike the majority of her fans, take her own advice? Certainly she would! She had implicit faith in herself, *implicit*. Very well then!

Dear Mrs. Marley, Am I mad? Yes or no?

She took the dangling strings, placed them on *Insane?* and *Self*. She stretched them across to *Yes* and *No* respectively. Where they crossed was the opening paragraph of the letter she would have written to herself, had she been somebody else.

My dear, it advised. *I am so sorry to hear that you doubt your sanity. Have you spoken of your fears to your mother, your medical advisor, some unbiased outsider? Personally, I feel – but I can only base my opinion upon the strange brevity of your letter! – that you should consult a psychiatrist. And – may I stress this? – AS SOON AS POSSIBLE.*

Egon started downstairs beaming, humming, clicking his fingers. He swung a briefcase containing enough work to keep him busy for a week, all of which would have to be finished that night, but he did not care. He had not felt so confident and jaunty since he had left school.

"Tell me, sir," he asked himself aloud with the air of gaunt integrity which he employed for interviews, "to what do you attribute your present lunatic grin?"

"Glad you asked me that, old man," he answered himself with the embarrassed little laugh employed by so many of his victims. "Quite a number of items, matter of fact. If you've got a couple of days to spare, I'll put it as briefly as I can. Lie down, won't you? Take your shoes off! Got your pajamas, shaving tackle, pemmican? Oh yes, quite a number of items, actually . . ."

Well, what were they? he asked himself silently, jumping down three steps at a time and, quite unable to contain his glee, faking a jovial left hook at the wall.

Item One was the fact that the Marley junket was at last under control – *his* control – and wrapped up to his entire satisfaction. If poor old Charlie was left with a fistful of loose ends and contradictory evidence which flatly refused to tie into any sort of conclusive knot whatever, not even a grannie, then he had only himself to blame. He should not have become a policeman in the first place.

Item Two was that the next six issues of *You* were already sold out and B.F. had voluntarily suggested another increase in the print order. He had also almost doubled Egon's budget, and J.L. had officially decreed that all indifferent material was to be off-loaded on to *Me*.

Item Three was the unswerving loyalty of his staff, every member of which he loved, respected, and trusted; every member of which – always, of course, with the exception of Enid Marley – was a staunch friend, a proven ally. His staff whose . . . whose footsteps he now heard above him in the corridor on the fifth floor.

Their voices rang clearly down the lift shaft, surely audible even to the janitor in the basement. Smiling, conscious of a surge of affection for them individually and collectively, Egon moved nearer, listening.

"Und me, I worked, I *slaved* to *gure* amnesia!" Doctor Feltz was saying, amazed. "*Why*? Am I mad all these years? Who am I to rob berhabs two hundred batients of their mosd briceles bossession? We loog ad the world doday, don't we shudder? Therevore, vor the world of domorrow, is id nod my duty as an analyst to engourage, to bresgribe, to *induce* amnesia?"

Paul asked with mild sarcasm, "On the National Health?"

"Bud yar," said Doctor Feltz. "Domorrow, amnesia musd be vreely available to *all* . . ."

"Tomorrow," said Mrs. Ryder shortly, "we shall need it. Business as usual." She sighed and added, "*Fritto Misto*. I have to use up the rotten fruit from the Natural Beauty spread, and what else that's photogenic can I cook with all that muck on a perishing primus?"

Jimmie stopped whistling through his teeth and said, "You know we're going to miss Murder and all that. Oh well", he said philosophically, "back to the salt mines!"

"I liked Both best," remarked Doon. "Then Suicide."

"I never really got *enough* of Suicide," complained Rex. "Like caviar, if you know what I mean."

Paul said through a loud, prolonged yawn, "Murder was my baby. Like a dog, I followed it, faithful and true."

"Superficial, that's me," said Ellie. "Incapable of sustained emotion. Until an hour ago, I was mad about all this lovely Perjury. But now I know it's going to become an integral part of my life, I've completely lost interest . . ."

Egon, about to shout up the shaft for silence, was overcome by a fit of coughing. He stood spluttering, alternately shaking the banisters and thumping himself on the chest.

Above, Doctor Feltz said gently, "Now berhabs we should shot our drabs. Aggousdics, you know."

"Security and that," agreed Mrs. Ryder. "Nothing like it."

There was a brief pause, then Jimmie started to whistle again, somebody sneezed, and Doon said, "Darling, did you remember the bread?"

"Oh God!" said Rex. "Haven't we got any Ryvita?"

Still coughing, Egon went on downstairs. *Marvelous people*, he told himself firmly. *Splendid chaps, salt of the earth. Real, warm, pulsing, human people. Perhaps a shade too human now and then, a little on the salty side occasionally, but what did he want, an office full of zombies?*

Between the third and fourth floors, Kidder crouched in the lift packing a suitcase, drinking whisky, and chewing an unlit cigar. He looked up, saw Egon, and said, "Oh, so it's you, is it? I just heard that your mob of Regular Complainers have taken the *Echo*, to put it mildly, by storm. They've left my office in a couple of million pieces."

"Too bad," said Egon sympathetically. "Tough."

"Tough hell!" Kidder grinned and tossed a pair of pyjamas into the suitcase. "You know something, a deep truth? Drop me out of outer space, and you know where I fall? On my feet. Chum, I tell you that around that joint, I'm *king*. The Old Man loves me like a son. They're going to run front page pix of the wreckage and build me up as The Most Unpopular Man In Fleet Street. I'm *made!*" He kicked open the gate of the lift. "Come on in and let's give *You* a shot in the arm."

Egon climbed into the lift and sat down on Kidder's suitcase. "There's been a new development," he said, reaching for the whisky. "Misadventure's out, dead as mutton. Enid's agreed . . ."

"Yeah, I know."

"*How* do you know?"

"Shamus on the Third knew."

"Carstairs? How did *he* know?"

"How do *I* know?"

"I know. Snooping."

"He burbled something about trailing you for Sister Toothache and her for you, and he figured as you were closeted together, you'd each know where the other one was, so he's gone to the movies with the Hungarian photographer." Kidder leant sideways to drop a handful of corks and an empty cigar box down the lift shaft. "A Garbo fan."

The feeble voice of the janitor floated up from the basement. "'Ere! Now you stop that droppin', Mr. Kidder! She's 'ad quite enough, thank you very much!"

Kidder ignored it. "Then I won Woodman, with Kayes in tow. Know what he gives me?"

"Yes. 'No comment.' "

"Big blabbermouth!"

Egon pulled at a thread dangling from his cuff, realized that it was something to do with the buttonhole, and tucked it up his sleeve. "How are we going to play it? I'll give you an exclusive on the Kayes stuff if you can laugh off the Marley caper."

"It's a deal," said Kidder, reaching for his notebook. "Let's take it from the roof chase."

"Mmm? What roof chase?"

Kidder said impatiently, "Look, pal, you've got a roof, haven't you? All we want is a chase, which *I've* got. Why not? Adds tone."

"Sure," said Egon. "Okay!"

"*Okay!* So you come down from this roof. He's chasing you. His eyes are bloodshot, he's . . ."

"No," said Egon. "*I'm* chasing *him*."

"You are?"

"Less, obvious, more plausible, Okay?"

"Okay! So he pounds down the corridor, footsteps ringing on the concrete. He's gibbering in some unknown lingo. He stops, turns. For an instant, you think he's going to charge. You trip, fall, gash your knee . . ."

"To the bone."

"Of course. You pick yourself up. You're badly shaken, the blood's gushing down your leg, soaking into your sock. You ignore it. He whirls, flees. You dash after him, breathless, determined, your heart pounding against your ribs. Cigar?"

"Thanks."

"You know that the red-haired colossus ahead of you's a killer berserk, no longer a man, but an animal at bay, desperate, cornered. Yet do you hesitate in your headlong pursuit?"

"No. Match?"

"Thanks. Not on your life! Courageously, you . . ."

"Fearlessly."

"Recklessly?"

"Check."

"Okay, what did you do recklessly?"

"Knowing full well that I was taking my life into my hands, that I was facing a death so horrible, so repulsive . . ."

"Look," said Kidder, "they're holding the front page. Give it to me straight, will you? I'll fix it."

Egon scowled at his shoes. "I tried to crown him with this bottle of champagne," he admitted reluctantly. "I missed and clobbered Doc. So Kayes wheeled on me, his eyes . . ."

"*Straight!*"

"Oh, I don't know. He cuffed us around generally, tried to strangle Enid, tore my jacket, socked Jimmie slap in the puss, and went like a lamb when Woodman showed up and said, 'Good evening.' You see? It just won't *do*. It has no drama, no climax, no impact! That's been the trouble all along. I kept on and on thinking at last I'd got my teeth into something or other, and I kept on and on being forced to the conclusion that I was just biting myself."

"I like it," said Kidder. "It's real. Goddam it, it's almost human." He pulled his transmitter set towards him and tapped out his call signal. "We'll kick it around a little, scrub the roof chase, maybe completely re-angle the whole works. How, for instance, about a Kayes-the-kid-from-an-Occupied-slum slant, a story that would wring a tear from every one-eyed mother in the country?" He blew a cloud of smoke and waved it away impatiently. "Kidder calling, Kidder calling! Stan? Over."

His smile faded as he listened. "Oh, no!" he cried. "Oh, no, no, *no!*" And then, "Oh, you fabulous oaf! *Now! At this stage!*" He looked at Egon, shook his head in the manner of a punch-drunk boxer, and asked, "In the name of all that's lousy, how do you like that?"

"What?"

Kidder said with unnatural calm, "This moonchild has finally produced a stiff! A real honey of a stiff! Two big shots in the City, a beautiful, wanton wife called Laura. Buckets of blood, bags of sex, sadism, wealth, glamour, class, and an old deaf dog from a broken home! Everything, all we ever wanted! The lot, on a tailormade plate! Even the name ties up."

"How? What with?"

"The corpse," said Kidder, raising his eyebrows, inviting Egon to share his frustration, "answered to the name of Marr-Leigh."

"No, he didn't," said Egon. "I won't *have* it!"

"Chum, you've got it," mourned Kidder. "Marley, Marr-Leigh, Marr-Leigh, Marley. *He* was City, like *her* husband. God what I couldn't have done with this yesterday!" His eyes glazed. He sat holding his cigar as if it had been a spear. "You know how I'd have led into it? *Toga!* This dame called this stiff Toga. WHY?"

Egon said, "Well, slap off the top of my head, I'd say . . ."

Kidder interrupted. "Ah, what's the point? It's too damn late." He tapped a finger on his transmitter set. "It's now, that's when this yokel tells me, *now!* Isn't life disgusting?"

"Bawl him out," suggested Egon. "Fire him! *Now!*"

Kidder's shoulders sagged. "How can I? He's the Old Man's nephew."

"Oh." After a long, baffled pause, Egon rallied. He gave Kidder a sympathetic slap on the back. "Okay," he said. "There goes the Marley caper! So okay, so what? You want to know what? Okay, I'll tell you what! We count up to four million, then we give each other a great big, shifty smile, and we say to hell with it! *Mmm?*"

THE END

The first three books by Pamela Branch, *The Wooden Overcoat, Lion in the Cellar*, and *Murder Every Monday*, are also available from The Rue Morgue Press and can be purchased from the same bookseller who sold you *Murder's Little Sister*. The Rue Morgue Press reprints classic mysteries from the 1930s to the 1960s. For a catalog write: The Rue Morgue, 87 Lone Tree Lane, Lyons, CO 80540, or see our website: www.ruemorguepress.com